Brian Thomas, educated at Pengam and Bournemouth Schools, served in the Electrical Branch of the Royal Navy from 1954 to 1968. He joined the Submarine Service in 1962, attaining the rank of C.P.O. As a civilian, he joined a multi-national company, eventually managing a service branch in both the City and Westminster areas of London.

Always interested in art, Brian left the bustle of business and moved to Devon to become self-employed and to find time to paint and to write. He considers writing to be the greatest of challenges and studies while he writes, but still finds time for his cats, his garden and cooking.

CARLOTTA'S DAUGHTER

Brian Thomas

CARLOTTA'S DAUGHTER

Vanguard Press

A CIP catalogue record for this title is
available from the British Library.

ISBN 978 1 84386 458 5

*Vanguard Press is an imprint of
Pegasus Elliot MacKenzie Publishers Ltd.*
www.pegasuspublishers.com

First Published in 2009

**Vanguard Press
Sheraton House Castle Park
Cambridge England**

Printed & Bound in Great Britain

Dedication

This book is dedicated to my sister, Audrey, for her unstinting and selfless caring of her husband, Ron. Royal Marine Sergeant, Ronald. C. Biles, took part in the assault of Port Said during the Suez Campaign and is now fighting another battle against the dreadful Alzheimer's disease.

Acknowledgement

Thanks go to my dear wife, Pat, for tolerating the click clack of my keyboard and my vagueness when engaged in normal conversation.

Sincere thanks to David Morgan for reading the manuscript and advising on the intricacies of computer technology – also for his work on my design for the cover.

CHAPTER 1

COCK OF THE FLEET

Quietly, slowly, the unlit motor launch made its way across the dark waters of Malta's Grand Harbour towards the lights of the British warship. The occupants of the small boat, sweating from the lingering and oppressive heat of the departed day, nervously passed missiles amongst each other. Closer now, the rumble of machinery deep within the hull of the looming warship reached their straining ears. With a few yards to go, the coxswain signalled to the engineer to cut the engine. To the men in the boat the slap of tiny wavelets sounded too loud as the boat glided towards the alien gangway. Hardly daring to breathe, each man stared anxiously up at the grey ship's side to the rail above; to be discovered now, this close, would be curtains.

James Davis, dressed only in shorts and sandals, crouched in the well of the boat, sharp and ready to erupt into action. His taut young body, damp in the humidity of a high summer night, glistened from the reflected lights of the fortress all around. Taking his share of missiles he grasped them to his bare stomach. The stench attacked his nose as his fingers sank into their putrefying skins. The bowman, stretching forward with his boat-hook, secured a hold on the gangway as the small vessel entered the light from a lonely lamp suspended above the ladder. Collectively the men held their breath.

Then without warning, like the first clap of thunder in a silent storm, all hell broke loose. Shouts and screams, mixed with klaxon hoots filled the night. Faces appeared above where there were no faces before. Missiles rained down upon the startled attackers.

"Back, back." Stokesy, the engineer, fumbled for the engine starter. In his blind panic, he failed to find the button.

"No we don't," screamed the coxswain. "On you go lads, up the ladder."

Two of the bravest scrambled onto the wooden platform at the bottom of the gangway, but arms held above their heads offered scant protection from the hailing missiles.

"Where's the Cock?" came a voice from the boat.

"On the top 'o 'B' gun turret." The bowman held manfully onto his boathook despite being a key target from the defenders above.

The men on the ladder, under terrific assault, made some progress up the steps. Jamie, with his head tucked under the rear of the man in front, gained a foothold on the shaking, creaking ladder.

"Give 'em support lads; get those spuds going," shouted the coxswain from the stern.

"It's bloody hopeless," screamed Stokesy. With one arm held above his head the engineer fiddled with the engine panel. He managed to restart the engine. "Back – get back – we're leaving."

The engineer's shouts went unheard – lost in the shouting and cries of pain as potatoes, flung by both sides, found their marks. The defenders, superior in position and numbers, gave no respite.

Minutes passed before the first of the attackers reached the top of the ladder – only to be met by an impenetrable group of howling banshees who grabbed each assailant, frogmarched them for'ard and threw them overboard. Suddenly two men appeared from the destroyer's fo'csle with a deck-wash hose held between them. Its powerful gush of water hit the topmost attackers, tumbling them back in a flurry of arms, legs and curses. Those further down the ladder retreated into the launch and some, like Jamie, jumped into the water.

Pushing off, the bowman shouted defiance to the cheering crowd lining the rails of *HMS Dunness*. "You load of tossers. You can stick your bloody Cock right up your…"

A well aimed rotten potato shut him up; the stinking mess splattered over his face and dripped down his shirt.

Jamie trod water until the launch picked him up. With the taunts and cat-calls from the *Dunness* defenders ringing in their ears, the boat made its way back to the friendly lights of *HMS Demon*, a British destroyer that had that day taken part in the 1956 Mediterranean Fleet Regatta at Marsaxlokk Bay – and lost to her sister ship, the triumphant *HMS Dunness*, the Cock of the Fleet.

The symbol of that triumph, a fully plumed figure of a cockerel, proudly sat unsullied on top of *Dunness's* 'B' gun turret, to mock the attempts of other ships to steal it until she sailed out of Grand Harbour two days later.

Back on board *Demon*, Jamie made his way along the Iron Deck to his workshop. Being responsible for the ship's batteries, the small battery charging workshop on the starboard side of the Upper Deck provided him with his own private space. He needed a smoke, a shower and a sleep. Recovering his blue working shirt and tobacco tin from the tool locker, Jamie leaned on the wire guard-rail and gazed at the silhouettes and lights of Valletta. He rolled an ample tickler and lit up – the saltpetre in the pusser's tobacco flaring as he drew in the smoke.

'Latch would have enjoyed today,' he thought. Jamie contemplated on the many good times he had shared with Derek Latchbrook but as usual lately, the image of his friend as he had last seen him – head shaven and being led away by Naval Police – broke through. Mentally Jamie shook away the image, preferring to think of Latch in happier times. Jamie smiled. 'That slippery so-and-so would have got through to the Cock. Somehow he would.'

Enjoying the quiet of the moment, Jamie retraced the day – it had been a memorable day, starting with the regatta and finishing with the expedition to steal the Cock of the Fleet trophy.

Jamie had been a reluctant oarsman in the miscellaneous mess's whaler – press-ganged, as were most of the others, by Petty Officer Gordon Grundy. On paper, the crew appeared favourites, but fortune deserted them. Instead of winning the coveted Cock of the Fleet trophy, *Demon*'s secret weapon, held in reserve for the final, came in last. But, as PO Grundy had tried to explain to their Divisional Officer, it wasn't their fault; Dusty, the giant, ex-Field Gun Crew heads cleaner – whose strength should have ensured a good result – caught a crab at the start of the final race. The mishap caused the huge stoker to fall back, banging his head on the thwart behind. He spent the rest of the race suffering from a coma and was taken to the military hospital at Bighi.

Wet shorts cooled by a night breeze that rippled the black surface of the harbour brought a shiver to Jamie's naked torso. He put on his shirt. Without seeing, he watched drunken bodies on Custom House Steps falling into their respective liberty boats.

'Tomorrow,' he mused. 'Tomorrow I have a date with Nell.' The contentment of the moment dissolved with the thought, giving way to a persistent niggle – an uneasy feeling in his stomach that returned each time he thought of the girl.

"Nelleee, Nelleeeee," he mouthed the words in a whisper.

The shrill pipe on the Tannoy cut through his thoughts.

'Pipe down and my hammock yet to sling.'

He shut the battery shop door and hurried for'ard, deciding on a quick wash now; a shower could wait until morning.

Sunday dawned bright and cloudless; the clear, calm waters of the harbour reflecting, in rippling images, the sand-coloured ramparts and buildings encircling the ship. Early morning, the freshest part of the day after a night free from the burning Malta sun, caught the smells and sounds of Malta's historic cities. Church bells chimed from all directions adding to the waking sounds of the ships packed into the anchorage.

After Church Parade on the fo'csle, Jamie, dressed in his white cotton duck-suit, lined up in the canteen flat for his issue of grog – necessary, he felt, to settle his rebellious stomach.

"Hiya, Jamie. Are you going swimmin' this aftie?"

Turning in surprise, Jamie found Dusty Miller behind him in the queue. Dusty, with his dark complexion that the sun had turned into a patchwork of shades, always managed to look as if he needed a good scrub. Towering at least six inches above most other men had given his head a permanent downward bend. Today he sported a white bandage, but still visible was the shorn patch where his scalp had been stitched.

"I thought you were in Bighi," said Jamie.

"One night in that place is enough." Dusty ruefully touched the back of his head. "Some blood-sucker of a medic looked into my eyes, gave me two tablets and let me out this morning."

"No swimming for me today, Dust. I'm off ashore."

"Okay, I'll come. I could do with getting pissed after yesterday."

"Sorry, mate. I'll be meeting someone."

"Not Carlotta's daughter? You jammy bastard."

Carlotta, a far from young bar-girl who worked at the Lucky Horseshoe – a garish bar halfway down the Gut – had taken a shine to Jamie and had promised him first go at her eldest daughter. The pink drinks the girls of the Horseshoe managed to persuade their clientele to buy them contained nothing more than coloured water, but matelots didn't complain. The promise of other benefits, however misguided, proved too strong to resist.

Jamie smiled at the face above him; Dusty's mottled skin looked dirtier than ever against the white bandage.

"I might see you in the Horseshoe later."

In the three months since attaining man status, Jamie had grown used to his rum. He had little trouble downing the tumbler of grog expertly issued each day by a stores rating under the eagle eye of the duty officer. Anxious not to be late he headed out on deck to muster for inspection before boarding the liberty boat at 12.30.

At Custom House most of his shipmates headed for the cool, dark doorways of the bars set into the stone walled ramparts opposite the quay. Jamie walked past them up the hill to the bus depot at Valletta. Recalling the instructions in the note he looked for the name of St Paul's Bay amongst the destinations on the collection of busses lined up at the terminus. The note, scrawled untidily in faint pencil, had been passed to him at the Lido a long, nervous, week ago, by the woman who sold cold drinks from an ice-box at the kiosk. Finding his bus he boarded the empty old Bedford and asked the driver to let him know when the road out of St Paul's Bay split to Ghajn Tuffieha. The note had asked him to wait at that junction and the prospect of a picnic date with a girl who had haunted him and his best friend for two years filled him with excitement, but more than that – deep inside, Jamie felt a foreboding that bordered on fear.

Settling on a hard wooden seat in the bus, Jamie thought back to the previous Saturday. Together with other members of his mess's water-polo team, Jamie had embarked on the ship's motorboat, bound for the Lido, a recreation spot accessible only from the water. Motoring almost to the breakwater at the entrance of Grand Harbour they entered a small, deep-water cove that provided a natural swimming area, ideal for diving from the rocks and with plenty of space for water polo. Jostling for position the impatient swimming party scrambled out at the small concrete quay and raced up the steps cut into the limestone rock to grab one of the few sun beds on the sunny, walled patio. Jamie arrived to find all of the beds occupied. He and his friends settled for a spot on the flat-topped boundary wall – a good place to sunbathe.

"Who is that?" Pedlar Palmer, a fellow electrician, lived his life cursed with an over-active sex drive that had landed him in trouble more than once. Setting his towel on the wall, Jamie undressed down to his swimming shorts and looked to see what had taken Pedlar's attention.

At the far end of the Lido, past the refreshment hut, a group of three people occupied sun beds, a fact not unnoticed by the crowd because two were graced by girls. One of the girls, sitting on the edge of her sun bed, peered out from under a shading hand. She waved towards Jamie. He recognised the hair first; then the legs – he had seen those legs before. The shock of recognition prevented him from acknowledging her wave.

"It's you – she's waving at you," said Pedlar.

"Shit'n it, Pedlar." Jamie looked away.

"She wants you to go over, Taffy," said Dusty. Hardly able to conceal his excitement the stoker's head protruded from his shoulders like a vulture. Jamie, giving up hope of avoiding embarrassment, sidled over to the girls as nonchalantly as he could, which proved difficult as the hot concrete slabs burned his feet. He stopped in the welcome shade of the refreshment kiosk a few feet from the group.

"James," welcomed the girl. "What a surprise. Beth, Mark, this is James. I knew him at Chatham. What are you doing here?"

"Oh, you know," he mumbled, "cruising around – on *Demon*." With a loose sweep of his arm he indicated the general direction of the ships in the harbour. "But what on earth are you doing here?"

"Ah, *Demon*." The girls' male companion interrupted before Nell could reply. "Old De-Fotherinham. Give him my regards, will you."

Jamie, surprised to hear his captain referred to in such a familiar way as 'Old De-Fotherinham', glared at the man.

"Mark – Lieutenant Tuey – is on Daddy's staff." Nelly's speedy interjection did little to ease Jamie's instant dislike of the lieutenant. Mark stood, arms folded, with one flip-flopped foot on Beth's sun bed. A cigarette moved in his mouth as he spoke, his eyes screwed against the curling smoke. Apart from an initial glance at Jamie the young officer's gaze held steadfastly on a small spindly bush growing from the rocks behind the kiosk. Even without the introduction, Jamie would have recognised an officer – the affected stance; the overlong white shorts that accentuated the spindly nature of the pale legs – but most revealing – the clipped, direct speech that all together added up to an attitude of superiority that Mark Tuey did little to hide. A zonal change from white to red where his collar usually covered him up to the neck confirmed this man's officer status. For a brief and confusing moment Jamie felt a pang of jealousy. With as black a look as he could manage, Jamie turned his back on Mark Tuey and spoke to the girl.

"How are you," he mumbled.

"I'm fine, thanks."

The girl's blue eyes, direct and unblinking, locked with his and he suddenly lost all sense of time and place. In the silence, when it seemed that every eye and every ear on the Lido was poised for the next word, Mark Tuey coughed. Jamie felt the heat of a blush rising in his face – the reddening hidden from the others by his deep tan.

"Well, good to see you." Jamie indicated the polo ball wedged under his arm. "The lads are waiting – we've got a game. Bye."

Without waiting for a reply he backed away – running a gauntlet of barely subdued hisses and taunts. Needing desperately to escape he hurried to the cliff edge and, followed by his noisy companions, he dived into the cool, crystal clear water.

With a water-polo game well underway, Nelly's party descended the steps and boarded a Dghajsa, which had been waiting off the jetty. As the boat sculled through the swimmers, Nelly waved, Beth smiled and Mark Tuey pointedly stood in the bow holding on to the high, brightly painted prow. If the young officer had not been staring forward, as if modelling for a ship's figurehead, he probably would have avoided the ball. The polo ball, thrown by Dusty and apparently slipping from his large paw, hit the officer with some force on the side of his head. Dusty sank out of sight leaving hardly a ripple and the girls giggled uncontrollably.

In the hot, bouncing Bedford bus, Jamie smiled to himself as he recalled the incident. Reaching inside to the breast pocket of his tight duck suit top, he extracted his pay book wallet. Carefully he slipped out the small piece of paper, unfolded and read it for the umpteenth time. The faint pencil and spidery writing couldn't mask the directness of the message – a directness Jamie had seen in the girl before – it simply asked Jamie to meet her for a beach picnic with the time and place and was signed 'Eleanor' – and, typically, it left little or no room for refusal.

Tense and apprehensive with the uncertainty of the coming reunion he reflected on his unlikely acquaintance with the girl so different in station to himself and the fate that had brought them together.

CHAPTER 2

HMS COLLINGWOOD

The entrance to the sprawling expanse of Hampshire countryside occupied by HMS Collingwood surprises travellers who come upon it on the country lane between Fareham and Southsea. In July of 1954, the Royal Navy's electrical school, sweltering beneath a hot summer sun, busied itself turning out increasing numbers of young men – men competent and able to meet the challenge of an increasingly technical navy. Emerald green lawns, edged with the whitest of edging stones, lined the wide road from the main gates to the broad expanse of the parade ground. Surrounded by rows of dark wooden accommodation huts, sheds and red-brick featureless buildings, the hot tarmac took a pounding from rectangles of blue recruits being drilled like soldier ants remotely controlled by large-voiced instructors.

Junior Electrician's Mate James Davis and Electrician's Mate (Second Class) Derek Latchbrook, shouldering heavy World War Two Lee Enfield rifles that bounced painfully on raw shoulders, halted, breathless in front of a tight-faced Chief Petty Officer Instructor after twice doubling around the circumference of the parade ground.

Dressed in full uniform including webbing, gaiters and boots, their new entry class had been drilling for over an hour. The bike sheds at the perimeter could have provided some shade but the chief kept the party fully exposed to the high sun. Sweat rolled down adolescent faces, stinging skin unused to close morning shaves freshly applied by naval issue razors. Legs, constricted by tight khaki gaiters that reached to just under the knee, itched from the rough blue serge of unfamiliar uniforms.

"Inhuman bastard," Derek had said.

"Inhuman bastard," Jamie had concurred.

"This parade ground," the Chief had said, indicating, with a broad sweep of his short arms, the square of tarmac disappearing in a heat haze into the distance, "is the largest in the Royal Navy. You two are about to measure it – twice round at the double."

The statement confirmed to the two recruits that new entries should be seen and not heard, and that instructors possessed Superman hearing. As the offenders completed two gruelling circuits 'Stand Easy' sounded on the Tannoy. A mobile NAAFI canteen, parked on the road between the rows of accommodation huts, had opened its shutters and the classes of heavy-booted new recruits had been dismissed to cluster around the tea and sticky buns on offer. Gasping for breath, the two offenders joined the rear of the queue.

"You two," screeched the Chief. "Why have you stopped?" The instructor, a diminutive, slightly round person, sported rows of medal ribbons any Yank would have been proud of. "Did I tell you to stop?"

"No, but you said twice round…" started Jamie.

"Did I ask you to count?" enquired the Chief. Before either of his victims could reply he continued. "No I did not ask you to count. You will stop running when I tell you. Well, now I'm saying twice round again. At the double – move!"

"But…" protested Jamie.

"Shut up," said Derek. With Jamie following, Derek sped away like a hare with the added incentive of making it back before the canteen closed its shutters.

The two had joined the Service at the Navy's extensive electrical school together. Derek, older by two years, shared the same birth date with his younger classmate. Jamie, a shy 16 year old, measured two inches taller than Derek, but the Londoner carried himself with a self-assurance that bordered on cockiness – a state that Navy trainers found challenging. Despite a regulation haircut, the man from Harrow on the Hill managed to maintain a blonde quiff that popped out when he pushed his cap to the back of his head. As unlike poles attract, the two young men hit it off very quickly but, as Jamie found out, Derek didn't care too much for rules. Consequently Derek found himself pounding the parade ground or washing piles of greasy aluminium pans frequently. One evening in the accommodation hut Derek approached Jamie. He found the young Welshman busily forcing Cherry Blossom boot polish into the toecaps of his newly issued boots with the plastic handle of his newly issued toothbrush. Most of the class members lay on their bunks, enjoying a rare evening free of activity, but for the mandatory writing of a letter home.

"D'y like dancing, Taff?" Leaning on Jamie's metal locker the Londoner tried unsuccessfully to comb his heavily Brylcreemed, but severely cropped, blonde hair back into the style he had joined up with.

"Not a lot." With a shudder, Jamie remembered back to his only experience of dancing – a few awkward steps at the Trebarry Methodist Hall, which the Rev Tucker had put on some Wednesdays after Bible Reading.

"Have you ever been to the Palais – Hammersmith?"

"Hammersmith? I've never been to London."

"Never been to the Smokey? Bloody 'ell."

Derek fell silent for a while as if letting that momentous fact sink in. Jamie elbowed Derek out of the way and carefully slotted the shining boots into the bottom of his locker. Closing his locker doors, Jamie straightened up and looked at his new-found friend.

Derek Latchbrook, a muscular young man with a fresh complexion, enjoyed the advantage of never looking as if he needed a shave. In contrast with Jamie's dark features, Derek's skin seemed flawless. Blessed with a generous mouth and ever ready with a grin, the Londoner identified his East End roots each time he spoke.

"Shouldn't you be writing home?" Jamie nudged himself some room and sat alongside Derek.

"Writing letters? Who me? Me Ma probably doesn't even know I've left the house. Anyway, forget about letters." Derek lowered his voice to a whisper. "I could do with a run ashore. I hear there's a gap in the fence – up behind the boiler house. D'y fancy coming?"

"We're not allowed ashore, you know that."

"Allowed? Don't you ever do something unless you're allowed?"

"What you're suggesting means going AWOL – and that would be stupid."

"You're stupid. Who would know? Two or three hours; a couple of pints and we'd be back."

"Yeah, and what happens if the chief from hell lands us with a surprise – like the last letter night – he had us going over the obstacle course in the dark."

With a sigh of resignation Derek cuffed the youngster gently on the ear and returned to his bunk leaving Jamie to wonder if his newly found friend would really have jumped ship, a risk Jamie would never think of taking. The young Welshman, brought up in a tight, religious community, found no reason to do anything else but conform. Even so he readily embraced the swearing, smoking and prideful set his new life offered. As opposites attract, Jamie liked Derek and enjoyed the older man's talk of girls and of London and the world of Teddy boys and big bands and weekends in Southend. Untroubled in his upbringing by threats of violence or danger, Jamie listened

25

but only half believed some of Latch's tall stories of fights and gang clashes – until the evening when his new friend *Demon*strated his determined and fearless character.

Eddy Higgins, a classmate from the South Riding of Yorkshire, had great difficulty in maintaining personal cleanliness. Tall and gangly with a shock of dark, curly hair, he avoided showers and clothes washing despite direct orders from the instructor and progressively increasing pressure from his peers.

"A bath? Once a week, us," he would say when challenged, "and that was if we needed it or not. Wears thee out – all that scrubbing."

After four weeks his bar of yellow soap, issued at day one for washing clothes and bathing, had hardly been touched and his new toothbrush could look forward to a long and easy life. With canny Yorkshire guile he kept spare underwear folded and untouched for locker and kit inspections; the remaining set he wore constantly.

Mal Kelly, a loud self-important man, picked on him at every opportunity – wearing everyone down except Eddy.

One evening after a day of square bashing and violent exercise in the gymnasium the exhausted class members crashed out on their beds. Eddy disappeared to the heads – a cold echoing brick building containing washbasins, showers and toilet cubicles attached to the rear of the huts. Jamie, not quite comatose, noticed Kelly gathering three of his friends and following the Yorkshire man toward the toilets. The shiftiness and the lifting of a stiff broom from the cleaning cupboard on the way out worried Jamie. After a short while he quietly shook Derek.

"I think Kelly is up to something in the heads."

"Dirty bastard." Derek turned over and closed his eyes. "If he's not careful he'll go blind."

26

"No, you idiot – they're after Eddy – I think. They took the stiff broom."

"He deserves it. He's overdue a bath."

"The stiff broom, Latch. They'll kill him."

"Oh, you bloody do-gooder. Go and do some good then, leave me alone."

"There are four of them."

"For Christ's sake." Derek heaved himself up. "Come on."

Once inside the rear corridor the sound of high pitched cries of anger and hurt confirmed Jamie's fears. At the wide entrance to the heads one of Kelly's group stood guard. Beyond him they could see a naked Eddy being held by the other two assailants under the full-on spray from the showerhead in the far cubicle – and from the absence of steam, Jamie knew that the water would be cold. Struggling and sobbing, the young Yorkshireman pulled against his captors, doing his best to twist his body to protect his privates from the vicious needle sharp bristles of the broom. Mal Kelly, grinning from sheer enjoyment, pushed hard against his victim with the brush, vigorously scrubbing the white skin wherever the opportunity arose. The fourth tormentor, the largest of the group, spread his long arms across the entrance and glared. "Piss off, you two."

Derek beckoned to him and whispered something in his ear. As Derek talked, the guard's face changed from threatening to concern – then, without a glance behind, he left.

Entering the heads Derek shouted, "Kelly."

Kelly dropped the head of the broom to the deck and spun around.

In a voice just loud enough to be heard above the hiss of the shower, Derek continued. "There's three of us and three of you. I suggest you stop skylarking and leave before I stick the handle of that broom up your arse – sideways."

Lifting the broom to meet the challenge, Kelly pointed the bristles at Derek. "Piss off, Latchbrook. He needs a bath and he's getting one."

Maintaining eye contact with the now red-faced Kelly, Derek dropped to one knee and slowly removed a lace from his canvas shoe. Looping each end around his fingers he tested its strength between two hands.

"There's only one person here who knows what I can do with this," he said quietly, "and he is sworn to secrecy. Taffy, you know what I taught you. Get your garrotte."

Jamie, still dressed as were the others in PE gear, bent to undo the lace in his gym-shoe.

"You're fuckin' mad, you are." Kelly threw the broom to the bathroom floor. "Fuckin' mad."

Keeping Derek and Jamie to his front, Kelly sidled away. The two others released Eddy and quietly left also. Shivering uncontrollably, Eddy moved from the shower.

"I could have managed," said Eddy.

"Yeah, I could see you were getting the better of them," said Derek. Bending to retrieve a grey looking vest from the deck he handed it to Eddy. "And while you're here you may as well give these a scrub."

"Aye, may as well." Eddy gathered the rest of his sodden clothing and dolefully watched his rescuers leave.

"What did you say to the one on guard?" asked Jamie, as they followed the trail of wet footprints back to the hut.

"I told him to move his arse from there or I would tell the class that they were queers and that I'd found them together in the toilet."

For a reason only known to their Admiralty masters the itinerary for each new entry member included a climb up the high mast at HMS St Vincent. To anyone entering the main gates of the boy seaman's training base at Gosport, the dreaded

28

mast could not be missed. Dominating all, it towered impossibly high into the Hampshire sky. Standing square on the parade ground, the 120ft mast represented the ultimate challenge to each would-be sailor. With a week to go to the end of their initial training course, Jamie's class found themselves facing the dreaded obstacle.

"My Gawd," said Derek. Reluctantly he vacated the safety of the navy blue RN bus. The class, usually full of noise like a cage of parrots, became subdued as they surveyed the towering obstacle. Jamie, daring to look up to the tops, where the white masthead tapered to nothing, felt a trickle of fear that quickly turned into a flood, churning around his insides.

"I can't get up there," he said to no one in particular.

"You don't climb the mast; you don't finish the course," said the Chief Instructor with simple Chief Instructor rationale.

At the start of the climb the mast mainstays, spliced with crossed steel wires, provided good foothold. The keen and the agile members of the class raced up and through a gap in the safety net – a web of braided steel wire designed more to protect the parade ground from falling bodies than to save potential victims. With a dry mouth, Jamie forced his shaking limbs to move. He started upward.

"What ever you do, do not let go with more than one hand and do not look down," the Chief had said.

So far Jamie had managed the first but could not resist the second – his attention taken up by the instructor shouting into the ear of a sobbing classmate whose feet remained firmly planted on the ground. Jamie decided the mast was the less unpleasant option and continued the climb. Far too quickly Jamie, followed close behind by Derek, reached the halfway point – a circular wooden platform effectively barring further progress like a rat collar on a ship's hawser. Jamie desperately looked for a way through but, with a sinking feeling, he knew that to reach the upper mast he would have to climb out under

29

the platform and over its edge. Without hesitation Derek gripped the wire ladder and started out, clambering upside down, towards the edge, eight foot away. Jamie, alternately wiping his sweating palms on his trousers, followed until the full realisation of his precarious position hit him and he froze, hanging like a fly on a ceiling.

"Derek," called the terrified youngster. Frantically willing his brain to keep functioning he withstood the urge to look down. Derek, who had disappeared on to the top of the platform, reappeared.

"Go back, you silly sod."

"I can't."

"Well, come on then, you stupid idiot. Grab my hand."

"I can't, and don't call me stupid."

The insult freed Jamie's mind. Taking a deep breath, he gathered his reserves and moved. By concentrating intensely on the parts of the structure within inches of his face he blocked out the fear that threatened to rob his strength and deposit him onto the very unsafe safety net fifty feet below. Threading his arms alternately through the wire ladder, and with a steel grip support from Derek, Jamie managed to inch his way up and over the obstacle. With a head made light with relief, he slumped against the upper mast.

For a moment he couldn't speak but eventually he gathered himself and looked up to thank his friend but Derek was already on his way up to the mast head.

Each step of the climb down brought elation to Jamie's heart – he had achieved the impossible – but his sobbing classmate still stood on the ground, both hands firmly gripping a wire stay. Surprisingly the chief had stopped shouting and was comforting the lad. The next morning the recruit remained in the accommodation hut while the others mustered outside. When the class returned to the hut later that day the failure's locker had been emptied and no one spoke of him again.

At the end of the following week the class passed out with a full parade, guard and band. Being at attention for a long period on a warm day the rating immediately behind Jamie collapsed in a heap, his rifle clattering onto the tarmac. Jamie instinctively bent to help.

Chief Super-ears screamed, "Leave 'im."

Derek said, "Inhuman bastard," out of the left side of his mouth.

Jamie said, "Inhuman bastard," out of the right side of his mouth.

Long after the parade had cleared, the two were again measuring the circumference of the largest parade ground in the Navy – at the double.

CHAPTER 3

HMS PEMBROKE

Jamie dragged his gear into the canteen of the Union Jack Club in the heart of London. By some accident of fate or by design, Derek Latchbrook and Jamie Davis found themselves drafted together to continue training at the Electrical School at HMS Pembroke, Chatham. The pair, pleased to know that they would be together for the next six months, had arrived at Waterloo Station late on a warm autumn Saturday afternoon. Jamie had to continue the second leg of the journey alone – Latch had permission to visit home and report to the Naval Base the next Monday – leaving Jamie alone to wait until the next day's connection to Chatham. At the wide entrance to Waterloo Station Derek said goodbye and pointed the young Welshman in the direction of the UJC before disappearing underground to ride the tube to Harrow. Weighed down with a full kitbag, a rolled up hammock and a gas mask, Jamie had decided it would be easier to wear his heavy greatcoat than to carry it. By the time he reached the imposing grey stone building he was hot and very tired.

The canteen, a large cream-coloured room with a high ceiling and cold tiled floor, echoed with the noise of clattering dishes and conversation from the servicemen occupying the many tables scattered about the room. Jamie found a space on a bench against a wall and dumped his gear. From the pocket of his greatcoat he pulled out the remains of a squashed bag meal given to him before leaving Collingwood. Sorting out some pennies he bought a steaming mug of tea from a woman in a wrap around pinafore and settled to wait out the night.

Time passed very slowly but he rejected the idea of taking a walk. Leaving the club meant asking someone to watch his gear and anyway, London was a large place to get lost in, as his view from the train earlier had confirmed. From the carriage he'd looked out at miles of grimy factories, tenement blocks and streets of dirty houses joined together and cut through by the blackened railway – this was not the capital he knew from books – so he stayed put, loosened the laces of his boots and amused himself by counting the variations in the servicemen that came and went.

"Hiya, Jack." A soldier stood in front of Jamie with a suitcase in one hand and a cup of tea in the other. With a tired sigh the man in a khaki uniform slipped his gas mask from around his shoulders and threw the pack under the bench. "Bloody nuisance, these things." His accent identified him immediately as North Country.

Jamie mumbled a defensive hello, unsure of what to say to this older man with a stripe on his sleeve.

"Room for one more?" Without waiting for an answer the soldier sat himself down. "I've been on leave and missed my connection. I'll catch the one in the morning."

"Won't you be adrift?" enquired Jamie. The fear of the consequences for anyone being late had been well installed into the young recruit from his first day.

"No. I'm going back early anyway. I ran out of dosh – too much beer and not enough women – how about you?"

"I'm on my way to Chatham but I can't get a train until tomorrow," said Jamie. He added, "bastards," without really knowing who he was blaming.

"Right then, Jack, call me Corp – cards it is." Without waiting for a reply, the lance corporal produced a pack of playing cards from his suitcase.

"I've no money for cards," said Jamie.

"Matchsticks is all I've got too, lad, so stop worrying. Ten matches – one ciggy, okay?"

As they played Jamie warmed to the North-Countryman and chatted freely.

"My Dad was a soldier," said Jamie.

"During the war?"

"How did you guess?"

Corp looked over the spread of cards in his hand, "You're what – seventeen?"

Jamie nodded, "Nearly."

"That puts him a young man at the start of the war – and besides, you told me your dad was a soldier. So why the Navy?"

"My father has four brothers; three of them were pong… sorry, I mean soldiers. My Uncle Delwyn was in the Navy. The others used to gang up on him so I took his side. I think he liked me for that. He used to tell me stories. I liked the sound of it – much to my Mam's disgust."

"Quite right." Laying down another winning hand on the bench between them the Corporal claimed more of Jamie's matches. "So you joined despite her?"

"She died," said Jamie.

"I'm sorry," said Corp.

"They took her to Ponty – that's Pontypridd Hospital – for an operation – opened her up but it was too late – so they said."

"Cancer?"

Jamie nodded and looked into the angular face of his companion, realising that this was the first time since that awful time a short four months ago that he had talked to anyone about the death of his mother. Somehow it was easier with a total stranger.

"It was so… unexpected. One minute she was there – as always – fussing around Dad and me and my sister – then she was gone. My father was the ill one. He spent most of the war

34

in a prisoner-of-war camp, on the Polish border, mining coal for the Germans."

"Bastards." Corp laid down his cards. "How did he get captured?"

"D'y know – I'm not sure. He's not one for telling us anything. I think he got himself separated at Dunkirk. He mentioned Arras, but I…"

"What was his outfit – Welsh Guards?"

"How did you know?"

"Elementary, my dear Watson. You're a Taffy, and your Dad's regiment fought at Arras. May, 1940 – just before the Dunkirk evacuations. You must get him to talk, you know. It would do him good."

"I know that he was taken back through Germany to Poland," said Jamie, defensively. "Marched most of the way."

"So what happened?"

"The work he did – down the mines – the dust knackered his lungs."

"Bloody Krauts."

"He tried to work when he got home; took a job back in the pits, but not for long. He got so that any effort made him breathless. He spends his days sitting in his chair by the fire. He cuts up newspapers into squares…" Jamie laughed but he felt like crying, "…for the toilet – and spills to light his pipe. I love the old chap, but I couldn't stay anymore." Jamie's face reddened; the words sounded wrong. "He has my sister," he added hastily.

Late into the night they gave up the cards and slept on and off, propped against their kit, until the sounds of Sunday morning awoke them.

Jamie made his way by an almost deserted tube to London Bridge where he eventually boarded a train to Chatham. A much diminished Sunday service meant a wait until mid-afternoon for a rickety old puffer, pulling a cold non-corridor train that stopped at all stations on the Medway route. He arrived at 1730 to find a 'Royal Navy' truck waiting at the station. The civilian driver, in no hurry to leave with only one passenger, waited a fruitless hour. Eventually, with a huge sigh of resignation, he started the engine and moved off.

The main gates of HMS Pembroke appeared at the end of a long high-walled road that continued on to Chatham Naval Dockyard. The naval base gates, two imposing ironwork barriers set into the wall, blocked the inward and outward sides of the road. Through the gates Jamie saw, for the first time, a Dickensian scene of huge, red-brick buildings that flanked the right hand side of the road. The driver directed Jamie through the smaller pedestrian gateway to the door to the Guard House on the left. Jamie gathered his kitbag and hammock from the back of the truck and dumped them outside the green painted door and entered.

Behind a high counter, a leading hand sat polishing the brass buckles of his white belt. At the back of the room, a petty officer stood at a filing cabinet. He raised his eyes from some papers, glanced at Jamie and returned to his files.

"J.E.M.2. Davis reporting, Leading Hand."

"Leading Regulator," sighed the killick. "Give us yer papers."

For what seemed an uncomfortably long time to the tired Jamie the guard wrote laboriously on some forms then looked up and handed over a card.

"This is your temporary station card. You'll be back to see us tomorrow on your joining routine."

Looking at the clock behind his head he said, "Have you eat'n boy?"

Jamie shook his head.

The PO snorted and boomed. "Speak up lad. You were asked 'have you eaten?' Now stand up straight and answer the Leading Regulator."

"No, Leading Regulator, I haven't eaten."

Then, like a machine gun firing, the killick rattled off a burst of instructions. "Right, leave your gear here; go to the second block on the right; get your tea if you're lucky. Come back here pick up your things and go to the transit block, third building on the right, up the stairs to the first floor and sling your hammock there. Breakfast is at 0700. Be back here at 0800. Dress No.2s and gas mask. Off you go."

In the dying light of a dreary September evening Jamie trudged up the main road of HMS Pembroke. Preoccupied with finding the galley he took little notice of the imposing architecture of the place. Unlike Collingwood, with its wide open spaces and low utility buildings, this historic establishment crowded in an array of aged structures. Edging the left hand pavement of the main road a low wall afforded protection from a deep twenty foot drop to a wide space of a parade ground. Jamie would get to know that parade ground and the motley buildings that flanked the perimeter on the opposite side. To his right, he passed a succession of large red brick accommodation blocks to find the galley building. Dragging his feet, he climbed a flight of granite steps to a huge hall – a high-ceilinged room filled with rows of tables, but empty of people – except for two white-clad chefs cleaning up behind the serving counters. With a sigh, but not a word, a tired-looking cook chose some edible bits of cold meat, placed them on a large white plate and handed it to Jamie. At the end of the servery he picked through the remains of a stack of sliced bread, some dry and curling at the edges, and spread margarine on two pieces. At a large urn he filled a mug with luke-warm tea and sat at one of the long tables in the empty hall to eat. Placing the meat between the slices of bread he took a bite and felt revulsion.

The hole in his stomach could not be filled with food. The ache he felt inside cramped his belly and parched his mouth, turning the dry bread to cardboard. For the first time in his young life he felt the effects of homesickness. He managed a mouthful of tea, cold and gritty, then he left to pick up his kit.

When he reached the transit mess he found the huge room empty – empty of anything. No lockers or beds; no curtains at the high windows – and no people. An expanse of brown, highly polished lino covered the floor. Iron hooks and bars hung in orderly rows from the ceiling; supporting pillars stood like sentinels on guard; the only sound, his own sound, echoed around the walls to remind him that he was alone.

Jamie unrolled his hammock. Separating the ropes and stretchers, he forced his tired brain to remember the knots and rigging. The new canvas and cords, stiff and unfamiliar, hurt his fingers. Fighting frustration he eventually managed to prepare and suspend his canvas bed – the musty smell of hemp catching the back of his throat. Wearily he undressed; glad at least to be out of the boots he had worn for more than two days. Carefully, he folded each item of his uniform and placed them on the cold, shining floor. Knowing he should wear his striped pyjamas he could not bring himself to unpack his kit bag. In vest and pants he walked, shivering, to the echoing heads. On his way back he switched off the lights and hauled himself into the hammock.

Listening to the silence, he fought the waves of self-pity invading his mind, each surge bringing tears to his eyes until they spilled over and he cried himself to sleep.

Jamie took flight that night.

"This cannot be – I am looking down. I can see my house and the chapel and Reverend Tucker. Look there's the quarry. I can dive down, skim the water – watch out for the stones – now I soar up; loop the loop. There's Bobby Hailstones, he can't catch me; can't tell my Mam for throwing stones at the allotment. There's the tip, Trebarry tip as black as Dad. There's Mam in the garden. No, she's in the house, on the bed. Her face is so white. I'm not flying anymore. I'm looking at her face and holding her hand. Her hair is black and grey and wavy. She's cold but she's flying with me now. Look, Mam, there's my school and me in the playground playing hopscotch. There's a girl. There's my sister. Where's my Mam, Gwyn? She's not flying anymore. She's there in her Sunday best. She can't fly anymore, but I can fly. I can fly alright. I can fly, up and up..."

Jamie awoke to the sound of a bugle blasting from a loudspeaker on the wall. Sunlight streamed through the windows catching cigarette smoke curling up from below. Jamie rubbed his eyes and looked around at a deck strewn with kit.

"Come on Jimmy, boyo."

Jamie recognised the balding head of Jock Dunlop – a married National Serviceman from Jamie's class at Collingwood.

"Where did you come from?"

"I spent the weekend with the wife. Just arrived..."

"Hands off cocks, you dirty little devil."

Derek Latchbrook, with a very welcome and familiar grin, gripped the side of Jamie's hammock, tipping the youngster to the deck. Somehow the brown lino seemed warmer this morning.

Jamie ate breakfast with a much-improved appetite. Afterwards he accompanied Jock and Latch on a tedious joining routine, registering with each department around the naval base.

In the sickbay an SBA in pristine white jacket with a watch pinned to the lapel told them to undress down to vest and socks. After weighing and measuring, he tested each man for a pulse. The SBA seemed to enjoy his job.

"De ye ken," whispered Jock in Jamie's ear, "yon tiffy. If he asks ye to turn your head and cough, it's yer knob he'll be after."

Feeling very vulnerable, Jamie watched and felt an overwhelming relief when the SBA knocked on an office door. An officer in rolled up shirtsleeves emerged, looked up and down the queue and sighed. Deftly, he engaged a stethoscope with his ears and waited. Jamie, first in line, stood ramrod straight in front of the doc.

"Open wide."

Shoulder epaulettes – double gold bars separated by red – identified the weary looking officer as a Surgeon Lieutenant.

"Good; say 'ahh' – good. Breathe deeply; hold it."

Jamie waited as the examination moved down his body.

"Look to your left and cough."

As the cold fingers touched his testicles, Jamie pulled back, covering his bits with both hands.

"Good God, man. Do you have a problem?" exclaimed the doc.

"No, Sir."

"Good," continued the officer, "then please be assured that I am not going to damage what little bit of tackle you possess so look left and cough. I would not welcome your germs in my face, now would I, lad?"

"No, Sir."

Jamie turned his reddening face left – coughed and moved on. Derek, next in line, whispered something to the lieutenant who called the SBA who pulled Jock out of the line and led him into an examination room. Looking worried and tugging his vest down as far as he could the Scot looked back at his colleagues until the door closed.

"What did you say in there?" asked Jamie to the chuckling Derek as they dressed.

"I just said that my friend was worried about a discharge and that he was too shy to mention that he experienced pain when passing water."

A very irate and highly suspicious Scotsman emerged later from the sickbay to join the others. "Bloody SBA; inspecting my tackle. I'm a married man, I am. Askin' me if I'd been with a pro – bloody cheek."

For the rest of the day the group plodded around the remaining offices becoming members of HMS Pembroke. Together they joined the class to go through the next six months training at the electrical school, a spillover from the overstretched facility at Collingwood.

A cold wind blew in from the North Sea across the flat east England landscape and up the Medway early that year. The long, hard winter, dark evenings and lack of money, kept Jamie in barracks. Being a junior he was also restricted to a 9pm curfew and chose not to join Latch who often went ashore for a drink. Instead, he took advantage of the entertainments put on to occupy the troops on board. This is where the two friends first encountered Miss Eleanor Henderson.

Jock Dunlop hailed from Thurso, which, as he never failed to mention, is almost as far north as you can go without falling into Scapa Flow. The newly married Scot filled most of his evenings writing letters to his wife.

One Wednesday evening in November Jock surprised his messmates. Instead of writing, the Scot washed, shaved and made ready to go out.

"Ay, Ay Jock." Derek watched the preparations with interest. "And where are we off to then?"

"Scottish dancing."

"Scottish dancing?" Jamie, lying on his bunk digesting his supper, sat up. "Any girls…?"

"Och, Aye, ye cannie dance wi'out girls," interrupted the Scot. "But it's not the girls – it's the music. They've got Jimmie Shand records an' all."

"Can we come?" Derek swung his legs over the edge of his bunk. "Where is it?"

"It's on the base – away up at the Church of Scotland Hall – but you two sassenachs wouldna' be interested…"

"No doubt it's free?" Latch winked at Jamie.

With a snort of derision, Jock left followed by the two friends.

Scottish dancing, new in Jamie's experience, proved to be less interesting than he first imagined. Finding a space at the back of the featureless wooden hut that belonged to the base Church, he and Derek watched the antics of the dancers. Dunlop loved it, dancing and whooping like a banshee, inspired by the accordion music played as loud as the record player would allow. With unbridled enthusiasm and despite the handicap of bell-bottoms and boots, the Scot repeatedly attempted the intricate steps needed to avoid the crossed sword blades of the sword dance. More often than not, the attempts deposited Jock onto his backside.

Very quickly Jamie decided that the 'girls' could not be the attraction he had imagined. Apart from a few Scottish WRNS, eager for the taste of 'home', the 'girls' turned out to be well-meaning officers wives doing their bit for camp morale. That was until a young girl, almost unnoticed by the cavorting dancers, slipped into the room. Avoiding the flailing arms and kicking legs the girl made her way to the back of the room and leaned against the wall, some feet away from the two friends. Derek nudged Jamie's arm, but Jamie had already found himself unable to look anywhere but at the newcomer. From his position behind Derek, Jamie watched the girl with great interest.

About 17, he thought, and lovely. Delicate high-heeled shoes lifted her to the same height as Derek. Her light-coloured hair had been tied back in a ponytail, exposing the delicious curve of her neck and some wispy strands in the nape. Dressed in a simple floral dress, and self-consciously holding a cardigan closed about her slim figure, the girl looked about her. The move allowed Jamie to see her full face; a face without, and not needing, make-up to mar her perfect skin; a face that glowed with natural health. For a few seconds Jamie met her eyes – eyes of deepest blue that transfixed him; held him motionless, then they were gone – gone to Derek, who had moved towards her.

At the end of the evening Jamie waited while Derek said goodnight to the girl. For a while, on the walk back to the mess, the two remained silent – until Jamie could hold himself no longer.

"You dirty, lucky bastard. Who was that?"

"Who do you mean?" said Derek.

"The girl, you so and so. You know…"

"Nelly, do you mean?" A self-satisfied smile spread across Derek's face. "Miss Eleanor Henderson. Her father is no less than Lieutenant Commander JG Henderson, the Base Entertainments Officer."

"Well, that puts her out of our reach – an officer's daughter."

"Don't you believe it, mate. She's already told me that she'd decided to stop going to the dances – her father had asked her to go but she didn't like it – until now."

"So you're going again?"

"'Course I am – and so are you."

Out of loyalty to Derek, Jamie continued with the Scottish Dancing evenings, taking up his usual position at the rear of the spartan church-hall while Derek danced and chatted to the girl. To Jamie, the most striking feature of the young girl was her eyes – not only were they blue and beautiful but the way she used them amazed him. From a direct, unblinking invitation to a withering dismissal, she could instinctively manipulate those around her with her eyes. Jamie fell under her spell too – but, with a realistic appreciation of their respective positions in the tight military hierarchy, he kept himself out of her way.

On the other hand Latch seemed oblivious of the station the officer's daughter held. He chatted and laughed with her in the same confident manner that he had used with girls at the fairground in Southsea. She responded with a look and a touch on the arm – her happiness obvious to all as she guided Derek through the intricate steps of Highland traditional dance.

After a few weeks Jamie decided that he could no longer stomach Scottish dancing – uneasy with his feelings about the girl and finding that the stomping and howling females were either too old for him or unavailable like Eleanor. The girl created mixed emotions in the young man. On the one hand he loved her shape and sound and movement, images he took back to his bed at night to relive and to feed his imagination. Without fully understanding, he realised that somewhere inside him was a building resentment; a dislike for the girl generated by her privilege and by the ease with which she commanded the attention of his friend.

Concerned that Latch's usual disregard for the rights and wrongs of life would lead the reckless Londoner into trouble, Jamie looked for the opportunity to speak up. A Saturday kick about on the camp's frozen football pitch resulted in a hurt knee for Derek. Returning from sickbay, Latch lay on his bunk staring into space, his knee propped up by a pillow. Jamie took his chance.

"How's the knee?" Jamie sat on Latch's bunk and passed him a cigarette. "I don't suppose you'll be going to Scottish dancing next week."

"Piss off, 'course I am." Latch winced from pain as he reached under his pillow for his lighter.

"You won't be dancing with that leg..." started Jamie but Latch interrupted sharply,

"You don't think I go for the bloody dancing, do you?"

Jamie fell silent for a moment. He knew very well what Latch meant. No one in the mess mentioned or teased Derek about Nelly but something inside Jamie needed to come out.

"That's an officer's daughter you're messing with."

"So what?" Derek's lips stiffened and his cheeks reddened. "That doesn't make her any different; or any better. We like each other, that's all – so keep your nose out."

The finality in Latch's voice stopped Jamie for a moment but he was not about to give up on the subject. Anger and frustration with his friend's stubbornness welled up until he could no longer hold back. "You stupid prick," said Jamie. "Don't you know what they'll do to you if you're caught?"

"Look," Latch leaned forward to emphasise his words, "as if it's any of your business – which it ain't – we're having a bit of fun and we don't intend to get caught..."

"The lad's right, you know, Latch." Jock stopped writing. "Pigs don't stand for the likes of us muscling in on their women – and you will get caught."

"Good God," exclaimed Derek. "Is everybody sticking their oar in?"

"And I thought you were smart." Jamie stood and faced Latch. "Don't you see, Derek? Jock's right. They'll crucify you, mate."

Struggling with the pain in his knee, Latch pushed Jamie away and stood up.

"What is it with you, Davis? Jealous?"

"I'm only thinking of you."

"Well, think of yourself, Mate, and mind your own business – and that goes for the lot of you."

Turning his back, Latch hobbled off towards the heads.

"Stupid bastard," said Jamie, under his breath, secure in the knowledge that he could outstrip Latch with his hurt knee.

"I heard that, you little Welsh plonker."

CHAPTER 4

THEATRE

During November Jamie spotted a note on the school notice board. The base theatre wanted an electrician to help with stage lighting. Seeing a way of avoiding Scottish evenings, Jamie applied and on the next Saturday morning he was shown the backstage workings of the theatre and accepted for the job.

Jamie enjoyed the theatre. He volunteered for the job of spotlight operator and spent each show in a cage high against the auditorium ceiling. From his vantage point he thrilled to the weekly variety shows put on for the ship's company.

Time passed quickly. Jamie saw little of Derek outside of school but Jamie knew from the whispers and undertone rumours circulating the place that Derek met with Nelly Henderson at every opportunity. In early December the theatre's autumn programme ended to make way for the Christmas pantomime. Amateur volunteers from the barracks made up the cast. The orchestra, members of the Royal Marine band, soon filled the hall with brassy sound. Derek showed an uncharacteristic interest in the panto: an interest that puzzled Jamie until the evening of the first gathering. Called together for a pep-talk from the entertainments officer, the theatre group filled the stage. Most of the speech went over Jamie's head until a familiar name took his full attention, "... and your director has asked my daughter, Eleanor, to take the role of Prince Charming."

The Lt Cdr reached into the crowd behind him and a shy Nelly Henderson stepped forward. Jamie hadn't noticed her before but instinctively he moved his eyes across the group –

sure enough he spotted Derek, perched on a dais at the rear of the stage.

"...and I am sure you will give her all the help she will need and I am also sure that this year's pantomime – Cinderella – will be as good as ever."

The group politely clapped; the most enthusiastic being Derek, whose eyes never left the demure figure of the Lt Cdr's daughter.

Jamie studied Nelly's father. Tall, thin and with the gaunt look of a man used to suffering, the officer stood back to allow the cast to congratulate his daughter. As he moved, Jamie noticed with fascination that the Lt Cdr limped quite badly; the left leg beneath the smart navy trousers appeared bowed and obviously malformed.

"Good stuff, this theatre lark, Jimmy boyo." Latch had caught up with Jamie on the short walk back to the mess.

"What happened to the Scottish dancing?"

Derek ignored the question. "I tried for a singing job but the old voice box ain't up to it – they've given me a job shifting props."

As usual, Jamie realised that Derek had no intention of being drawn into a conversation that could lead to discussions about Nelly.

Jamie tried another tack. "What's up with Henderson's leg?"

"Tut, tut," said Derek. "Lieutenant Commander Henderson, please – or Hoppalong to his friends – dunno. Some kind of war wound."

"How can he do his job with a leg like that?"

"They keep him behind a desk – so I believe – but how would I know?" Latch finished the conversation by bounding across the parade ground and up the steps towards the accommodation block. As Jamie watched him go he recalled the entertainments officer's face and couldn't help but wonder if his pal realised the risk he was taking.

Nobody could mistake the obvious pride that Lt Cdr Henderson felt for his daughter; or that he would have disapproved profoundly of the association she had struck up with a brash and common sailor. Shaking his head, Jamie dismissed the thoughts and followed his friend back to the mess and turned in.

The rehearsals and the panto proper, being full of lighting effects, proved a busy time for Jamie. Nelly took to the role of Prince Charming with enthusiasm: charming everyone with her full, naturally low-key voice. Wearing impossibly high-heeled shoes, her legs seemed to go on forever; legs that were very much responsible for the hoots and whistles from the full theatre each night. Despite Derek's involvement in the panto, Jamie saw very little of his friend and almost without exception Latch and Nelly had left the theatre before Jamie had finished securing his lights. Often the exhausted youngster was asleep before Latch returned to the mess.

Christmas came with a rush and closed the school for Christmas leave; it also ended the panto but not before the theatre group gathered on the stage to celebrate the end of the last show. While Jamie sipped a beer from a plastic cup he was surprised to find Nelly at his side.

"Well," said Nelly. Heavy stage make-up exaggerated the ever-present twinkle in her eye. "Mr Spotlight. I've never seen you down here amongst us mortals."

Jamie, feeling a rush of embarrassment, looked around the chatting company. He spotted Derek sharing a joke with other members of the cast.

"No. I, er, I'm usually up there. I see you, though. You were very good…"

"Praise, indeed," Nelly deliberately moved to block Derek from Jamie's line of sight, "from someone who doesn't like me."

Still made up for her role and dressed in the costume of her panto character the girl commanded the full attention of all of Jamie's senses. It took a few long seconds for the comment to sink in.

"Like you? I like you." Jamie dragged his mind from the spectacular form in front of him to the need to answer a statement he barely understood.

With hand on hip Nelly tossed her head and stole a glance back to Derek. "Then why do you look at me the way you do?"

"Look?" said Jamie.

"I know a disapproving look when I see one, James. You are Derek's best friend, yes?"

"I like to think so."

"Then good friends shouldn't judge."

Jamie, taken aback by the unexpected truth in Nelly's words, searched for a response. Aching to spell out his fears, Jamie struggled for a reply but before he could find something to say she had turned on her heel and left.

Christmas leave meant travelling to Wales to be with his dad and sister but the holiday was not the happy time he remembered from the past. The change in his father stunned Jamie. From the day he returned from the war Maldwyn had appeared thin and drawn – but the change since Jamie had last seen his father shocked his son. Hunched in his chair beside the fire, Maldwyn stared out from sunken eyes. The flesh on his face had receded leaving the bones protruding; his skin, almost yellow in colour, stretched like parchment over his skull. Maldwyn tried his best to join in the celebrations, particularly on New Year's Eve. He sent Jamie out to buy in some beer, but his father's tortuous fighting for breath, alleviated only by a mask connected to an oxygen bottle, prevented any celebration. Gwyneth had given up her job to look after their father and Jamie felt a deep unease that his sister shouldered the burden alone. He offered to leave the Navy but she would hear nothing of that sort of talk. Nevertheless, he could not rid himself of the feeling of guilt, so he did all he could to help out until the end of leave. Each morning he awoke to the familiar surroundings of his small bedroom, waiting for the call to breakfast from his mother – a call that he quickly realised would not come. Each day he longed to return to Pembroke – despite the hardship of life in the cold Dickensian buildings – for that was where his friends were.

A week or two after Christmas leave had ended Derek Latchbrook's bravado brought the Londoner to the attention Nelly's father. From the first day of joining up, Jamie, in common with his classmates, had been marched everywhere. The soles of Jamie's boots – both pairs – had worn down to a thin sliver of leather. Severely cold weather across the east coast of England marked the opening of 1955. Often Jamie awoke to find that snow had fallen overnight; snow that had to be cleared from the small parade ground beside the school – an activity that resulted in wet feet and discomfort for Jamie during the remainder of the day. Therefore a chance to earn ten shillings spending a Saturday beating for the local shoot became a rare and attractive opportunity to earn some extra cash. Jamie put his name down, together with Jock Dunlop and Derek Latchbrook, the youngster determined to use the money to repair his boots.

On a bright and cold Saturday morning the volunteers collected oilskins and sea boots from the slop room and bag meals from the galley. They and other ratings from the base climbed into the back of a canvas-covered lorry and settled themselves for the trip into the country.

'Snodland' the notice had said.

"It's a little place about five miles from here," declared Jock, who had asked a local.

Chilled by the cold and numb from the hard ride over country roads, the beating party disembarked into a leafless tree-lined lane. Raucous calls of disturbed rooks reverberated in the morning air. Further down the lane a group of shooters had gathered at the tailboard of a muddied Land Rover. Their leader, gun broken and crooked on his arm, beckoned the beaters forward and shouted out instructions. Latch elbowed Jamie and nodded towards the group of six or seven men fiddling with their shotguns and marshalling their dogs. Lt Cdr Henderson, tall and looking completely at ease in his country clothes, stood quietly watching the motley crew of beaters.

"If I'd known Hoppalong was here," whispered Derek from the side of his mouth, "I'd have stayed on board."

Positioning himself beside the taller Jamie, Derek pulled his oilskin collar as high as it would go.

"What's the problem?" asked Jamie.

"No problem," hissed Derek. "I don't want the old man to see me, that's all."

At that moment one of the shooting-party swung open a wooden field-gate and ushered the beaters through, handing out a variety of noise making tin cans and spoons. Deep mud around the gateway area pulled and sucked at the boots of the struggling beaters as they moved into the field and spread out facing a sea of tall green kale. Jamie, preoccupied with remaining on his feet, lost sight of Derek and found himself next to Jock Dunlop.

At a signal from the organiser the beaters, ten feet apart in a line, moved forward into the kale, shouting and clanging; scaring up game for the shooters. As they plodded through the muddy fields the curly cabbage leaves showered the men with stored rainwater, soaking their trousers and filling their sea boots. Despite the echoing cacophony of noise produced by the beaters very few birds took flight. Occasionally a flapping pheasant attracted calls of 'your bird' and the double crack of shot reverberated in the clear air.

At the end of the morning the call to halt came down the line. Relieved, Jamie joined Jock and the pair squelched wearily back to the rendezvous where they retrieved their bag meals from the lorry. Gratefully they sipped from mugs of steaming hot tea dispensed by a well-covered woman from an urn set up at the side of the road.

"If this is a sample of your countryside give me the Highlands anytime," complained Jock. He settled with Jamie into the relative cover of the rear of the lorry.

Cold and wet, the exhausted beaters ate their food and downed the steaming tea. The shooters, voluble and loud, stood around the tail of the Land Rover pouring amber liquid from silver flasks into their mugs.

"Have you seen Latch, Jock?" asked Jamie.

"Nope. He was with you."

Taking his time, Jamie carefully perused the gathering – confirming to himself that Derek was nowhere to be seen.

"How far is it back to barracks?"

"Dunno, son, a good five miles by my reckoning – why?"

"Well, either Latch has gone walkabout, or he's halfway back to his bed. Either way he's missing."

Sat on the tailboard of the lorry Jock rolled a tickler, licked the gummed paper and lit the cigarette – all the while scanning each group of beaters. Nodding his head he said, "I agree, Jamie. Nineteen – I make nineteen. There was twenty of us to start."

Jumping down from the lorry, Jamie circulated the men.

"Ain't seen him," replied someone.

"His bag meal is still up front," said Jamie returning to Jock. Scrambling into the vehicle he retrieved the brown paper bag from the transport's bench seat and opened it to find its contents untouched.

"What do we do, Jock?"

"Dinna ask me." The Scot stood on the tailboard to get a better view of the lane.

"You're senior," said Jamie.

"He's your mate," said Jock. "Tell Henderson."

"I can't do that."

"Don't be stupid. He could be out there somewhere – lost."

"But Henderson? Latch wanted to avoid old Hoppalong. I'll probably drop him in it."

"Report him missing, Jimmie. If you're any kind of mate you can't take the risk. That stupid townie could be caught in a bog or an animal trap…"

"Okay, okay." Jamie made his way reluctantly towards the shooters.

As Jamie reported the missing Latchbrook he watched the tall officer's face but saw no adverse reaction to the name. Very quickly and with much shouting Lt Cdr Henderson organised the men into a search party. Retracing the route of the beat, the gullies, copses and fields resounded with Latchbrook's name. This time pheasants took flight all over the place, eliciting a heartfelt, and very un-officer like, "Fuck!" from the gunless Hoppalong who had joined the line.

"Do you think he's been shot, Jock?" asked a worried Jamie.

"Nae, mon. He would have shouted 'ouch' or something. Did anybody hear an 'ouch'?" called Jock to those within earshot along the line.

"There ye are see," responded Jock to the 'no's' he received back.

Privately Jock thought that Derek could well have been shot but he didn't wish to worry the youngster.

By mid-afternoon clouds gathered, fading the light and tentatively releasing sleety rain onto the miserable beaters. Hoppalong called off the search. The shooter in charge handed out the ten bob notes before the subdued group of forlorn beaters, wet, cold and hungry, climbed into the transport for the trip back to barracks. Jock took charge of Derek's money, just in case he hadn't been shot or lost down a bottomless slurry pit. The journey back lacked the banter that usually occurred between the men on similar trips – each man depressingly quiet and lost in his own thoughts.

"What do you think they'll do, Jock?" asked Jamie as they washed and dried off in the heads.

"Can't do much tonight, Jimmy. They'll probably ship us out there tomorrow to search again."

"Poor bastard."

"Aye," sighed Jock. "I fear he may not survive. Poor bastard a'right."

Later that evening, while the lads lay on their beds recovering from supper, Derek ambled in still clutching his oilskin and boots. Without a word and humming a little tune he started changing his dry and un-muddied clothes. Jock stepped down from his bunk, the colour in his normally white face turning pink; his breathing noticeably quickening through flared nostrils.

"Well, there ye are then, lad," welcomed Jock.

"Hiya, Jock."

"Did ye have yersell a nice day?"

"Triffic!" Latch beamed as he removed his No.8 shirt, apparently insensitive to the heavy sarcasm in Jock's voice. "I didn't fancy the beat so I walked down the lane. A farm lady took me in and give me dinner... and tea."

"Och, dinner *and* tea was it?" The skin on Jock's face tightened and mottled with anger.

"Yeah, and she had a lovely log fire going and... she brought me back... and..."

"You, you... sassenach!" With a shriek Jock bounded forward grabbing Latch's vest with his left hand. "D'y no ken what trouble we went through to look for you? You're supposed to be missing or shot and all the time ye're being fed and kept warm by a, a... farrum lady."

With his usual disarming laugh, Derek managed to keep Jock at arm's length – until he suddenly realised that the stocky Scot was serious. A vicious right fist caught Latch behind the ear as he struggled to pull away. Stumbling, he lost his balance and landed on the deck with Jock sitting on his chest. Latch held his arms up as the Scot squared up to hit him again. Jamie and Tommo reached the Scotsman before the blow landed and dragged him away. They couldn't stop him though when Latch raised himself from the floor and declared, "Sorreee. Um, did anybody think to bring my bag meal back?"

Later that evening Jamie accompanied Derek to the NAAFI canteen.

On their way across the parade ground Derek ruefully rubbed his bruised cheek. "That bloody Scotsman – he's mad. They're all mad – those Jocks."

"What did you expect? We spent all afternoon looking for you – and we didn't even get to finish the only hot cuppa we'd had all day to do it. And all the while you were being entertained by a..."

"Entertained, nothing," interrupted Latch. "I was entertaining myself – in a bloody barn."

"But you said..."

"I know what I said. I couldn't let on to that lot that I was hiding away from old Hoppalong – now, could I? Have you got your ten bob?"

Instinctively, Jamie patted the outside of his blue serge jerkin and felt the reassuring outline of his pay-book wallet that held securely the ten shilling note he had worked so hard to earn.

"Good." Latch pushed open the large wooden doors of the arched entrance to the canteen. "You'll have to lend it to me."

"Get lost," said Jamie, "I had to..."

"Look, Jamie." Leading Jamie to a table in a corner of the almost empty canteen Latch turned to face his friend. "It's pay-day next Friday. I haven't eaten all day – I'm hungry; thirsty; and I have to report to the Guard-House tomorrow morning. Cough up the ten bob for me to get something to eat and I'll forget that you shopped me to old Hoppalong."

"How do you know...?"

"Never mind how. I'll be stuck inside this prison for at least fourteen days for this – so cough up and I'll buy you a sticky bun."

With a sigh of resignation Jamie handed over the note. He lit up a cigarette and watched as Derek headed for the canteen servery. Wriggling his cold toes inside his damp boots he mourned for the new soles that had almost been his – repairs would have to wait another week.

The following Monday morning Derek received fourteen days number 11's punishment, which confined him to barracks and committed him to a variety of onerous chores every evening for two weeks. More worrying to Latch, his name and face had been identified by the officer bringing the charge – Lt Cdr Henderson – the very thing he had wanted to avoid all along.

Jamie saw nothing of Nelly after the panto and very little of Derek outside of the classroom. He knew that Derek met the girl often but Jamie had learned that any mention of the girl's name or any reference to the relationship would be met with a stony silence.

The course at HMS Pembroke finished in February. With a week to go the class gathered around the school notice board to read the list of drafts.

"There is a God," said Derek with glee. "Reserve Fleet, Chatham..."

Jamie traced his finger down the list. "They're sending me to HMS Drake – where's that?"

"Guss," said Jock. "That's the naval base down in Devonport."

"That's a good draft for you," said Derek as the pair walked away.

Jamie glanced at Derek. Unable to control a feeling of loss, he realised that his friendship with this rascal of a man was about to end – and that at this moment Derek's broad smile showed that he was happy not be leaving Pembroke – and Jamie knew why.

"Cheer up, mate," continued Derek. "You'll be much nearer home."

"I suppose so." Visions of his sick dad added guilt to his gloominess.

"Do you know we haven't had a run ashore since we got here," said Latch. "How would you fancy a few pints – just me and you?"

"Where shall we go?" Turning up the collar of his Burberry, Derek led Jamie through the main gates and headed towards the bus queue. Jamie dug into the deep pocket of his great-coat and pulled out a small packet handed to him when they'd lined up for liberty-men inspection.

"Put that away, you plonker," said Derek. "Do you want to shock those ladies?"

He nodded toward the ladies standing at the bus stop; some anxiously peering up the hill; some stamping their feet and hugging themselves against the cold damp of the evening.

As the bus arrived, Derek asked, "Where do you want to go – Gillingham or Chatham?"

"I've never seen Gillingham."

"Right, Gillingham it is."

Climbing to the top deck of the bus the two friends sat in the front seat.

Intrigued by the unfamiliar feel of the little packet, Jamie studied it. "What's the point in this? I won't get to use it."

"You never know, Jimbo. See that pub? I had a knee trembler round the back of that place before Christmas."

"You liar."

"Yeah. I know. But I did hear of someone that had a knee trembler behind that pub."

"He was probably lying as well."

"Probably."

By the time they reached Gillingham, drizzling rain had crazed the view through the bus window. Leaving the bus depot they hurried along the main street and ducked into a large, impersonal drinking house that smelled of trapped smoke and stale beer. Dim wall lights, some on, some off, struggled to illuminate the Victorian interior.

"Evening Jack." The bar man interrupted his preparations for the Saturday evening trade to come. Jamie, ill at ease in unfamiliar surroundings and conscious of being underage, found a table at the rear of the room while Derek bought two pints of mild.

"Cheers." Jamie sipped the dark liquid.

"Here's to the beginning of the rest of our lives." Derek downed a quarter of his pint in one satisfying draught.

For a while the two sat in silence, savouring the beer as it warmed their insides.

"I wonder where we'll be in a year's time," said Jamie.

"Where do you want to be?"

"Dunno. Maybe the Far East – on a small ship. Hong Kong will do. I've heard things about Hong Kong. The girls there do everything for you and you live with them like wives."

"Hold on, mate. Seventeen and you're talking about living with girls like wives."

"I'll be eighteen in a year. Anyway, I probably won't get the Far East – everybody volunteers for that draft. Where do you want to be in a year?"

Derek took another sip. "It's got to be small ships." He paused, "I fancy a survey vessel or something like that – something different. Down in the Antarctic or somewhere. They go to all parts of the world that warships don't usually go – with less bullshit and all that discipline stuff."

"Yeah, that would be good." Jamie, caught up in the dream, allowed his imagination to wander along undiscovered coasts and tropical islands.

"Well, get your name down, then Taffy, boyo."

"Why – have you?" enquired Jamie. A shadow crossed the fresh face of his friend.

"I volunteer for nothing, that's my motto, mate. The bastards always give you the opposite to what you want anyway, so what's the use."

"If you don't ask you don't get," said Jamie.

"Yeah, well. I don't really want to go anywhere," said Derek, cheerlessly, "I wish… I wish…" he stalled.

"Wish what, mate?"

"Oh, nothing."

"The girl, is it?"

Derek studied his young friend for a while. "Do you know this is the first time we've been ashore together since we got here?"

"Yeah, I suppose it is."

Derek shook his head. "Sorry, mate, I haven't been much of a pal to you these past few months."

"Yes you have," protested Jamie. "You don't have to go ashore to be mates."

"Well, maybe not – the time's gone so quick – we should have had a few runs, though."

Derek finished his beer; Jamie's glass remained half full. A few people filtered into the pub to stand at the bar. Jamie took both glasses for refills.

"Cheers," said Derek, downing a mouthful of mild, "just the job. You know why I haven't been around much, don't you, Jamie?"

"Yeah, I think so."

"Well, you're right. I see Nelly every chance I get. By the way, I should have congratulated you. You did well on the course."

"Thanks," said Jamie. "It's just like school – I'm still used to sitting in classrooms, I suppose – but you did okay…"

Derek interrupted. "I'm in love with her, you know?"

Jamie waited while Derek lit a cigarette. As the smoke from the first puff cleared he continued, "I can't get her out of my head; she's always on my mind. Stupid, ain't it?"

Jamie shrugged, not knowing what to say.

"We've been making plans, you know – silly plans like, er, getting married."

Jamie spluttered into his glass.

"Stupid, ain't it?"

"No, not stupid – more like difficult, I would say."

"Difficult you say. Difficult isn't the word, more like sodding impossible – and bloody stupid. An officer's daughter and me – what would old Hoppalong have to say?"

"He could do nothing once Eleanor's twenty-one."

"Nothing? Now you're being stupid. He could have me sent to bloody Siberia or even Wales, which is worse."

Jamie laughed, but he recognised the seriousness of Derek's feelings. "Does he know about you?"

"Know about me? You're joking. I'm still here, aren't I? If he even got a sniff that I'm seeing Nelly he'd go ballistic. My feet wouldn't touch…"

"How do you get to see her, anyway?" asked Jamie.

"The old man – old Hoppalong – spends most evenings in the wardroom – he likes his gin. They have a house – less than a mile from the base. She's always on her own. It's dead easy…"

As if realising he had said too much, Derek stopped, stubbed his cigarette out and emptied his glass.

"You're slow."

"I guess I'm not used to it."

"What I said, Jamie – about old Hoppalong's house – forget it. The less you know the better. Anyway, drink up. We'll find somewhere else. It's a bit dead in here."

Outside the rain had stopped. Puddles remained on the wet pavements to reflect the streetlights and headlights of passing vehicles. A large store window featured a wooden cabinet with its doors open revealing a flickering Cathode Ray Tube. Jamie stopped to watch a group of singers mouthing undecipherable sounds on the screen.

"Haven't you seen one of them before?" asked Derek.

"Television? 'Course I have," said Jamie, "hasn't everyone?"

"Bloody liar."

Ducking into a smaller, brighter pub the two blinked to get used to the light. An ornate jukebox filled the place with tinkling music and a group of men created more noise at a darts board on one side of the bar.

"This is better," said Derek, loudly. "You'll have a bottle this time, I think."

Finding a space away from the darts the two friends joked and chatted and observed the other patrons; the time passed swiftly.

Derek leaned forward to talk into Jamie's ear. "See them there?"

"The Teds?"

A group of three youths, dressed in full Teddy boy outfits had taken up a space further down the bar.

"Yep, I used to dress like that, would you believe?"

Jamie laughed. He tried to imagine Derek in drainpipe trousers, knee-length jacket and thick, crepe-soled shoes.

"I had my suits made special – velvet collars; string ties; the lot."

"Hair?"

"Yep, I had some of that as well."

"We'd better get moving," said Jamie. "I have to be back at ten."

Opposite the pub the stark white lights of a chip shop blazed like a beacon. They bought a bag of steaming hot chips each and stepped out for the bus station. Rounding a corner Derek hesitated, clutched Jamie's arm and said, "Take off your coat and put it over your arm."

"You what?"

"Do it," snarled Derek.

Catching the urgency in Derek's voice, Jamie hurried out of his coat and looked for the cause of the concern. Twenty yards up the street, under the watery light of a streetlamp, the three Teds from the pub lounged casually against a wall. Beyond them Jamie could see busses waiting at the deserted bus station.

"Say nothing; do as I do and use your boots if you have to," hissed Derek.

"What, the old 'garrotte' trick?"

"Idiot, kick 'em. Kick 'em in the balls if you can. Now just follow me."

As they approached the group the tallest Ted moved to the centre of the pavement to block their way. Jamie stopped; Derek stepped up to within a foot of the leader.

"Was you laughing at us back there, Jack?"

Derek smiled, "Laughing? No not me mate." He glanced back at Jamie. "Was you laughing, Taff?" but before anyone could say more, Derek heaved his packet of chips full into the threatening face, swiftly followed by a vicious kick to the groin. With a 'woof' of pain the Teddy boy doubled up – sinking to the ground. Derek, lips stretched back over his teeth in a maniacal grimace, followed with another kick to the chest, raising the grounded youth to deposit him on his backside some feet away.

"Run Taff." Derek leapt over the floored Teddy boy and started running. Before Jamie could react one of the remaining assailants came at him swinging something that caught him across the upper arm and shoulder. The blow sent his cap spinning from his head. Ducking low he managed to avoid a second swipe from the weapon. As he came back up he found himself level with the Ted's stomach. Instinctively he lunged forward, driving his head hard into the Ted's soft solar plexus. Out of the corner of his eye, Jamie spotted the third figure coming at him. Sidestepping the assault, Jamie mashed the packet of chips – that by some miracle he still gripped in his left hand – into the front of the pristine velvet collared suit. Stunned and outraged the third man jumped back, frantically wiping the greasy chips from his chest. Jamie grabbed his cap and took off after Derek towards the bus station. Diving behind a low, brick wall the two stopped.

"Are you okay?" Derek, breathing deeply, peered around the corner.

"I think so. The sod got me with something."

Taking deep breaths, Jamie willed his pounding heart to calm down. He felt his upper arm and winced with the sharp pain.

"It was a bike chain," said Derek. "The bus is over there – wait 'till the driver starts the engine and run for it."

After what seemed an age the driver of the bus marked 'Chatham Dockyard' appeared. He and the conductor prepared to leave. Keeping low the two friends crossed the open space to the bus and jumped aboard. Scuttling up the stairs to the top deck, Derek sat where he could see the depot entrance.

"Why didn't they follow?"

"They're probably chicken," said Derek.

"Why did we run, then?"

"Bloody 'ell, Taff, don't you know nothing? They were Teds – razors; bike chains; knuckledusters; they carry the lot. You have to get in first with them bastards. I know – I've done all that."

"You give that tall one quite a kick in the bollocks," said Jamie.

"I had boots on; they only had beetlecrushers. No contest."

Later that night, as Jamie lay on the thin mattress that had been his resting place for the last six months, he thought about the future. The pain from his bruised arm had settled to a dull ache but it didn't bother him. On the contrary, he felt quite proud of the pain; a memento; another memory to store away of the times spent with his rascal friend. Perhaps they would meet up again. Perhaps Derek would come to his senses and forget the officer's daughter. Jamie had no way of knowing if that would happen. What he did know was that he would miss Latch – badly.

CHAPTER 5

HMS DRAKE

Through the remnants of the winter and into the spring of 1955, Jamie billeted at HMS Drake, the Devonport Naval Base. Separated from the seniors, his accommodation hut sat alongside the black cinder-covered square of ground used by the Devonport Field Gun Crew as a training run. He doubted the sanity of anyone who would volunteer for such torment. He watched the brutal exercises avidly, convinced that sooner or later he would witness the amputation of a hand or a foot. Most of the rugby-shirted maniacs that careered around the course sported bandaged fingers and thumbs like badges of honour. Some miraculously survived the wickedly violent transport of the separate parts of a field gun, its carriage and cart, wheels and barrel, over walls and across chasms to be put together and fired under the doleful eye of a gunnery officer with a stopwatch. Jamie made a mental note that no matter the incentive or bribery, he would never, not even in a moment of weakness, volunteer for the Devonport Field Gun Crew. As he watched he had no way of knowing that a past member of that illustrious band of men was destined to share an adventure with him and become a firm friend.

February and March of that year proved reluctant to let go of winter's icy grip. He wrote two letters to Derek but received no reply.

Eager to move on, Jamie visited the Draft Office regularly until a draft to the destroyer, HMS *Demon*, came through. With the ship firmly in the hands of the dockyard, Jamie joined the naval advance party. Each morning he met up with the seniors to march through the dockyard gates to the ship. Sitting in a dry dock, Jamie found it difficult to imagine *Demon* as a proud warship. With her hull coloured patchy red and her decks festooned with cables, hoses and ropes, she sat trapped by thick timbers wedged between her and the dock walls. Jamie thought she looked miserable.

Dockyard workers swarmed over her like worker ants. Windy hammers rattled unceasingly, creating ear-splitting noise, chipping paint from metal bulkheads and deck fittings. Heavily protected welders burned and splashed with their crackling rods of fire while huge dockside cranes lifted machinery off and lifted machinery back on. Two of her 40mm AA guns sat dejectedly on the dockside, leaving gaps like pulled teeth in the ship's substantial superstructure.

Each day Petty Officer Electrician Gordon Grundy, who lived in married quarters in St Budeaux, came to work with his sandwiches and flask, neatly packed by Mrs Grundy into a small brown case. The case also contained his folded blue overalls, which he daily donned over his uniform on arrival at the ship. He also carried a copy of the *Daily Mirror* that he read on the bus and folded at the crossword before disembarking at Albert Gate. In his left hand he carried a rolled-up brolly, come rain or shine, just in case. This almost settled daily routine was the nearest Gordon had come to experiencing a proper job in twelve years. Gordon Grundy rarely smiled, sported a black, straggly set beneath a large nose and had recently signed on for a further ten years of service. At the age of thirty years Gordon considered leaving the Navy and maybe taking a job in the dockyard but, with two kids to support, Mrs Grundy said he should stay where he was.

In the small space allocated aboard as the Electrical Office, PO Grundy had hooked up a telephone, a one-bar electric fire and a single light bulb. Each day Jamie gingerly picked his way through dark, cable-strewn passages and hatchways to report to Gordon and to receive his daily task. Each day PO Grundy

67

looked up from his crossword and sent Jamie off to scrape the Asdic dome.

The object of his allotted task protruded from the for'ard part of the destroyer's keel and provided streamlined protection for the large, square submarine detecting transducer inside. Using the stone block steps built into the dry-dock sides, Jamie descended into the cold and damp depths of the dry dock and located the dome. Ducking beneath the huge belly of the hull – balanced, precariously it seemed to Jamie, on a line of wooden blocks – he began attacking the mottled and barnacled surface of the dome with his metal scraper.

"You can't use that."

A seaman, overalls smothered in paint, watched from the planks of a cradle hanging down from the ship's side.

"It's stainless. You'll 'ave to use wood."

"Wood?"

"Yup, 'ard wood. That there's a thin skin o' stainless – you'll damage the metal."

Embarrassed, but relieved to be away from the constant sound of running water – water that squirted in through the join in the straining dock gates – Jamie climbed the slimy stone steps and returned to the office.

"I have to use wood," said Jamie to Grundy. The petty officer sat with his feet on a desk under which an electric fire glowed. A biro pen, clamped firmly in his mouth, only just extended past his large nose. He looked up from the crossword.

"PO." Grundy shifted the pen to one side of his mouth to issue the correction.

"I have to use wood, PO. It's the stainless…"

"I knew that. I thought you knew that. Get some wood then."

"Where…?"

"Use your initiative, boy." Irritated at the interruption, but satisfied that another problem had been solved, Grundy settled back to work out the next clue.

Back on the sun-warmed dockside Jamie asked a dockyard worker where he might find some hard wood.

"There's them there wedges we use to wedge the shoring timbers, by." The docker pointed at some sawn pieces of wood strewn at the dockside.

"Are they hardwood?"

"Don't look very 'ard, do they? Try the wood store," he advised, "or if you see a chippie – he'll be the one carrying a saw, more'n likely – you ask him."

Jamie wandered off, searching the ground for hard wood and chippies while enjoying the warmth of the spring sunshine on his back. Skirting docks and quays the variety of craft fascinated him. The yard seemed to be filled with boats, ships, tugs, and vessels of all types in various states of readiness – some active and some laid up with their armament cocooned. At the northern end of the dockyard he spotted three submarines; three sleek and silent vessels as black as the coal piled high on the nearby coaling jetty. In contrast a huge frog-bellied Monitor, an old warship designed to sit on the bottom in shallow water to fire its huge gun, rusted away on the next jetty. The two barrels of the Monitor's giant gun, pointing threateningly at the Tamar Bridge, excited Jamie's imagination. Somewhere a clock chimed 1500, interrupting Jamie's daydreaming and reminding him that he needed to head back to the ship. At 1530 he fell in at the dockside to be marched back to Drake for tea. PO Grundy packed up his case and went home in time to play with his kids, bath them and put them to bed.

A few days later Jamie found a friendly dockyard matie who was interested enough, as he had a son in the Navy, to ask what the hard wood was for.

"Go to the paint store over there and ask for some paint stripper," he advised.

The paint stripper cost Jamie five of his blue lined, Navy-issue cigarettes. It took him a day to complete the job, but he did not tell the PO.

The lax routine came to an abrupt end when Lt Christopher Jollyman joined the ship. The Electrical Officer, a tall, thin man with a large head, soon gained the nickname of 'Joystick'.

More men joined as the advance party swelled its numbers. 'Scouser' Riley and 'Toffee' Hammer arrived as switchboard watch-keepers. Between them they manned the two switchboard compartments, one forward and one aft, to organise the distribution of electrical power as the ship's own generators gradually came on line.

One wet Monday morning it became obvious that things were about to change. PO Grundy stood at the gangway with the new officer, filtering out any ratings remotely associated with the Electrical Branch. Standing to attention in the rain, with white Blanco running from their caps, the Lieutenant spoke to each man in turn.

"Davis, isn't it?"

"Yes, Sir."

"And what section have you been working on?"

"Scraping the Asdic dome, Sir,"

"I hope you've been using wood?" he questioned.

"Yes, Sir," interjected PO Grundy. "I made sure of that."

"Well done, PO," said the officer. Grundy accepted the compliment without a glance at the young man's face.

CHAPTER 6

COMMISSIONING

A cutting north wind, picking up speed down the slopes of the snow-capped tors of the Devonshire moors, funnelled along the Tamar to slice through the 300 officers and men lined up on the dockside facing *HMS Demon*. The band of the Royal Marines played 'Hearts of Oak' and the First Lieutenant, Lieutenant Commander JG Worthing and a padre with a scarf hiding his dog collar, stood freezing on the dais. Showing a modicum of human kindness Lt Cdr Worthing ordered the men to double march on the spot, excusing the officers, who would have found their swords and things too bouncy. Jamie found this difficult too as he was standing on a railway line.

A large black car picked its way through the many dockyard obstacles, honking to clear a path through a group of dockyard maties gawping and taking the piss under a big crane. The First Lieutenant brought the ships company to attention and a very tall, four-ringed Captain unfolded from the car's rear passenger seat.

"Oh, Gawd," a voice piped up behind Jamie, "it's De-Fotherinham."

With a red face and a jutting jaw, and with only a short hesitation to show he had heard the comment, the Captain mounted the platform and took the salute. With a purposeful tap on the microphone he spoke.

"Why are these men wearing gloves, First Lieutenant?" Without waiting for an answer he ordered. "Get them off, *if you please.*"

Unphased, the Jimmy gave the order, "Ship's company, off gloves," as if it were an everyday sort of order, which it wasn't.

Those who wore gloves removed them, complaining among themselves, fidgeting to find a place to stow them – up jumpers, down jumpers and even under caps.

"This is fine, I must say. It's bloody freezing. Where are you going to stow yours?" asked a Leading Steward next to Jamie.

"I told you he was a bastard. He was our Jimmy. Right masochist he was," said the voice from behind.

"Sadist – he's a sadist," corrected the steward.

"Oh, you know him too."

Captain Norman De-Fotherinham watched with disbelief, his jutting jaw growing noticeably.

Unable to stomach the embarrassment, the coxswain moved forward. "Ship's company." The assembled men stopped fiddling with their gloves. "Attention. Shut up. Shut up and stand still."

The dockyard maties cheered and the sailors stood stiffly to attention. In a clipped, deliberate, monotone the Captain spoke into the microphone.

"Your First Lieutenant and your coxswain addressed you as 'Ship's Company'. Well – from where I am standing I don't see a ship's company. I see a disjointed gathering of discordant people." He paused and scanned the assembled ranks from one end to the other.

The dockyard maties stopped their banter and remained silent.

"From here I see a rabble – but – I promise you, you *will* become a ship's company. You *will* become worthy of this magnificent ship no matter how long it takes or how hard it gets." A ripple of applause from the dockyard maties stopped as the skipper threw them a withering glance. Straightening up to his full 6ft 4ins he finished up with, "You'll see."

Another, slightly larger, black car arrived and a civilian dressed neatly in a suit and wearing black-rimmed spectacles stepped out. Being the Secretary of War – or someone of that standing – he accompanied the skipper and First Lieutenant on inspection of the troops. Stopping at a rating in the middle row the civilian enquired the significance of the unusual arm badge sewn onto the sleeve of his jacket.

"I am a Coder, actually," said the shivering, slightly-built young man, "Paul Smitte." Smitte's nose, red and pointed, protruded from a bony face. At its tip a drip threatened to drop but for a timely sniff. "It seems that people call me Smithy."

"Oh, yes. Languages?"

"Seven, actually; three naturally – father is Swiss. The others I read at London."

"National Service?"

"Yes, actually – just started. Looking forward to the experience."

"Well done." The civilian passed on allowing the Captain to point out to the Jimmy who pointed out to the coxswain that Smithy was wearing a scarf – navy blue, wool and neatly tucked under the lapels of his single breasted fore and aft rig jacket.

The coxswain, nicely warmed up by his anger, stood toe-to-toe in front of Smithy. "Do you know who that is?"

"Yes, the gentleman in question is the Royal Navy's political representative in the house."

A look of shock passed briefly over the Chief's face with the unexpected response. "Chief," was all he could think of to say.

"No, I'm not a Chief, I'm a Code…"

"Remove that item of non-uniform, lad," said the coxswain, recovering his authority, "and permit me to study your face. I want to remember your face. You are mine for two years, and at the end of it you will know, in seven languages, how to say 'Sir' when addressing your superiors, do you understand."

"Yes, er, Sir."

73

"Coxswain."

"No, I'm a Coder."

"Oh, my God," sighed the coxswain, giving in and moving on.

"You're right in there, mate." A large able-seaman standing next in line spoke in a stage whisper. "You know what they say – the hand that wanks the coxswain rules the ship."

The commissioning ceremony continued without further mishap, including a very quick tempo rendition of 'God Save the Queen' by a very cold Royal Marine band. Finally the crew said goodbye to the civilian with a rousing three cheers. A very relieved Jimmy dismissed the crew and followed his Captain aboard. A Royal Marine bandsman nudged Jamie as he passed by. "And the best of British luck to you, mate, you *will* need it."

With the commissioning ceremony over, the chaos of settling the crew into their quarters began. After eight months as a member of the ship's advance party, Jamie had become familiar with the vessel's layout. Willingly, he answered questions and helped move in those who were new to life on a ship. A large proportion of the lower deck messed on the space below the fo'csle – immediately beneath the turrets holding the double barrelled 4.5inch 'A' and 'B' Guns. For'ard of the canteen flat; from one side of the ship to the other and up to the bow; the whole area seethed with men jostling for a place to stow gear. As he worked, Jamie became aware of a giant of a man quietly helping out and arranging the growing amount of hammocks and kit-bags into their allotted cages. He seemed to be settling himself into the area of two tables on the port side of the messdeck demarked as Miscellaneous – Jamie's mess.

"You're a stoker," said Jamie.

"Very observant." The man lifted a hammock with one huge, gnarled hand and rammed the rolled canvas bundle into its cage.

"Sorry," smiled Jamie, "but I thought stokers lived over there – on the starboard side."

"They've given me a special dutyman's job," said the stoker. From his vantage point of a head's height above everyone else he looked across to the other side of the messdeck. "Seems there's not enough room for me over there – so here I am."

Detecting that the big man was not entirely happy with the arrangement, Jamie changed tack. "Don't I know you? You seem familiar."

Turning to face Jamie, the stoker looked the youngster up and down. "Is this your first ship?"

Jamie nodded.

"Did you watch the Devonport field gun this year?"

Again Jamie nodded, recalling the hours he had spent earlier that year watching the practice runs from his accommodation hut next to the field gun crew's training ground at HMS Drake.

"Then you must have seen me. I was one of the idiots carrying a wheel – Miller, Dusty Miller."

Dusty held out a hand – Jamie grabbed it and felt the strength in the handshake.

"Jamie Davies – Jamie; Davie; Taff – take your pick."

The killick of Jamie's mess, Leading Electrical Mechanic Mick Quinn, a soft-spoken Northern Irishman, appointed E.M.1 'Badger' Bates as the man in charge in his absence. Badger, a hairy, ginger man, sported three good conduct badges on the upper arm of his left sleeve indicating that he must have kept his nose clean for at least twelve years. Short and square, the lines on his freckled face showed that smiling was not common to him. How long Badger had served no one knew but it was rumoured that he was once a PO and had lost his senior rating status during the war.

Taking advantage of Jamie's knowledge of the ship, Mick quickly sorted out the members and billets in his mess. Jamie enjoyed showing people where to stow gear, and he took pride from Mick's, "Ask Taffy, he'll know."

Externally the ship sparkled. Inside the crew worked hard, cleaning and painting; clearing away the dockyard dirt.

A few days after completion of the commissioning ceremony Jamie called in at the mess to pick up his overalls from his locker. Being mid-morning, Jamie expected the messdeck to be empty so he was surprised to find Badger busily brassoing the mess gash bucket.

"Skiving, Badger," teased Jamie as he stepped over the watertight-door sill. Badger looked up with a frown but said nothing. Standing and deliberately placing the Brasso tin and cotton waste onto the newspaper-covered table he moved towards Jamie. Without warning the three-badgeman clenched his fist and delivered a vicious blow to the young man's stomach. Gasping for breath, Jamie dropped to the hard deck, unable for a moment to understand what had happened. On his knees he clutched his aching midriff and looked up into the grim face thrust inches from his.

"Listen, you Welsh sheepshagger. This is *my* mess. What I do is none of your fucking business. I don't like Welshies and I don't like you."

Still breathless and unable to speak, Jamie crawled to the bench seat and hauled himself up. Badger stood over him and continued. "You'll keep your place and stay out of my way in future. Got it?"

"I only..." started Jamie, but a voice interrupted his answer.

"Hello, hello, hello. If it ain't Jimmy Davis."

Instantly recognising the voice with its London accent, Jamie spun his head around.

"Latch, you bastard," winced Jamie. "What are you doing here?"

Derek Latchbrook stepped into the messdeck and deposited kitbag, hammock and gas mask at Jamie's feet. He flipped off his cap, revealing the blonde quiff that had grown into a lock falling almost into his eyes.

He spun his cap expertly onto the table. "What's up with you, Jamie boy? Got the dog?"

"Yeah, something like that." Jamie realised he still clutched his aching midriff. "What on earth are you doing here – are you joining us? I thought you were Chatham."

"So did I mate; so did I. This is what you get when you have friends in high places – and I have some – sending me on me holidays away from the wicked Smoke. Anyway, time to talk later. Where do I sling me hook?"

With effort, Jamie restrained himself.

"Sorry, mate, I have to turn to. Badger there will put you right. He's in charge of the mess. I'll see you later."

"Please yourself, mate. Bugger off then."

"Yeah. Good to see you too."

Jamie, feeling a mixture of self-disgust at not responding to the attack and elation at seeing Latch, removed his overalls from his locker and left. Derek shook hands with the man who had just violently established authority over his best friend and settled in for what was to become a short but eventful stay.

Despite their previous friendship, Latch and Jamie failed to get together during the few weeks of hard work preparing the ship for its work-up. Each time Jamie broached the subject of Derek's move to Devonport something came up to interrupt. A rare opportunity arose on the day *Demon* left the dockyard for sea trials. Most of the dockyard workers had left the ship; some carrying their upholstered toolboxes; others dragging the last of the umbilical cables and pipes with them. A few remained –

77

mostly experts needed on board to test operational equipment at sea.

On a cold, bright December morning, Jamie, neatly dressed in full blues, fell in next to Derek on the fo'csle amongst the others lining the guardrails. Further aft lazy white smoke from the ship's two smoke-stacks turned to serious blue as newly lined boilers tuned up, and for the first time the crew felt the power of steam turbines vibrate through the ship. On the fo'csle the PO in charge of the cable party waited for orders from the bridge relayed by an ordinary seaman manning a telephone behind 'A' gun turret.

"Wa's at?" shouted the telephone man. "Come agin."

"Was that an order?" enquired the PO.

"Say agin, will ye," shouted the seaman into the phone.

"What a load of bollocks," said Derek.

"Single up." The Skipper's faint shout could be heard from somewhere overhead. "And where is that bloody megaphone?"

"Single up," echoed the PO.

Dockers standing by on the dockside released the heavy springs while on board straining seamen hauled the ropes inboard.

"Wa's at?" screamed the telephone operator, "say agin, will ya?"

Vibrations increased markedly as the ship moved away from the dock. The hawser holding the bow to the dockside stretched and creaked as the ship attempted to pull away. The dockers waiting at the bow rope scattered to hide from the threat of the straining rope.

"You know we are about to be killed, don't you. Jimmy?" said Derek.

"Stop complaining," said Jamie. "You never used to drip so much."

"I was never this far from civilisation before. I planned to die in the Smoke," said Derek.

"Shut – up." shouted the PO.

"Was that an order?" asked the telephone operator.

"Not you – you idiot. What's the bridge saying?"

"Dinna ask me. I dinna ken a word," answered the operator.

The PO strained upwards to see the men on the bridge. Then, among a cacophony of megaphone feedback, the Captain's voice split the atmosphere. "Let go for'ard. Let that line go."

"Too tight," shouted the PO Seaman. "Give us some bleedin' slack – Sir."

"Say again," came the electronic reply.

"Slack, for God's sake, slack," screamed the PO.

"Christ. If that rope parts we're dead," said Derek.

Very slowly the bow rope stopped singing its protest and sagged tiredly. A brave docker in canvas gloves dashed forward, unlooped the hawser from the bollard and ran back to safety. Slowly, the ship pulled away from the jetty into the Tamar River and turned her nose seaward.

Passing Flagstaff the crew lining the rails stood to attention to salute the Commander-in-Chief. From Plymouth Hoe a few individuals, braving the weather, watched as the ship gathered speed and moved through the Sound to head out to sea. Clearing the Breakwater and with the lazy roll of the hull that was to become so familiar to the crew the Tannoy announced, "Fall out harbour stations. Sea dutymen close up. Passage routine. Petty Officer Grundy report to the bridge."

A tense Grundy caught up with Jamie later that morning in the Amplifier Room. Situated in the bridge superstructure, the Amplifier Room contained the banks of amplifiers and telephone boards for internal communications -- allocated as Jamie's part-of-ship.

"Two things," said Grundy with a scowl.

"Yes, P.O?"

"The phones were working perfectly, I knew that. It was an Irish twit on the bridge and a Scotsman at the other end. They couldn't understand each other."

"Yes, PO – and the other thing?"

"Fix this – Latchbrook will help you."

"But – it was working. I heard the Skipper…"

"It was working until the Skipper bounced it off the bulkhead next to the Irish twit so just mend the bloody thing."

Derek entered as Grundy left.

"Shut the door – keeps the warm in," said Jamie.

"You're a jammie git." Derek sat on Jamie's toolbox. "How did you land this cushy number?"

"Me and the PO – we're like that," joked Jamie, crossing his fingers.

"You're lucky – old Joystick won't give me a section. I feel like a spare prick at a wedding."

"Well, you're not exactly the life and soul, mate – and it doesn't take a genius to work out why."

Derek sat quietly for a moment while Jamie started to strip the loudhailer.

"Have you ever had a girl," said Derek. "A proper girlfriend I mean?"

"I've kissed a few," said Jamie, "at school. I took a girl to the pictures once – she passed out on me when I felt her tits. Turns out she was prone to fits when she got excited. Her mother told everyone in the village that I was some kind of monster. I didn't bother after that."

"Do me a favour," said Derek, smiling despite his obvious depression. "I mean – a proper girl…"

"Like Miss Eleanor what's-her-name?"

"Henderson," said Derek. "Don't tell me you've forgotten Nelly – and her father Hoppalong – the bastard."

"So he's your friend in high places?"

"Oh, yes, you can bet on it."

"What happened?"

"That time – when I went missing from the partridge beat – remember?"

"I remember you half-inched my ten-bob note."

Derek ignored the remark. "I knew I should never have stuck my head above the parapet... cost me that did – and more than your bloody ten bob."

"What happened, for God's sake?" said Jamie.

"Hold your horses," snapped Derek. "I'm coming to that. It was only a few weeks ago. I'd been to see Nelly. Old Hoppy should have been his usual pissed self in the wardroom – but that night he came home early..."

"He didn't catch you in his house...?"

"Shut up – let me tell you. No – he didn't catch me in his house. It was a close thing though. I'd only just left and was on my way back to the barracks – along his street – he passed me in his car; recognised me and turned around to find out what I'd been up to."

"Why should he do that?"

"I'm not sure – I haven't been able to speak to Nelly since. There are only a few houses in that road and I suppose he could think of no reason for me being there. Once he recognised me I was done for."

"What did you tell him – about being in the road, I mean?"

"Oh, I made up some story about losing my way or something but it wasn't my best effort. I didn't for one minute think he would place me with Nell."

"So – he knew you'd been to see Nelly?"

"I told you," said Derek impatiently, "I haven't spoken to her – you'd better get on with that hailer. Grumpy will be back shortly..."

"It's okay – the battery connection had come off. I fixed it a moment ago."

At that moment the ship's Tannoy system announced stand-easy.

Derek stood. "Let's get a cuppa..."

Jamie remained where he was. "You can't stop now. Here, have a ciggy. What happened? How did you land down here?"

Jamie expected an objection from Derek but instead the Londoner lit his cigarette and sat down again.

"Nelly had told me her father was becoming suspicious – I dunno, little things probably gave us away. I wouldn't be surprised if he'd planned to come home early that night."

"But a matelot walking on a street – you could have been on a message or anything..."

"He recognised me – got quite mad. Called me a bad lot and asked me right out what mischief I'd been up to – told me to get back aboard. My feet haven't touched the ground since."

"Clever bastard," said Jamie "He must suspect something to send you down here. He knows this ship will be safely in the Med by next February."

"With me on it – well, if he thinks he's put a spoke in between Nell and me he's got another think coming – come on, we've still got time for a cuppa."

By mid-December the dockyard finished with the ship. Faced with an intense and stressful period working up, the crew welcomed the Christmas break. Jamie and Derek fell into the half of the ship's company that took first leave – a fortnight that included Christmas Day. Jamie planned to help his sister as much as possible but within hours of arriving home he felt ill and spent long and boring days in bed sweating out the flu. By December 28th Jamie had returned to the ship, together with a rough-looking lot of unenthusiastic men, to take over the duty from the New Year half.

Knowing the depressed state of mind that Derek had been wallowing in before leave, Jamie half expected his friend to do something stupid like staying away – but, to Jamie's relief, Latch returned on time. The break had done little to lighten Derek's mood. With most of his pay still burning a hole in his pocket, Jamie decided to ask Derek ashore. Leaving the Dockyard gates, they started up Albert Road hill towards Aggie Weston's. Jamie had often called in at Aggie's to take advantage of the facilities offered by the charitable group in the imposing Victorian building run for the benefit of young sailors. Apart from the cheap food, Jamie loved the sheer luxury of lounging on upholstered chairs – such a contrast to the basic furniture he had lived with since joining up. This evening they failed to reach Aggie's.

"Have you ever tasted Scrumps, boyo?" enquired Derek as they walked past a deserted food van parked on a recently demolished building site at the side of Albert Road.

"Scrumpy? No."

"Well, I know just the place."

Taking the lead, Derek turned into a side street. Poorly lit by old-fashioned cast-iron street lamps, the small terraced houses on either side showed little signs of life. As they walked, Jamie guessed that the narrow street ran parallel to the river.

"How do you know where we're going?" said Jamie. "You're Chatham."

"Your friend Badger told me."

"Badger?" said Jamie, "he's a bastard."

"Yeah, I noticed you two aren't the best of mates. What did you do to him?"

"Bugger all – sweet FA – nothing. He doesn't like me for some reason – calls me a sheepshagger."

"Well, you are," teased Latch, ducking to avoid the swinging punch.

With the smell of low water strong in their senses, the end of the street widened to reveal a ramp: shining wet under a solitary lamp light, sloping away into the black Tamar. In the almost total darkness Jamie noted the huge chains anchored at each side of the ramp.

"If we've come the right way then that's the ferry – Torpoint Ferry," said Derek, "and that must be the place."

Crossing the wide road Derek made for a building at the end of the row of houses opposite – a building that identified itself as a pub with an illegible hanging sign.

"Here we are," announced Derek. "The Sign of the Hanging Tit, on the Street of a Thousand Arseholes."

"Very cultured," said Jamie.

Ducking through the low doorway they entered a sparse room, its walls and low ceiling the colour of smoked haddock. Old yellow photographs of ferries and moustachioed ferrymen hung unappreciated among plaques of RN ships past and present. A well-worn carpet covered most of the wooden floor, its paisley pattern long since lost to its hessian backing on the route to the bar.

A stout mine host welcomed them. "Evening, Jack. What'll it be?"

"Two pints of your best scrumpy, please," ordered Derek, removing his cap. Jamie had already doffed his to get through the door.

"Scrumpy?" A flicker of concern passed across the landlord's florid face as he looked from Derek back to Jamie. "You don't mean cider?"

"Scrumpy, please." Derek re-enforced the order by slapping a half-a-crown onto the sticky surface of the bar. Jamie, feeling self-conscious under the gaze of the landlord, made for an unoccupied table at the rear of the room. The landlord reached for two straight pint glasses and placed one carefully under the tap of a blackened wooden barrel marked NO.2 in chalk. The four other patrons watched with interest as the liquid trickled into the glass with no bubbles or other signs of life apart from small white particles that slowly sank to the bottom. The landlord patiently waited until the residue had almost settled before starting on the second.

"Scrumpy, b'aint it Jack?" A slightly built man leaned on the end of the time-worn bar. "Strewth, that there is strong stuff, that is."

"Yeah, I know," said Latch, licking his lips.

"Scrump-'eads drink that there." The man sucked the last life out of a tiny dog-end – his slack cheeks caving in with the effort.

"Thank you, Bosley," said the landlord. "You should know. You drink enough of it."

"You're right there, Governor." Bosley grinned, revealing a toothless mouth. "And I'm only twenty-one."

The old timer burst into laughter at his own joke. Quickly the cackle ended with a racking cough, which he quenched by downing the last of his drink, white bits and all.

Sitting next to each other on the bench seat the two sailors surveyed their murky drinks.

"What's the white bits?" Jamie followed the tortured progress of some debris as it settled to the bottom of the glass.

"Pure apple juice, that is, Taffy. There's no added stuff in there, boyo, so that must be bits of apple. Come on – down the hatch."

"Cheers." Jamie sank his first mouthful of fermented rough Devon apple juice. "Well, that was easy." Warmth spread around his insides. "A bit yucky, but easy. It's like drinking Corona."

The second pint tasted rougher than the first, but Derek continued drinking with apparent relish. "They sent me down here to get me away from Nelly, you know."

"Yeah? I thought that might be the reason."

"Yup – she writes to me without that dad of hers knowing."

"What about the plans?"

"What plans?"

"You know, the plans you had to get married and that."

"There's not much chance of that now, is there? Not with me down here and she up there. I'll bet you a fortnight's pay her dad organised that – the pig."

"Yeah – the pig." Jamie felt himself becoming tingly and paternal. "It's not as if you have, you know, carmel intentions, is it."

"I have, though," said Derek, seriously. "And, you're the only person in the world to know this, she has too. I discovered this at Christmas."

Jamie rolled a tickler with great difficulty. Every paper he pulled from the packet broke apart as he folded in the tobacco. "Well, that is a privilege, mate."

"What's a privilege?"

"You telling me."

"I know." Derek finished off his second pint and tipped the residue out to investigate the white bits. Bosley paused on his way to the gents and stood swaying in front of the two sailors. Placing one hand flat on their table he prepared for the anticipated relief by undoing the bottom buttons of his well-greased waistcoat and the top button of his trousers.

"Awright, Jack? 'pee New Year to yew." Steadying himself he continued. "Was Andrew meself – in the war."

"Lying bastard," said the landlord as Bosley swayed off. "He's worked in the yard all his life."

"Near enough." Derek sorted out some change and pushed the coins to Jamie. "Get 'em in again, mate."

Jamie gathered the money, stood and fell back into his seat. On the second attempt he managed find some balance to reach the bar.

"Two pints, please," said Jamie.

"Where's your glasses?"

"Glasses? I don't wear glasses."

"The glasses I gave you to drink out of," said the landlord with a sigh.

Jamie turned and pointed to the table across the swaying room, hoping the landlord would appreciate the difficulty. "Two pints, please," he persisted and was rewarded with two fresh glasses of cider. He delivered the drinks one at a time for safety sake.

Bosley visited on his way back from the toilet and rolled himself a tickler from Jamie's tin.

"Long time since I 'ad one of these," he said, borrowing a light for the thick cigarette he had deftly produced. With the tickler well aglow and puffing serenely he called a tête-à-tête with his new friends.

"What do you think of 'er?" He indicated a woman sitting alone at the table under the window. A colourful headscarf tied tightly around her head and a plain overcoat buttoned over an ample bust seemed to say that she wasn't stopping, but an ashtray full of dog-ends said otherwise.

"Er, very nice," said Jamie.

"She's just like me old Dutch," said Derek.

"You can 'ave one off'n 'er if you want. I knows the maid. I'll go and ask for yer."

"That's very kind," said Derek. "Very kind, ain't it, Taffy?"

"Yeah, very kind, Bosley."

"Yeah, and we would too, wouldn't we Taff. But we've just got out of Stonehouse Hospital and we mustn't exert ourselves, must we Taff?"

"Nah, it's the stitches see."

"No problemmo," said Bosley, "'ad stitches meself – during the war. Nasty buggers, stitches."

Bosley suddenly became thirsty and made his way to the toilet. He hesitated at the door marked 'Gents', and turned back to the bar. Before he'd reached the bar the couple from the table next to the motherly woman leaned across and whispered something to her that resulted in her rising and swiping Bosley across the back with her handbag. Bosley cackled with mirth and continued to prop up the bar, and to enjoy his pusser's tickler and his pint.

Glowing with goodwill and totally relaxed Jamie said, "This time next month we'll be in the sunny Med."

"Bollocks," said Latch, "and it's two months."

"Yer right. This time next two months we'll be in the sunny Med. Here's to the Med."

"Are you trying to upset me?"

"But it's the Med, Latch. Gib, Malta..."

"Yeah, but she's not there, is she?" Derek focussed as best he could into the depths of his glass. Jamie tried to think of an answer but gave up and slumped back in the bench seat, curiously exhausted with the effort.

"I 'ad her, you know, Taff. More'n once."

"You..."

"Yeah, I did and I shouldn't ave. She's only seventeen..."

"Seventeen," said Jamie. "I'm seventeen. I thought she's older..."

"Seventeen," said Latch, sternly, "...but, oh, so sweet and..."

"...and an osiffer's daughter."

"Yeah, the pig," said Derek, "and now I'm on me holidays down here in the back of nowhere – getting pissed with a Welsh sheepshagger."

"Serves you right," said Jamie.

"Yeah, you're not wrong. But she is so... so... beautiful," was all he could say. "We couldn't help it, you know? The first time was in her house, after the shows, remember?"

"I feel sick," announced Jamie.

"Right there in old Hoppalong's house. He wasn't there though. My God, she was so beautiful. And then at Christmas…"

"I feel sick," repeated Jamie.

"I feel like a piss." Derek swayed to his feet and assisted the younger man to his feet.

"You look like a piss, a long streak a piss." The giggling lasted them all the way to the gents. In the heads Derek relieved himself and Jamie brought up his scrumpy followed by the supper he had eaten back on board. The bits of regurgitated meat pie and steamed pudding splashed over his shoes and onto his best bell-bottoms so they left, waving goodbye to Bosley and his missus but ignoring the snitch couple. They politely thanked the landlord, wished him a happy New Year and fell outside into the black street.

"Any Teds down 'ere, Taff?"

"Only Bootnecks."

"Marines? They're worrse."

Somehow they found the route back to Albert Gate. At about the halfway point Derek was sick and Jamie relieved himself against a wall. At the mobile chip shop, on a piece of waste ground opposite the dockyard gate, they each bought a bag of chips because they were hungry.

Once inside the dockyard Jamie felt confident he could find the ship but instead he found the dry dock; empty but for a lot of water. Wandering about in the dark they discovered anchor chains, bits of dismantled guns and rusty boiler pipes and eventually the ship. While they'd wandered they swore that they would never, ever, drink rough Devon cider never, ever, again. It also gave Derek time to say, "I didn't shag her, you know, James. I lied to you."

It didn't matter really because Jamie forgot everything about the evening anyway.

CHAPTER 7

WORK UP

A week later *HMS Demon* lay at anchor off Weymouth for the night, waiting her turn to be swung around in a 360 degree arc to facilitate the adjustment of the magnetic compass. Below decks, the messes, at their fullest during the hours between supper and lights-out, buzzed with chatter and the sounds of card playing. In the short weeks since commissioning, the Miscellaneous mess had settled into two factions. The table furthest for'ard attracted the older, crib playing members, while those at the other table favoured brag. Cigarette smoke lay in a blue haze above the sea of heads as ventilation systems were run on low to keep out the cold of an English Channel winter.

Ginger Long loved playing brag, probably the result of a lengthy spell in hospital recovering from a broken leg, fractured cheek and internal injuries he'd sustained while climbing a hill in Wales.

"Why do you always hold the bank, Ging?" Jamie counted the cigarettes remaining in his packet.

"'Cos I'm senior to you. Come on. Stop complaining, Taff, make up your mind."

"I'll have one," said Jamie – knowing that another two or more cigarettes were about to bite the dust.

"I just heard a buzz you'd be interested in, Taffy, boyo." Badger's voice, louder than necessary, reached Jamie from the crib school.

"Yeah, and what's that then?" Jamie contemplated raising another two cigarettes.

"Latchbrook was picked up today. I was in the office when Joystick was given the message. He's for the high jump for deserting."

"Bollocks." The delight obvious in Badger's comments angered Jamie. "He'll have a good reason for being absent without leave, you'll see."

"You can coco! He was picked up. That's desertion. He'll get a warrant. As sure as eggs is eggs, he will."

"Up yours, Badger." Angry and frustrated, Jamie threw down his cards and left the mess. Moving through the darkened canteen flat, he opened the watertight door and stepped out into the cold of the upper deck.

Leaning on the guard rail Jamie watched the lights of Weymouth flickering against the black of the land behind. To the left the imposing mass of Portland stood out granite hard against the lighter hue of the sky, a sky clear and cold and full of stars.

Hunching his shoulders against the chill, Jamie pondered the fate of his mate who had not returned from a run ashore on the previous Saturday.

Before leaving, Latch had confided in Jamie his plan to make for London to meet up with the girl. Jamie had expected to see him back aboard by Sunday but Derek had still not appeared by Monday morning. Derek's station card, deposited at the gangway as an indication that he had left the ship, had been removed from the Bosun's Mate's box so no one was aware he was missing until turn-to on Monday. PO Grundy, severely reprimanded for not checking his team over the weekend, lost no time in calling for the chief suspect.

Jamie shuddered as he recalled the meeting.

"Latchbrook is your oppo, isn't he, Davis?"

Grundy, sitting in the Electrical Office chair, fingered his beard worriedly as he looked up at the standing Jamie.

"I know him, PO."

"Know him? You joined up with him according to this."

A brown manila folder lay open on the desk. The only other occupant of the office stood watching from a filing cabinet at the end of the small space.

"Does he have to be here?" Jamie nodded towards Badger.

Grundy glanced over at Badger. "Give us a minute," he said.

As Badger squeezed past Jamie the older man made no effort to hide the smirk on his face.

"Well?" Grundy had continued. "You know this could ruin your career – if you were found to have helped a deserter? Did you know Latchbrook was planning on jumping ship?"

"He's not a deserter," snapped Jamie. "Latch – er, Latchbrook had some pressing business in London – but he said he'd be back..."

"London?" exclaimed Grundy, slamming the folder shut. "Did you think he could make London and be back by Sunday morning?"

"Trains?" said Jamie, lamely.

"What was this 'business' that was so pressing?"

"I don't know, PO."

"Did you remove his station card from the gangway?"

"No!"

Grundy stared up at Jamie. The youngster felt the heat rising in his face under the sustained glare.

"If I find out you knew something about this, Davis, I'll 'ave your guts for garters." The menace in Grundy's voice surprised Jamie. "Now get out."

Jamie gripped the steel wire guard rail and peered into the blackness of the sea. "Stupid, stupid bastard," he said aloud. "Why couldn't he stick to his own sort?"

"Talking about that oppo of yours?"

Startled, Jamie looked to his left to see the unmistakable bulk of Dusty Miller.

"Sorry. I didn't know anyone was there."

"What's the beef with Badger? Is he riding you?"

"I can handle Badger," said Jamie. "He's just a prick. One of these days I'll sort him out."

"I could do it for you. I don't like the man – just say the word."

Jamie peered into the darkness to make out Dusty's face. The sincerity in the direct eyes was clear.

"Thanks, Dust, but I'll manage. Anyway, he's probably right – Latch deserves all he gets."

The cold Channel air forced them back to the mess to find that Jamie's pile of matches had disappeared and no one owned up.

"Bollocks," he said and hated Badger even more.

A sickening crash woke Jamie. Gathering his thoughts he lay for a while in his swinging hammock. The creaks, bangs and violent movement of the ship told him that while he'd slept they had engaged the storm raging in the Bay of Biscay.

"Wakey, wakey, Taff." A head swathed in scarf and oilskin appeared below. "Come on you lucky sod. It's your turn. It's blowing a bastard out there. Red watch on deck, it's five to four. I wants me 'mick so don't delay."

Jamie swung himself down, timing his movement to the rise and fall of the ship to avoid crumpling onto the deck. Leaning against a bulkhead he pulled on his clothes, adding a woollen jersey against the cold he knew was to come. In the dimmed light he saw that a number of lockers had discharged their contents onto the deck. Crockery, some smashed and some still miraculously intact, rolled about underfoot.

"Bloody 'ell," swore Jamie. Struggling to stay upright he moved through the canteen flat like a drunk. Reaching the starboard passageway he found his opposite number among the dozen oilskin-clad men lining the bulkheads.

"You're relieved." Jamie accepted his oppo's oilskin and settled for a miserable four-hour watch as crew of the sea-boat. From his position he could see, through the open door, the heavy wooden whaler, secure in its davits, being lashed by the giant waves and screaming wind of the Bay.

With gratitude for small mercies, Jamie sat on the hard deck with his back against a ventilation duct – the metal warmed by hot air from 'A' boiler room – but before he could settle a figure approached.

"Davis, Kye," said the voice of authority from deep within an oilskin hood.

"Aw, PO," complained Jamie. "I'll lose my place by the exhaust…"

"Move yourself – and Turner – collect the mugs and go along with Davis."

Ordinary Seaman Topsy Turner struggled to his feet and collected the previous watch's cups from around the passageway. Holding on to each other to avoid being hurled against the bulkheads by the violent shift of the deck they made their way to the galley on the port side of the canteen flat. In the galley they found the thick bars of dark chocolate, tins of condensed milk and broken bags of sugar – the makings for the traditional Navy drink, Kye, beloved of cold and wet seamen the world over. With hot water from an urn they attempted to make the chocolate drink without getting severely scalded. Supporting each other they struggled back with the cups and the fanny of Kye – a very unsuccessful fanny of Kye. The undissolved lumps of chocolate floated on the surface of the dirty-coloured water like chunks of beef in an oxtail soup.

"…and fuck you too," responded Jamie to the volley of abuse his Kye generated, "…do it yourself next time."

Jamie sat on the deck a little way from the others bemoaning the loss of position alongside the ventilation exhaust. The effort to hold back the nausea of seasickness while working in the confines of the small galley left him tense and shaky. The hot drink helped settle his insides but his depression was not only from the effects of the heaving and yawing of the deck under him. Fresh in his mind was the memory of the reading of a warrant by the Captain, awarded to his best friend in traditional throwback to the days when serious punishment would be witnessed by all members of the crew. On the day before *Demon* left for the Med the ship's company assembled on the fo'csle.

Derek Latchbrook, flanked by two naval policemen, his boots free of laces, had slopped along the newly-painted non-slip deck to stand facing the crew. The offender, uniformed but without the usual trappings of collar, lanyard or silk, halted beneath the twin 4.5 inch barrels of 'A' gun. Bravely he'd faced forward, his eyes unblinking – but Jamie knew, from the reddening of his cheeks, that Derek was churning inside. Unable to witness his friend's discomfort, Jamie had focussed on 'A' gun turret, which shone pristine with its new paint and polish, each barrel plugged at the business end with a ship's plaque.

"Prisoner – one pace forward – march," ordered the cox'n. "Off cap."

Jamie had swallowed hard as the Skipper read out the charges of desertion and assault with a weapon.

For days leading up to that fateful day – busy days of exercises and tests of the ship's systems – Jamie had listened to rumours – many fuelled by the smug Badger.

'Resisted arrest; battered some shore patrol.'

'Deserted; on his way up north.'

'Someone on board helped him; whipped his station card from the gangway.'

'Got as far as London; didn't have a ticket.'

Jamie avoided the subject but deep inside he knew that Latch was capable of all the things being said. Despite this Jamie had clung to the hope that, by some miracle, his friend would appear back on board and explain away his absence. That hope had been well and truly dashed on the day the ship returned to Devonport to prepare for departure to the Med; the day that each and every man aboard stood witness to Derek Latchbrook's disgrace.

As the Captain read out the punishment, briefly and businesslike, Jamie allowed himself to look at Latch. 'Ninety days incarceration at the Naval Detention Centre, Portsmouth'; Jamie waited for the 'Dishonourable Discharge' that he was sure would follow, but it did not come. For a moment Jamie caught his friend's eyes and, with a shock that was almost physical, Jamie realised that Derek was smiling at him.

'Good for you,' Jamie thought, but then he noticed Latch's head. The blonde quiff, which Jamie had watched so often being combed and patted into shape, had gone.

"Prisoner – on cap." The coxswain followed his own order by slapping Derek's cap back onto the cropped head. As Derek adjusted the cap he winked at Jamie – but Jamie hardly noticed – his mind could not lose the image of Derek's shorn head.

"Good luck mate," said Jamie as Derek passed.

"Silence," hissed one of the escorts, then all three hurried across the gangway and into a van waiting on the quayside.

Hushed and thoughtful, the crew returned to the work of preparing *Demon* for her journey to the Med.

The crashing thump of another Atlantic wave brought Jamie back to the misery of the storm.

'I'd change places with that bastard Latchbrook right now,' thought Jamie as the ship dropped like a stone into another trough.

"Davis – Kye," shouted the Petty Officer of the Watch, "and this time you – Jonesy," he kicked the sole of an older AB, "go with him and show him how."

"Roll On My Fucking Time!" groaned Jamie with feeling.

"And ROMFT to you too," said Jonesy with feeling.

At 0800 Jamie made his way back to the mess. The strongest and most experienced hands had reclaimed some order from the chaos of their living area. The gash bucket bulged with broken crockery and the deck had been mopped and wiped over.

"Stow your 'mick and mash the tea, Taffy," said Micky. "We still have a few cups left. And see what's on for breakfast."

"Aye aye." Jamie braced himself against a locker while lashing his hammock. The nausea, which he'd suppressed all through the long four hour watch, returned with the thought of breakfast. He measured a handful and a half of tea leaves into the large aluminium tea-kettle and carefully made his way aft to the galley, grabbing any secure handhold to avoid being thrown off his feet by the bucking deck. Passing the washroom, the door swung open and a very pale Pedlar struggled out.

"Don't go in there, mate. It's disgusting."

From the door Jamie could see the white-tiled floor. Awash with spew, the evil smelling liquid swilled to and fro amongst the wooden duckboards in a grotesque dance with the rhythm of the tossing ship. A putrid smell hit Jamie's nose and he held his breath – too late; the contents of his stomach heaved into his mouth and he just managed to direct the spout past Pedlar to join the rest of the brew on the washroom deck.

"Bastard." Pedlar spun around and disappeared back into the washroom with one hand over his mouth.

Feeling slightly better and wiping his lips with his sleeve Jamie continued to the galley. At the serving hatch the steaming heat of the small space renewed the feeling of nausea.

"What's for breakfast, Chef?" asked Jamie.

Inside the hot room the duty chef, Wee Jock from Glasgow – Wee Jock because there was also a Big Jock – his white hat at an impossible angle, fought to keep two large, deep pans from sliding about on the electric range. Without taking his eyes off the pans he reached for Jamie's tea fanny and half filled it with hot water from a boiler.

"Rough weather gear," he replied, indicating the pans bubbling away like witch's concoctions on the stove. "Beans; stewed beef; you name it – good stuff. Bring a fanny and numbers. Hey, ye didn'a use my galley fer making Kye this morning, did ye?"

"Why?" Jamie hung on to the counter, wishing to be away from the smell of the galley.

"Because," said the chef, menacingly, "whoever used *my* galley left a hellaver mess, that's why."

"No, you don't say," said Jamie. "The sods. No consideration. Got to go, thanks."

Unable to face breakfast, Jamie joined other off duty men on the signal deck. Positioned aft of the bridge, the exposed semaphore and flag-raising deck, open to the furious wind hurling horizontal spray against stinging faces, helped stave off the worst feelings of seasickness. The angry sea, spume ripping from the crest of each huge wave, threw everything at the carbuncle riding on its back. To Jamie, the ship felt like a Barry Island ride as it dropped sickeningly into each deep trough to shudder and lift at the last second to climb the next impossibly high peak, reprieved and unbreached.

Time passed quickly and by mid-afternoon the ship gradually pulled out of the storm into brighter, calmer weather.

The following day brought warmer air, heightening the spirits of the ship's company. Dress of the day changed to white caps and a warm southern breeze blew in through open deadlights to ventilate and dry out the ship.

On the morning of the third day out of Plymouth a lookout reported the first sighting of Gibraltar.

CHAPTER 8

MEDITERRANEAN

.

The Rock of Gibraltar, standing high and bright in the southern sunshine, dwarfed the expanse of the dockyard and town buildings nestling below its craggy slopes. Eager to experience his first taste of 'abroad', Jamie joined Mick and Pedlar for a jaunt ashore. As he waited at the gangway he noticed another 'D' Class destroyer tied up on the berth for'ard of *Demon. HMS Dunness*, a clone of *Demon*, added to a number of other warships including two Town-class Cruisers and a Royal Fleet Auxiliary, resting at the outer jetty. A submarine, black and low in the water, sat almost unnoticed against the sea-side of the outer jetty. French and American ships, including a preposterously large American aircraft carrier, took up other parts of the dockyard.

Mick led the other two on the long walk around the dockyard's deep-water basins, and along a pretty, tree-lined residential street into the town.

"Just like Southsea in the summer." Jamie avoided shadows where he could, enjoying the warmth of the sun and the prospect of time away from the ship. Losing the company of Latch had unsettled Jamie. And the malignant presence of Badger took away much of his enjoyment of new experience.

As the trio passed the modest, but well guarded, Governor's house Scouser and Toffee overtook them at pace.

"What's the rush?" asked Micky.

"Can't stop," said Toffee. "We're on our way to La Linea. You can come with us – but you'll need your passport."

"What's La Linea?" asked Jamie.

"Across the border – it's the first town you come to," said Mick.

"You won't get nothing in Gib." Scouser waved a passport under Jamie's chin. "La Lin is the place. Cheap plonk and cheaper women."

"That's not all they'll get cheap." Micky watched the two hurrying away. "Them two will be lined up at the sickbay door in a few days…"

Pairs of British police, complete with helmets, sauntered benignly along the narrow main street of Gibraltar accompanied by white gaitered and belted Naval Shore Patrols. Elbowing his way through the crowds, Jamie took in the unfamiliar sounds and smells of his first foreign port. Pretty girls, dark-eyed and olive-skinned, pointedly ignored the appreciative looks from the many uniformed men milling about, and passed on. Large, cavernous bars, spewing brassy Spanish music sat comfortably alongside shops stuffed with exotic goods.

"Cameras, watches – why so many Asians?" asked Jamie.

"Duty free – Gib is a duty-free port – but first we'll get you kitted out for the Med." Mick ducked into an emporium festooned with shawls, fans and Spanish dolls. Inside the dark interior the musky smell of burning incense greeted them. After some intense bartering with the Indian proprietor each came out with sunglasses and some very colourful cotton shorts.

"That's your first lesson, Taffy, boyo," said Micky. "Never accept the first price; beat 'em down. Them cotton nicks will dry quickly and stop dhobi itch. Only one and sixpence each – I saved you a bomb so you can buy the first beers."

The rest of the evening passed by very quickly, the three moving from crowded bar to crowded bar; drinking British beer; clapping and singing along with the bands; fighting for a front seat to look up the skirts of castanet-clacking Spanish dancers.

The walk back seemed much shorter than the trip out. Jamie, not at all getting the hang of the pair of castanets he had bought for his sister, enjoyed himself trying anyway.

Demon left Gibraltar at dawn and headed out into the narrow straits – and into a squall. The wind and the short, steep seas caught the ship as she cleared the lee of the rock – but the older hands had seen it all before.

"I've seen it all before," said Leading Seaman 'Taps' Tapper, twenty years service and now proud to hold the special duty of Sailmaker. No one really knew what a sailmaker did but he kept a sewing machine in a special little locker and lived in the Misc. mess. The buzz that he sewed people into canvas shrouds when they died was supported by his habit of suddenly and for no apparent reason, whipping out a tape measure and measuring any unsuspecting passer-by. Being short he stretched a bit for the tall ones. Like a tinker displaying his wares, the sailmaker wore a custom-made belt carrying all the things seamen carried. Knife, spike, gloves, tape measure, all neatly sheathed in leather, hung around his waist like an American cop.

The breeze hit the ship as she cleared the lee of the Rock. The sea, running beam on, added to the force of the wind, tipping her over to an alarming angle. Crashing sounds mixed randomly with swearing came from most of the spaces below decks.

The Tannoy spoke up belatedly. "Rig for rough weather – properly this time. I will reduce speed for breakfast. Turn to at 0800. We are continuing work-up on passage to Malta. Be alert; know your stations and get it right."

"It's the shallow water." Taps busied himself making a sandwich with some bacon from the breakfast tray. He stored it in his locker in case things got bad enough to cancel lunch.

"If this is the Med, I'd rather stay at home," said Jamie.

"Shit'n it, Davis." Badger stuffed his face from a piled plate. "What do you know?"

"Leave 'im." Dusty, the large stoker, gripped a plate full of bacon and eggs with one hand. He stopped forking mouthfuls of food to look threateningly at Badger.

"Sprog," said Badger, but the comment held no conviction. He looked away and left the mess.

The next week proved very hard work for the ship and for her crew. Captain De-Fotherinham ordered drills and routines that tested *Demon*'s systems, and the men operating them, to the limit. Day and night, the ship's company spent long sleepless hours at the various stages of battle readiness – almost always called at the most awkward time.

'Fire in the Galley' caused chaos when piped at supper time; 'Action Stations' at 0410 brought curses from middle watchmen just about to sink into deep sleep after four hours of concentrated effort to stay awake.

Time after time Jamie stumbled, sometimes half asleep, to his action station in the for'ard switchboard, a cramped railway carriage sized space manned by people ready to switch supplies to or away from damaged areas or to control generators. Jamie squeezed in too, ready to be despatched to assist the damage control parties with a portable battery lamp: a heavy piece of equipment to lug up and down ladders on damage control exercises.

During the middle of the forenoon of the third day out of Gibraltar, Jamie found himself detailed to attend a jackstay transfer; a personnel transfer from a Royal Fleet Auxiliary out of Gibraltar.

"It'll be good experience," said Grundy. "And he's one of ours anyway – a replacement for your mate Latchbrook."

From his position amongst the hauling party Jamie watched as the awkward-looking supply vessel drew abreast to receive a line shot from *Demon*. With a brisk wind producing a choppy sea, both ships struggled to match speeds and stay perfectly on station. The line, looped through a pulley block and attached to a bosun's chair, looked very fragile and the water, churning and heaving between the two great grey hulls, looked very uninviting. Jamie listened intently to the instructions shouted out by the PO seaman in charge.

"Grab the rope. On my order, '2-6 heave', you run like hell," said the PO, "that way." He pointed, rather unnecessarily Jamie thought, for'ard. "And you do not stop until I order 'stop', understood?"

On the trial run Topsy Turner stumbled, bringing the hauling party down in a heap. The line dipped into the angry sea. A wave viciously sent the empty chair looping into the air before the RFA crew recovered the slack.

"Try that again." Jamie looked up to the Skipper leaning over from the bridge. "You *will* get it right."

Jamie spotted Taps, tape measure in hand, watching the exercise intently from a vantage point on the port for'ard Anti-Aircraft Gun platform.

The second dry run wasn't dry but not so wet as to postpone the inevitable. Derek's replacement secured himself in the chair and held on for dear life. Mouthing a little prayer, Jamie wiped his sweating hands on his trousers and re-established his grip on the rope. At about the halfway mark the two ships converged slightly causing the chair to drop perilously close to the raging water. Extra speed from the hauling team saved the day, smacking the chair and its occupant hard against the jackstay upright. As Joseph Ripley climbed out onto the fo'csle his legs gave way. A timely issue of grog restored the newcomer's power of speech and allowed him to introduce himself to the mess.

Winkle Ripley, fresh from maintaining equipment at HMS Rook, the Naval Base on Gibraltar, took over Jamie's job on Communications. Jamie transferred to Batteries and Motorboats. Thrilled to be trusted with caring for any battery aboard and all electrical systems on *Demon*'s small boats, he stowed his toolbox in the Battery Shop.

Jamie's first job as Battery King took him down into the heat and excruciating noise of 'A' boiler room to check the emergency lights. After an hour of clambering past super-heated steam pipes and squeezing along hot metal bulkheads, he climbed back up, staggered out of the air lock and headed for the water cooler. His No.8s clung to him, soaked with sweat from the intense heat.

"Bloody hell," he said aloud, "stokers must be very brave or very thick to work in that. Very thick, I think."

"What's that?" said a voice behind.

"Ah, not you, Dusty. Them down in the boiler room. Maniacs, they are. Phwor, Dust, what is that smell?"

"It's me. I've just unblocked the forward heads." Extending one arm he showed Jamie a brown smearing up to his elbow. His overalls were similarly decorated where he had wiped his hands and damp patches adorned his knees where he had knelt. The brown something was drying and flaking like the chocolate on the cakes his sister liked to make.

"Is that shit?"

"Yup, sure is. I'm on my way for a wash." He dropped the canvas tool bag and took a swig from the water cooler, wiping his mouth with the back of his hand.

"Gord, bloody stokers," said Jamie, ducking to avoid a shitty clip around the ear.

Jamie had grown to like Dusty; liked his sense of humour and his lack of airs and graces. In addition, Dusty disliked

Badger, who would rather Dusty slung his hook elsewhere. Tall and muscular, Dusty ate large amounts of food.

"I got the habit from the Field Gun Crew," he explained to Jamie one evening during supper. "Only the best for the boys at Devonport. Steaks as thick as your arm. All protein they used to feed us. Food and exercise; body-building stuff all the time. You wouldn't coco but I was an ordinary size before and I volunteered. I had to be completely re-kitted out when I left."

"You'll only get your share on *my* mess," interjected Badger who shut up when Dusty rose to his full height.

"Ignore him Dust," said Jamie, "he's not worth it."

Dusty came from Gloucester and cut his dark hair very short, 'to save on soap as I have to wash it so often.'

With so much activity no one realised the distance the ship had progressed, so a broadcast from the Captain came as a pleasant surprise. "You will no doubt be happy to learn that the first phase of our work up is almost over. Do not think that I am satisfied. I am not. We will continue after a short visit to Malta. ETA 0900 hrs tomorrow." The cheer from below decks could be heard on the bridge. "This afternoon I want this ship cleaned from top to bottom," the cheering turned to groans, "but as a last exercise we have just received a signal that a battlefield nuclear device has exploded ten miles away and the fallout is drifting our way. Secure the ship for nuclear attack."

Within minutes every orifice in the ship had been plugged; every watertight door, inlet and exhaust secured. Central control moved to the enclosed bridge – situated a deck below the open bridge. Water, sprayed from permanent pipes, covered the entire vessel. She must have looked like a sea going fountain but no one on board could tell, every man being incarcerated inside the unventilated, overheating, metal box. The spraying continued until the nasty nuclear particles were washed away and the decks tested by space-suited Geiger-counter operators who gave the all clear.

"I think I'd rather take me chances with Alpha particles than be slowly suffocated," declared Dusty at lunch.

"No decent Alpha particle would take up residence in you," said Badger with a rare attempt at humour. "Just stick you up top and they'd all piss off."

"Now, girls," interceded Mick. "Save your energy for scrubbing and polishing this afternoon."

After lunch Grundy popped his head into the Battery shop, interrupting Jamie cleaning the paintwork and brass fittings.

"When you fall out from 'Entering Harbour' tomorrow, don't change back into 8s. You're going to the Airport."

"Why? Am I going home, PO?"

"No such luck, we're stuck with you. You're picking up a parcel for the EA, that's all, and make sure those boat batteries are all fully charged. We're on a buoy."

"Yes, PO, three bags full PO," said Jamie to the departing Grundy, who turned to add, "…and don't forget the Captain's barge. Postie is using it."

During the rest of the day the crew turned to cleaning, scrubbing and painting. The sea had changed colour from the Atlantic's grey and murky soup to a deep, clear turquoise blue. The breeze, with them for most of the trip from Gibraltar, disappeared and the sea became glass smooth. The strengthening sun burned the shoulders of those lucky enough to spend time on deck. After supper Jamie and Dusty moved outside to the warm evening air and leaned on the rail watching the sea hissing past. Where the bow wave broke and effervesced into white foam, the surface twinkled and sparkled with a thousand fairy lights, jumping and shooting in all directions like fireflies in the night.

"Fluorescence," explained Dusty who had been to the Med before.

"That is bloody beautiful," said Jamie with a Celtic fervour. "Bloody beautiful."

"Have you been to Malta, kid?"

"Nope."

"I like Malta." Dusty took a last drag on his tickler and flicked it into the darkness. "Anchor beer; Marsala wine; Steak, Egg and Chips…"

"Triffic," agreed Jamie, solemnly.

"I got into trouble last time though."

"Yeah?"

"Yeah. I'd been ashore down Floriana – don't remember who with – but I'd downed a few sherbets. I got one of them there pony trap things to bring me back to the ship. There's a hill from Valetta down to the Custom House Steps where we caught the liberty boat. We got halfway down and the horse dropped dead."

"Grief," said Jamie. "Poor thing. Was it poorly?"

"No, dead."

"No, I mean what caused it to die?"

"I don't know. Old age I expect. Anyway, it made me late and I missed me boat. I was up before the Skipper next morning for bein' adrift."

"What happened?"

"Let me off, he did."

"Decent Skipper," said Jamie.

"Yeah, but the feller behind me tried the same thing after seeing me get off. ''Orse dropped dead, sir,' he said. The skipper must have been in a good mood 'cos he had a laugh and let him off too."

"Jammy sod."

"Yeah – then the Skipper said to the next one, 'I suppose your horse dropped dead too?'

'No Sir,' said the quick-thinking bugger. 'I couldn't get past for dead 'orses'."

Jamie glanced at his large companion, who gazed into the night with an unchanged expression. Not knowing whether to laugh or not, Jamie nodded sagely and said nothing.

CHAPTER 9

MALTA

Next day, after breakfast and 'clean ship', Jamie, dressed in white shorts for the first time, mustered for entering harbour. From his position on the starboard side of the fo'csle he watched the island of Malta taking shape. A slight breeze had blown up, taking the heat out of the sun and ruffling the surface of the water. The deep blue of the sea contrasted with the sandstone colour of the rocky land. Unfamiliar shapes, square, flat-topped houses and domed minarets, completed the landscape like children's sand castles on a beach.

With her crew lining the rails, *Demon* steamed around the southern tip of the island to the sheltered eastern side to approach the huge natural basin of Grand Harbour. Once through the entrance the expanse of the anchorage could be appreciated. Steeples and spires and domed square buildings captured the skyline. Impressive high stone walls and buttresses, witness to centuries of defensive necessity, enclosed the harbour. Slipping slowly past a high fortress to port another destroyer came into view sitting serenely at her buoy.

Demon manoeuvred for the approach to her allocated buoy. A flurry of activity further aft attracted the attention of everyone on the fo'csle. The whaler, suspended from her davits, had been lowered into the water by her stern. Anxiously the crew manning her hung on for dear life while the hand responsible for the for'ard release gear did his best to free her. It took a series of numbing blows from the frantic seaman before the gear responded. With a splash, the bow joined the stern in the water. With uncoordinated difficulty the men in the boat headed for the buoy, but the delay had allowed the ship to overrun.

With a clang the bow contacted the buoy. A swift order of 'full astern' brought the ship to a halt and amid a swirl of disturbed water she crept back.

As the buoy cleared the bow a brightly coloured Dghajsa, sculled by a dark, leather-skinned man in a beret, appeared. With practised ease the barefooted boatman stepped from his sculling position on the high stern of his small wooden craft and scooped up the line that had been thrown earlier. With equal ease, he passed the end of the line through the eye of the buoy. With a few sweeps of his single oar he dragged the line to the sea boat, handed the end to the coxswain and smoothly sculled out of the way. Interest from *Dunness* had grown and she had started to list noticeably with the numbers lining her starboard rails. Due to a mistake someone on her bridge accidentally pulled her steam hooter. The blast could be heard as far away as Gozo – but worse, it incensed Captain De-Fotherinham.

The remaining procedure went without mishap. The anchor party doubled up on her bow lines and the Captain ordered main engines shut down. Passage Routine changed to Harbour Routine and the Skipper sent 'my compliments to the First Lieutenant and would he please report to my day cabin – immediately'.

The Dghajsa man, quiet and unassuming, later attached himself to the ship to become the authorised taxi service. The position also entitled the barefooted boatman access to the leftover food from meals. With undented dignity Spiro appeared in the mess after each meal. At precisely the time the gash was about to be discarded, he padded silently in, filled a spotlessly clean tin can with potatoes, vegetables and any intact meat with his bony, parchment fingers and left. No one ever questioned or commented on the act but many wondered at the destination of the food.

Jamie, following Grundy's instructions, joined Postie in the first boat ashore.

"There will be Maltese Navy transport at Customs House to take you to the airport. Show him this." Grundy handed Jamie a slip of paper. "The spare part should be waiting for you at reception. Come straight back and no skiving, understood?"

Stepping onto firm ground at Malta's Custom House steps gave Jamie an uneasy feel after weeks at sea. A pungent smell of heat, dusty and heavy, hung in the air. The few people moving about progressed slowly, hugging the diminishing shadows to avoid the morning sun. A Maltese naval rating emerged from the darkness of an arched opening in the stone wall opposite the landing jetty and led Jamie to a Navy Land Rover parked on the road. Jamie jumped into the cab to find the windscreen bizarrely festooned with beads and religious items. Pulling away, the vehicle approached the hill leading up to the town. Unable to resist a smile Jamie imagined the road covered with downed ponies.

Outside of the city many of the dusty roads sported half-built two or three storey houses supported by rickety timber gantries. Beige-coloured stone blocks stood in piles, ready to be used in the buildings.

"Many bombs from the war," said the driver in a rare comment. "Now we make-a the house for our self – brother help brother, you understand?"

"Good system," nodded Jamie.

Approaching the airport the road skirted a fenced runway where a BOAC aircraft, looking huge with its four propeller engines, sat on the tarmac near a low terminal building. The Land Rover stopped and Jamie entered the wide entrance and enquired from a khaki-clad guard the whereabouts of reception. With a disinterested gesture the guard pointed into the cool spacious lounge – toward a man arguing heatedly with a smartly dressed girl behind a counter. Jamie stopped and watched.

"My transport should be here," said the man in the slacks and white shirt.

"I am sorry, sir," said the flustered girl. "I'm sure it won't be too long now. Please take a seat and I'll try again."

"I've sat here for an hour. How long does it take, for God's sake? I could walk this island in an hour."

Jamie doubted that the man could walk anywhere in an hour because he limped, in a very familiar gait, back to a row of seats opposite the reception desk – and to a stack of luggage.

For a moment Jamie could not believe his eyes but the name, printed in unmissable black letters on a suitcase, confirmed that here sat Lt Cdr 'Hoppalong' Henderson.

While Henderson busied himself with lighting a cigarette Jamie approached the girl. She looked up, briefly smiled at Jamie, and continued speaking into a telephone. As she finished the call Jamie produced his slip of paper and collected the parcel, which he signed for. Thanking the girl he moved away, keeping his eyes averted from the seats and from their only occupant. After a few yards he thought he was clear but a voice, loud in the echoing hall, stopped him in his tracks.

"Excuse me, son." Jamie looked around to see Hoppalong approaching. "Just a minute. Do you have transport?"

"Sir?"

"I'm in your mob; I am Lt Cdr Henderson."

Jamie saluted, self-consciously but smartly. Hoppalong held out a passport with one hand while loosely returning the salute with the other.

"And I need a lift to Valetta. Are you going my way?"

"Er, yes, Sir, but—"

"That's a good lad. Help me with my bags. Let's get out of here. *Demon*, ay?" Hoppalong had glanced at Jamie's cap band. "De-Fotherinham. How is the old boy?"

"Fine, Sir, I think."

"Good. I'll put a good word in for you when I see him. What's your name, son?"

"Davis, Sir. EM Davis."

Hoppalong stopped at the entrance and slapped a wide-brimmed floppy hat on his head.

"Davis? You seem familiar. Do I know you?"

Jamie dropped the bags. "I don't think so, Sir. Wait here – I'll get the Rover."

Hoppalong took the front seat. Jamie sat with the luggage in the rear, glad to be out of conversation range. The officer, sweating profusely, occasionally glanced back at Jamie. The boy desperately tried to look nonchalant, wondering when the penny would drop. Skirting the bus depot in Valetta, the Lt Cdr directed the driver through wide gates and along a flower-lined drive to the front door of a large, ornate hotel. White coated attendants hurried out, took the luggage, and led the limping officer to the main entrance. Jamie, much relieved to see the back of the father of the girl his best mate had gone walkabout for, nimbly hoisted himself into the front seat of the Land Rover and slammed the door shut, almost trapping a foot in his haste. For one heart stopping moment, the Lt Cdr, who had almost reached the hotel door, turned and came back.

"Davis."

"Yes, Sir?" Jamie felt light-headed.

"My compliments to your captain, if you please, and tell him I will be in touch shortly. Will you remember my name?"

"Oh, that I will, Sir." Jamie elbowed the driver in the ribs to get him going. "Goodbye, Sir."

"Er, yes, goodbye. Are you sure we've not served together…?"

Jamie sighed with relief as the Land Rover responded and accelerated away leaving the white-shirted man standing in the drive, hat in hand, with a puzzled expression on his face.

Back on board, Jamie delivered the spare part to the Chief E.A. and returned to the mess to change. A letter from his sister awaited him, which he read while eating his lunch.

'Please don't worry,' Gwyneth wrote in her almost print-quality handwriting, *'Dad was taken into hospital last week...'*

'God, that was two weeks ago', thought Jamie.

'...to the Pneumoconiosis Unit at Cardiff. He had a touch of double pneumonia...'

'Double? Don't worry, she says.'

'...but he's responding to the treatment. He had to have a needle in his back to draw the fluid from his chest.'

Jamie paused in his reading. 'Oh, Dad, you poor old bugger.'

'Lucky I get a lift from John to go see him. The busses don't go anywhere near the hospital.'

'John? Who the hell is John?'

'When he comes home he will have to have oxygen. All my love – Dad sends his as well.

Gwyneth.'

Jamie promised himself that he would sit down later and reply – but the plan had to be shelved when Dusty Miller, keen to share his knowledge of Malta, organised a run ashore.

Straight Street rarely sees the sun for the high, ornate balconied buildings crowding in on each side. Centuries old, the street miraculously survived the bombs of World War Two to continue its long tradition of supplying young, mainly naval, visiting men with the means of forgetting their troubles, wives, girlfriends or mums. Running parallel with the main thoroughfare of old Valetta, the street known throughout the seafaring world as The Gut, hid its shame and contained its activities away from local view.

Dusty, Jamie, Pedlar and Mick arrived at the top of The Gut hot and breathless after the climb from the harbour. Dusty's pace proved difficult to match on the incline to the high central part of the city. At the entrance, where the street dropped down away into the distance, Dusty stopped the group to survey the view. White-clad sailors walked or staggered up and down the narrow street, falling in and out of gaudily decorated entrances of bars and eating places, resisting or succumbing to calls from the sirens adorning each doorway.

Dusty sniffed a long sniff. "Smell that, can't you?"

"Smell what?" The others sniffed in unison.

"Anchor beer. I've been waiting two years for that smell."

"All I can smell is sewage," said Jamie.

"Yeah, that's it," said Dusty, "Anchor beer. So make sure you ask for a drop of lemonade in it. Hides the taste."

"Jack, ey, Jack. You buy me dreenk?" A buxom lady, in a wrap-around top and tight black skirt, called out to the foursome as they passed the first bar. Self-consciously they ignored her and the sound of 'Blue Suede Shoes' booming out from the bar's jukebox into the warm evening air.

Further down the street large double-sized doors with a brightly lit sign above announced itself brashly as the Silver Dollar.

"This is the place," said Dusty. Gently but firmly he cleared a way through the gang of girls adorning the entrance.

Inside, the heady atmosphere, thick with smoke, alcohol fumes and noise, stopped their progress. Jamie, feeling small and awkward, removed his cap and scanned the unfamiliar scene from behind the bulk of his large shipmate. Groups of matelots in various stages of intoxication lounged at the Formica-topped tables scattered about the room. A dishevelled able-seaman, the flap of his bells unbuttoned, swayed in front of a huge chrome and plastic jukebox. Tears streamed from his eyes; cigarette smoke bled from his mouth as he sang along, "I'll be home, my darling," to the record booming in almost visible waves of sound from the loudspeakers.

"Looks like we're too late," shouted Dusty over his shoulder.

Pedlar strained to see past Dusty. "Why? No room?"

"Nope," shouted Dusty, "it's full of Dung'eads…"

Before the sentence had finished Anne Newton's silvery tones faded away, allowing Dusty's insult to be broadcasted to the whole room. After a few silent seconds a group near the door responded.

"Well, if it ain't the *Demon* boys," said one. "You know, lads," he shouted to the room, "the ones who can't park without knocking the shit out of a poor innocent buoy."

Jamie cringed and pushed Pedlar back into the Gut, tugging Dusty as he went.

"We wouldn't drink in that trough anyway," shouted Dusty back into the bar. "It's infested with rats, great big two-legged ones."

"You idiot," laughed Jamie hurrying away. "They outnumber us umpteen to none."

"That's the worse cesspit in the street," complained Dusty. "And that lot of idiots have taken it over. Bastards."

"There's plenty more." Pedlar pointed to the many neon lights further down the well-trodden street.

Dusty chose 'The Lucky Horseshoe'. The bar, not quite as bright – as loud – or as large as the Silver Dollar, satisfied Pedlar too. Almost before the three had sat at a round table next to the bar a woman had eased her high-heeled feet off a stool and with an exaggerated sway, had sidled up behind the seated Dusty. Another woman rubbed her well-padded thigh against Pedlar.

"Ah, Darleeng boys. You buy me dreenk?"

"I'm married," said Dusty. "Four Anchor beers – cold ones."

"Oh," whined the woman. "You buy Carlotta dreenk." She tossed a disdainful look at the barman. "He throw me out, you not buy me dreenk."

"For pity's sake, buy her a dreenk," said Mick. "I'm after dying here."

Jamie sat back and watched in awed silence as the bargirl, bending forward to expose a broad expanse of cleavage, delivered the drinks.

"How old you?" Carlotta placed a bottle of beer, sweating with condensation, onto the table in front of Jamie.

"Me?" said Jamie.

"He's a cherry boy," said Pedlar, gleefully. "He's never had it."

"Shit'n it, Pedlar," said Jamie.

"Cherree boy." The woman stood back. "Ye-es. Now I see. I like Cherree boy."

With a wink to the others and a wicked smile on her face, Carlotta took Jamie's hand and placed it firmly on her breast. The others hissed and clapped with delight as Carlotta resisted his attempts to pull away.

"Whoa, yer in there, Taffy lad," said Pedlar.

"No, I too old you." Carlotta released her red-faced captive's hand. "I have lovely dotter. I save her for you. You marry her and take her back to Blighty, yes?"

She moved away to welcome other patrons from *Demon* and soon the place was full and loud and drunken. Occasionally Carlotta returned to sit next to Jamie and touch his groin, which responded with an instant bulging erection. Everyone at the table knew she was doing it by the look of cross-eyed ecstasy that came over the young man's face. In return she received another glass of pink water until all his money was gone.

"Shit 'ot place, that," said Jamie as the group fell out into the street.

"Yeah, you would think that, you dirty little bastard." Micky had downed two bottles of Marsala and could only progress by leaning heavily on Dusty. As they approached the Silver Dollar Dusty passed Mick to the other two for support.

"I won't be a sec." With a furtive glance up and down the street the big man disappeared through the swing doors. The three friends continued up the steps of the narrow alley backwards, watching for Dusty to emerge.

"Gone for a piss, 'spect," said Pedlar.

"Brave bastard, 'im," said Mick, falling onto his backside.

When Dusty emerged he had one hand up his jumper. In short steps, not quite a trot, he rejoined the others. Glancing back he removed his hand from its hiding place.

"Spoils of war." Dusty shook out a handful of cap tallies, each bearing the gold-embroidered name of *HMS Dunness*. "One each."

"You mad bugger," laughed Mick, but he grabbed one anyway and slipped it over his head like a trophy. With Pedlar to lean on the two led the way to the harbour each singing his own song and picking each other up when they fell.

"You were doin' okay in the bar, youngster." Dusty looked behind for signs of pursuit.

"Yeah, but they don't do it, do they, Dust? The girls, I mean." Jamie manfully tried to focus on the street ahead and on keeping a straight course.

"They do if you promise to marry them."

"She promised me her daughter – when she's old enough."

"Be a good shag, I 'spect. Make good wives, Malts," said Dusty. "Catholic, though. Are you Catholic?"

"C of E. – but I went to Chapel. It was closer to where we lived."

The two continued silently for a while, Jamie reliving, with a rueful touch to his groin, the feel of a female hand on his penis, even if it was on the outside of his trousers.

"Can I ask you something, Dust?"

"Depends on the question."

"Do you, you know, er, how do you, you know…"

"Spit it out, for God's sake, Taff. Do I what?"

"You know, when you feel randy. Do you, you know, do you go with women? Do you, you know…"

"I gather, from your idiot ramblings, that you are trying to ask me if I visit the ladies of the night. Am I correct?"

"Well, er, yeah."

"Nope, not any more – I'm married. But I did go with one prostitute – years ago in Liverpool. Mary her name was – they called her one-eyed Mary – due to her only having one eye."

"One eye?"

"Yeah, but she saw me off. Then when I was leaving she said she would keep an eye out for me."

For a long minute the story struggled through the fog of Jamie's brain until the penny dropped.

"You bastard," said Jamie, swinging and missing.

"As for the other, young man," continued Dusty. "If you bash your bishop too much you'll go blind. A couple of times a day is enough, but watch out for the hairs that grow in the palm of your hand. That's a dead give away."

The big man started running before Jamie, glancing at his palm, had time to realise that the mick was being taken.

In a fortunate instance of timing, *Demon*'s 2300 liberty boat pulled away from Custom House just as a group of gesturing matelots tumbled down the steps from the town onto the quay. Safe in the stern of the pinnace Dusty gathered his team to hoot and wave their trophy cap tallies at the incensed rivals left dancing and shouting obscenities on the quayside.

Long hours and hard work marked the weeks that followed – weeks of exercises with other ships interspersed with short breaks back in Malta. The men from *Demon* adopted the Lucky

Horseshoe as their favourite watering hole, avoiding the Silver Dollar – unless the rival ship happened to be away. At the beginning of April *Demon* buzzed with the news of a visit to Italy. To Jamie the jolly promised to be especially exciting as the dates coincided with his eighteenth birthday – a day when the Royal Navy considered that he had reached manhood: a day when he lost the title of 'Junior'.

CHAPTER 10

CIVITAVECCHIA

On the Tuesday of the second week in April, *HMS Demon* berthed alongside, close to the centre of the old town of Civitavecchia. Adjacent to the quay a busy road bustled with swiftly moving traffic. Trucks, cars and little motorised bikes honked and hooted their way along the wide thoroughfare. On board, the excitement of a visit to a new place affected all but the most seasoned travellers. Jamie and many other crew members, even some white-faced stokers who hardly ever saw the light of day, found excuse to carry whatever they had to carry across the upper deck. Despite the exhaust fumes hovering over the road, the air, cooler and fresher than the oppressive heat of Malta, smelled sweetly of spring. Colourful flowers and green foliage spilled from window boxes attached to red-tiled buildings across the thoroughfare. Jamie, on his way to the amplifier room had found time to take it all in from the flag deck – until a hand fell onto his shoulder.

"There you are," said Mick.

"I was just on my way…"

"Never mind that," said Mick. "Come with me."

Hurrying to keep up with the surprisingly nimble Irishman, Jamie followed Mick to the ship's office.

"What's up?" asked Jamie.

"Just wait." Mick pretended to fix the clamp on a battery-operated emergency lamp attached to the bulkhead next to the notice board. Inside the office a writer sat behind a desk. Dressed in his white shirt and black tie, the writer exuded an air of superiority only those with absolute power could match.

Within minutes the writer came out and pinned a number of sheets to the notice board. Micky hastened to look, along with others jostling for position around the notices.

"Invitations to jollies," said Micky. "You've got to be early to get the best ones."

As they scanned the sheets the Tannoy announced that invitations and trips had been posted and a crowd gathered swiftly. Mick, at the head of the melee, read the offers.

"Expatriates requests for two sailors – no good – prob'ly puffs," he muttered. "Coach trips – too bleedin' expensive. That's the one," said Paddy from the side of his mouth.

Jamie followed Mick's finger to the notice.

'12 required for tour of Rome, hosted by the Australian Consulate, Saturday. FREE, F.C.F.S.'.

"Hang on," Jamie pulled on Mick's sleeve, "I'm duty EM on Saturday."

"Never mind that." Mick scribbled his and Jamie's names onto the sheet. "We'll get you a sub. There's always plenty of spare at a Consul do and you're the good looking one – so you can come with me."

"What's F.C.F.S.?" queried Jamie, ducking out from the scramble.

"Free Cunt For Sailors," offered a voice from the crowd.

First Come, First Served," piped up the office writer from the office, raising his eyebrows in a gesture of contempt for the ignorance all around him.

By lunch time the mail that had been waiting for *Demon* on the quay had been sorted and issued to each mess from the mail office. On this occasion Jamie found two letters waiting for him. He instantly recognised his sister's handwriting, the address neat and clear on the front of a blue airmail envelope. The originator of the scrawl on the second envelope eluded him. Curious, he opened the small white envelope. The first few words, typically full of enthusiasm, told Jamie, even before looking at the signature, that the letter was from Derek.

'...they've put me on a diving course (no doubt hoping I'll drown myself). My Divisional Officer says it will be the making of me – Ha-ha. It's good, though – seems they need divers with a trade. And I get to use my superb body instead of my brain...'

As Jamie read on he realised that Derek mentioned nothing of his detention time, but equally it was obvious that Nelly was still on his mind.

'... I haven't seen you know who,' he wrote, 'and she hasn't written. She must be wondering about me but I expect old Hoppalong would have put his oar in – they don't know me, do they Jimmie, lad? By the way, I'm sorry I didn't stop to say cheerio to you that day on the fo'csle, but my two friends seemed in a hurry!'

The letter pleased Jamie, particularly the self-confidence oozing from the page about the diving.

'Good for you, Latch, you haven't let those bastards grind you down,' thought Jamie. He carefully folded the letter and slipped it into his No 8's breast pocket, but still, at the back of his mind, he could not shake the feeling that Derek's stubbornness would be his undoing.

Pedlar, sitting at the end of the mess table, groaned. "Oh, no, not another bloody Dear John."

Pedlar received more than his share of letters and more than his share of Dear Johns.

"Listen to this," said Pedlar. "It's from my Wendy. *I still love you but I think it's only fair to release you from your undying commitment. As a young attractive man...*' Hear that? She says I'm *attractive*. '*...you will need to sow your wild oats, especially abroad.*' Bloody 'ell is there no loyalty?

'*Besides, I have met this stoker who has one more stripe than you. Rodney is based at Raleigh, which is a ship that doesn't sail away like yours, and we will be getting engaged soon.'*

Not a stoker," groaned Pedlar. "Gazzumped by a friggin' stoker called Rodney."

With a sigh of resignation, Pedlar stood and pinned Wendy's letter with the other 'Dear Johns' on the notice board in the canteen flat. If he had looked he would have seen another with similar writing and the same signature. 'Wendy' was obviously clearing her portfolio in preference for the two-badge stoker.

Not knowing whether to smile or to commiserate with Pedlar, Jamie inspected the letter from Gwyneth – it contained a very small and simple birthday card, which reminded Jamie that today was the day before his eighteenth birthday.

Jamie arranged to swap Duties with Winkle from Saturday to Friday but this being Tuesday a trip ashore was organised for Wednesday, which was also Jamie's eighteenth birthday.

On Wednesday morning Jamie visited the ship's office. Excitedly he exchanged his old U/A station card, carefully checking that the new one categorised him as a G – a man in the eyes of the navy, and entitled to an issue of grog each day. Minutes before 'Up Spirits' sounded he took his place in the queue, watching with interest as a stores rating ceremoniously measured out – from the caramel depths of a wooden barrel – the sweet-smelling golden spirit. Under the eagle eyes of the duty officer and the coxswain, the stores rating deftly dispensed the rum from a copper measure and added two similar measures of water into each eagerly waiting man's glass. Feeling self-conscious with the eyes of his older mates upon him, Jamie shakily accepted his first issue of grog. Copying the routine from the others before him in the queue, he toasted 'The Queen, God bless Her' and gulped the drink down in one.

Coughing and spluttering from the unfamiliar burning in his throat and cheerfully accepting the punches and slaps on the back, he ran the gauntlet to the mess and sat at the table while the heat in his stomach subsided. Pedlar and Mick joined him and the trio set off to explore the town.

Pedlar, taking Wendy's advice, eyed every golden-limbed female they passed.

"Fancy that Wendy party sending me a 'Dear John'," complained Pedlar as they walked.

"But you have loads of girls."

"Yeah, but she was alright. And a two-badge stoker called Rodney – that's what really hurts."

Mick reckoned the best way to get the real feel of a place was to take the side and back roads, which they did – but not for long.

The back street buildings, with their shuttered windows and orange-tiled roofs, offered nothing of interest. Occasional food shops, closed in this, the middle of the day, displayed windows festooned with hanging sausages of all sizes and colours, from black to white and reds in between. Nothing stirred.

"Bloody fine way to spend my birthday," complained Jamie. He licked his dry lips, thirsty from the warm day and the effects of the rum.

Turning a corner the trio found themselves in a wide piazza lined with cafes, restaurants and shops. Jamie sat firmly on a white painted chair at a white painted table under the striped sunblind of a café. Pedlar positioned himself for the best view of the pavement and Mick moved to the doorway to look inside. A large female in a grubby pinafore confronted him and ushered him back to the table. With ample arms folded over an ample bosom, the lady waited for Mick to settle before searching inside her grubby pinafore pocket for a small pad and an even smaller pencil.

"Beer," said Jamie.

"Wine," said Mick.

"Red," said Pedlar.

"White," said Mick. "It's cheaper."

Then, in a nonchalant, leaning back in the chair worldly-wise manner, Micky engaged the café lady.

"Seeenora, we'll have a bottle of your house wine, white, and three glasses," he lifted three chubby fingers.

From her gestures and the expressive shrugging of her shoulders she indicated that she understood nothing of what was being said.

"Mamma, mia," said Pedlar, impatiently. "Wine, vino, blanco and three," he put up three fingers, "glasses, for us three."

"Si, me Mama," said Mama. "Tree beer, yankee doodles, GIs."

"Oh, Christ," groaned Pedlar. "She thinks we're Yanks. I wish we were down the Gut drinking Marsala."

"Ah," exclaimed Mama. "Marsala! Vino, vino."

"My God, she's got it." Mick nodded vigorously at the woman, "and make it bianco."

As she headed for the café Micky added, "and we're not bloody Yanks either."

The wine arrived in a large, cool bottle – water droplets condensing on the glass and soaking the paper serviette on its tray. Being much smoother than the two shilling variety sold in the Lucky Horseshoe, it disappeared very quickly. Toasts to Jamie's birthday and to Pedlar's last birthday and to Mick's next birthday emptied the litre bottle swiftly. The second bottle seemed to hold more than the first. The sun moved the shadows further into the street where leathery old men on upright bikes, ladies with baskets, and young, precocious girls passed in growing numbers.

"It's the hair," decided Pedlar. "It's all dark and thick, and their legs are different to our English parties, and their hips are so…"

"Pronounced," said Mick, helping out.

"That's it – pronounced. Their hips are so pronounced – or it's their dresses. Our parties would be wearing big heavy coats now…"

"Right," said Mick, "now we've sorted that, shit'n it. Get your mind off what you can't have and onto what you can. Get us another bottle."

Without exception the young women dressed in cotton dresses ignored, in a head tossing, haughty sort of way, the calls and whistles aimed at them by an appreciative Pedlar.

A group of young men dressed in smooth, olive-green uniforms, some with their caps folded and slotted into their epaulettes, arrived and sat at a table next to the three sailors.

"Eyetie pongos," stated Mick.

"Young, ain't they?" The now eighteen-year-old Jamie watched as the new arrivals downed small glasses of red liquor and tucked into steaming mounds of spaghetti – turning and twisting their forks expertly to load up the white pasta.

"Spaghetti," stated Mick.

"I'm hungry," slurred the birthday boy. In fascination he watched the white tails disappear into laughing mouths.

"So'me I," echoed Mick, "but if you think for one minute I'm gonna try ordering that stuff from that woman you can get knotted. 'Sides, we don't know how to eat that wormy stuff."

"Try asking those Eyetie pongos," suggested Jamie.

"Na, I'm not talking to that lot," said Mick. He looked pointedly at the other group. "Besides, bloody Eyeties no speeka da Eenglish."

One of the Italian soldiers looked over at them, his face breaking into a white-toothed smile. "Wanna peezza?" he asked.

Taken aback the trio whispered among themselves.

"Was 'e mean, 'peezza'?" enquired Jamie, quietly.

"He means pizza pie," decided Mick. He nodded affirmation to the soldier who jabbered to the café lady who looked over at the Eenglish haughtily before retiring to the café.

Ten minutes later Mama delivered a large, round, cheese covered pie. After the food had been consumed, much raising of glasses, together with half smiles, passed between the two groups. Eventually the English speaking Italian soldier stood and came over.

"Eenglish?" he enquired.

"Breetish," replied all except Pedlar, who nodded and pointed to his cap ribbon.

"You wanna come Mama's?"

"Another Mama's?"

"He wants to take us home," suggested Jamie, "to his Mum's."

"Mum's? I wonder what for."

"Geegajeeg." The pongo rolled his dark eyes and wriggling his hips to the delight of his friends behind him.

"Jigajig," perked up Pedlar. "P'raps he wants to introduce us to his Mum or his sisters."

"Dirty bastard," said Mick.

"My name Pepino – Pepe. I show you; you come?"

Pedlar jumped nimbly to his feet, grabbed his cap and followed before the others had gathered themselves.

"His prick's in charge again," said Mick, supporting Jamie who had discovered, when he stood up, that he had lost a percentage of leg control.

After a few streets the buildings seemed larger and older, with balconies and overhanging windows almost blanking out the light from above. Pedlar, walking with Pepe and his mates, stopped to let Jamie and Mick catch up.

"Its okay" said Pedlar "It's a brothel – Mama's is a brothel."

"I can't go there." Jamie stopped in his tracks. "I can't, I haven't enough money."

"Shit'n it," dismissed Pedlar, pulling him along. "Pepe says it's clean and cheap. This is the chance to break your cherry; besides, you're eighteen now. I'll lend you the liras as a birthday present."

Up ahead the group of Italians stopped at a pair of large carved wooden doors and waited for the sailors to arrive. Nervously, Jamie allowed himself to be ushered along with his two mates, into a cool, high ceilinged hallway. Dozens of young Italian soldiers sat on benches lining the walls, as in a doctor's waiting room. All eyes turned to the British visitors and the chatter ceased – which did nothing to calm Jamie's nerves.

"You a-first." Pepe generously pushed the three sailors through the wide hallway, their steps echoing on the coloured tiled floor.

"Na, that's alright. You go first," offered Jamie. He forced himself to concentrate, struggling with how to get out of this situation.

"No, you a-first – you a-pay weeth ze lira. I no pay. I haf ze pass." With a flourish Pepe flashed a white ticket from his breast pocket. "Zees ees free geegajeeg one time every week. Very good, very clean. You go a-da first. You pay."

Jamie looked along the line of Italians. Each man clasped a white piece of paper. As he contemplated his fate a female, the first they had seen in the place, appeared from a doorway at the end of the hall. Clad in a white frilly blouse and tight black skirt, the busty, middle-aged woman sat herself behind a reception desk at the bottom of a wide staircase as if taking a booking for a hotel room. Pedlar talked to the woman – money and white tickets changed hands. During the conversation he pointed back at the reluctant Jamie – the youngster doing his best to appear unruffled by leaning on the wall in a nonchalant way. His efforts proved to no avail when the matron said something in Italian loud enough for all to hear which caused a ripple of mirth around the hall and the colour to rise in Jamie's face.

"What's she saying?" asked Jamie out of the side of his mouth.

"I think Pedlar's telling her you're a cherry boy." Mick laughed, enjoying the younger man's crimson-faced discomfort.

That's your room number." Pedlar handed Jamie a white ticket. "Yours is special, seeing as it's your first."

Within a blessedly few minutes Jamie, who had begun to wish he hadn't eaten so much pizza, realised that the reception woman had called out his number. Keeping his head down in a futile attempt to hide the blush that had exploded into his face Jamie started up the stairs followed by a ripple of applause from the sensitive Italian audience.

His trepidation heightened at the allocated room door. He knocked and waited until a voice bade him to enter. Slowly, and with a clammy hand, Jamie turned the door knob and pushed open the door. Dazzled by sunlight from a window across the room, Jamie narrowed his eyes. At first he saw only a large double bed until a surprisingly small woman moved towards him from the dark part of the room. She wore a white dressing gown: a loosely tied drape that gaped open to her waist and exposed one breast. Jamie moved into the room. Politely he removed his cap and closed the door – automatic movements that allowed him to continue to stare at her left breast. The aureole around her nipple, huge and swollen, drew Jamie's gaze like a magnet.

"Hello." Jamie attempted to speak but only a squeak came out. His head felt light as blood rushed to his groin. The woman smiled reassuringly and held out her hand to lead the boy to a washbasin.

"You wash," she indicated the bowl. Jamie took a bar of soap from a soap-stand and started to wash his hands.

With a giggle she touched his lower reaches, now bulging and straining inside the flap of his bells. "No-no. Thees, you wash."

Jamie removed his top and bell-bottoms, thinking only that he was glad to be wearing Chinese cotton shorts. With a deft tug the woman pulled down his pants allowing his hot member to spring out.

A shock curled his toes and shot up to his head as the woman washed his hot member with cold water, brushing his back with her breasts. With a firm pull she turned him to face her and dried him with a rough white towel, all the while making little appreciative noises with intakes of breath, a skill honed by the countless initiations that she had been responsible for. Jamie struggled to focus and found the girl to be older than he first thought.

"My name ees Gina, but all my bambinos call me Mama. Thees ees yor first time, no?"

Jamie nodded and allowed himself to be pulled, like a dinghy hauled by its painter, towards the bed.

"I lova my bambinos," she purred. "I am very nice, no? Mama weel take much care of bambino. You remember Mama Gina rest of your life, Okay?"

The high double bed sat hard under a tall window mostly covered by a slatted wooden shutter. White towels covered each side of the sheeted mattress and up over both pillows. Gina lay on one and Jamie on the other. The late afternoon sun, streaming through the slats above them, hit the far wall providing a dim light.

"You lika da spaghetti?" She wet her lips; pursed them and sucked as the pongos had done when eating spaghetti at the café.

Jamie nodded, shook his head then nodded again. He shuddered as her lips, dark against her white teeth, engulfed his knob.

"Zees my spaghetti," she mumbled from the side of her mouth.

Just when he thought he could withstand the sucking no longer she stopped, slipped off her gown and lay back.

"You a-all time theenk of you first time, no? All a-you life you remember so, I take care my bambinos. Now you fock me."

As she guided him inside her with a practised hand Jamie gave up his cherry, happy and enthusiastically, to join Mama's exclusive family of bambinos.

Jamie, the first of the British contingent to reappear from their allotted rooms, skipped through the foyer, ignoring the jibes and hisses from the Italians as he passed by. Outside he lit up a DF. Minutes later Pedlar and Mick tumbled out.

"Well, Taffy, boyo. How did you like that?" laughed Pedlar. He grabbed Jamie round the shoulders.

"Hang on, Pedlar," said Mick. "What's up, mate?"

"Oh, you know, Mickey." Jamie dropped his cigarette end to the paving and crushed it with his foot.

"Don't tell me you didn't like it," said Pedlar. "What did they do to you in there?"

Jamie took in an exaggerated deep breath and looked miserable. "I, er, lost something."

"What, you were robbed, you mean?"

"Yeah, Mama took my cherry." A slow grin spread over Jamie's face. "And I bloody loved it. The best birthday present I've ever had."

"You bastard," shouted Pedlar as the trio ran, whooping down the road to sample another bottle of vino and maybe a plate of spaghetti.

CHAPTER 11

ROME

On the following Saturday morning Jamie joined eleven of his shipmates on the jetty. The mixed bag of ratings – seamen, engineers and others, including the office writer – stood in groups, impatient to get started on the tour of Rome.

Within minutes a small convoy of vehicles led by a small and very noisy red Fiat appeared. One after the other the vehicles pulled off the thoroughfare and stopped. A large woman eased herself out of the leading car – shouting to make herself heard above the popping and spluttering engine.

"Hi, there," said the woman in a loud, unshackled Australian voice. "My name is Margaret. I can take three."

Andy, a National Service radio mechanic, who swam for Scotland, together with Jamie and Micky, allowed themselves to be herded into Margaret's small, upright car. Jamie, with his long legs, and Mick, with his portly figure, fitted uncomfortably into the rear. Andy, being a university student, chose the front seat. Along the wide carriageway to Rome the little car responded well under the heavy foot of the driver. Surprisingly the ear-splitting engine and gearbox noises inside the car proved no competition to Margaret's powerful narration. Andy received the full blast of the Australian's running commentary, which she kept up untiringly for the full hour of the trip. Facts about the buildings, roads and river came thick and fast. Jamie and Mick nudged each other, glad that they weren't university students qualified to sit in the front.

"Now, you fellas," shouted Margaret over her ample shoulder. "We're close to Rome. The road will become busy but no worries – I do this everyday."

True to her word, as buildings crowded the road, traffic filled the lanes and Margaret stiffened her grip on the steering wheel. Hunkering down in the straining seat the determined woman grimaced and increased the speed of the little car to keep up with the other determined vehicles passing on either side.

"No worries," shouted Margaret. "You just don't give way. That's the secret."

Andy, his swimmer's barrel chest heaving, sat holding the sides of his seat with his eyes firmly closed. Jamie, not wishing to look forward, peered out of the side window at the other drivers passing by or being passed. Many gestured wildly with one hand, or sometimes both. Horns of every timbre honked and blasted all around, including Margaret's, which she hit constantly with her large fist.

With a screech of tyres, the little car crossed several lanes to swerve and bounce through an open high iron gateway into a yard where it stopped. The small Michelin clad wheels smoked and smelled of burning brake linings.

"Australian Consulate," she announced proudly. Holding the front seat forward she allowed her very relieved passengers out.

"Mad cow," breathed Mick. Sweating profusely he gave a helping hand to the shaky Jamie.

"Cuppa first." Margaret shepherded her charges through the main door. "Nice cuppa Rosie Lee then we'll show you the sights."

In the cool, echoing foyer of the large house Mick, Andy and Jamie found a window ledge to recover on. Ten minutes later the others trouped in looking far less stressed.

Margaret, obviously in charge, fussed among the guests, shaking hands and welcoming all.

"Trust him to bag the good jollies." Micky indicated the Office Writer. The haughty admin clerk chatted animatedly with two women. His starched collar, white and stiff, seeming to push his neck up at a snooty angle.

A girl, cute in tight pink trousers that finished halfway down her tanned calves, offered Jamie's group tea and biscuits.

"Are you the ones that came with Margaret?" she asked. A broad Australian smile lit up her face.

"You mean the *Demon* driver?" confirmed Andy. "Can't you tell from our pale faces?"

"She's traumatised a few in her time." The girl laughed; a forthright unencumbered laugh. "You should have come with me – I only had the officer in my car."

A loose cream blouse, knotted above the waist, revealed a tantalising region of golden midriff and a peek at a tiny belly button. Disappointingly the blouse was not over strained by the breasts it contained, but this fact did not deter the men from staring at her beautifully-formed rear that swayed alluringly as she walked away to help serve biscuits.

"Officer?" queried Jamie.

"She means the Office Writer twat," explained Mick.

"I'd bet she's been to university." Andy watched the girl's every move, clenching his fists in time with her walk.

"She's Australian," said Mick. "They probably don't have universities."

"'Course they do," said Andy. Without a further word he attached himself to the girl. Looking around, Jamie realised that the other hostesses behaved uncannily like the officers' wives at the Scottish dancing evenings back at Pembroke. The thought sent a shiver down his back. Wearing a little smile of satisfaction Jamie watched the girl as she swiftly passed Andy on to one of the older women. He wondered at the untaught skill of her gender.

"What are you, Taff?" asked Micky. "A tit man or an arse man."

"Both, I reckon. But in this case I'd forego the tits for that."

"I'd forego all of it for a drink," complained Mick. "A big glass of the black Irish stuff."

"I tried a bottle of it once, in the Lucky Horseshoe," said Jamie. "My God, it's awful – it's like medicine."

"Y'right, my boy. Medicine it is. Medicine for the soul, and good for what ails you – Liffee water, so 'tis."

"Where's the girls?" complained Jamie. "You said there'd be girls."

"There's that one; the one with the trousers."

"Yes, she's nice but one won't go very far, will it?"

Margaret interjected with her big voice. "Now you sailors – we'll walk from here."

Jamie choked back a cheer, relieved at not having to re-enter the little car.

"And don't forget to make a wish at the fountain and if you want postcards buy them in the Vatican post office – they have their own stamps. If you have any questions our willing helpers will be glad to answer them. No worries."

"Yippee," said Mick. "A full day of culture – just what we need." The young girl returned to collect the cups. "I have a question. Where can we get a drink? A real one I mean."

"No worries," she replied. "This evening Margaret will be giving a buffet party. There'll be plenty of *real* drinks then."

Micky groaned. "This evening. That's hours away. Can't you put a word in with the mad Margaret?"

"Why don't you tell her yourself? Mum's very approachable – for a consul's wife."

The day passed surprisingly quickly. Mick eased his need for a drink by slipping away to a café while everyone else threw coins into the Trevi fountain. At St Peters the party became fragmented. With so much to see, the party split up with the instruction to meet at 5pm on the centre spot of the square, where Margaret had *Demon*strated the way the multi columns around the square merged into singles when viewed from there.

Inside the huge entrance doors to the cathedral Mick grabbed Jamie.

"We've got to do something, Taff. I can't face a bleeding buffet with that lot of do-gooders. And I certainly can't get into that hearse on wheels with the good Mrs Consul again. You'll have to be sick. We'll go back by train."

"I can't do that, Micky. I'm not sick."

"If I say you're sick, you're bleedin' well sick and that's an order." He pointed to the anchor on his left sleeve. "Besides, maybe we can grab a quickie at Mama's back in Chivvy. What do you say?"

"Ah, now you're talking."

"Okay, sick it is."

They found Margaret on the centre spot, shuffling around in a circle, *Demon*strating in her strong voice to a group of total strangers.

"Mad as an Australian hatter," whispered Mick as they approached. "Ah, excuse me ah, Mrs Con... Margaret. Jamie here is sick and I'm afraid I'll have to take him back."

Jamie blushed with the lie.

"Mmm. He looks a little flushed. Got the dog, have we? I've had some of that in me time. Don't move too much, that's the secret. Now, if we were in the bush I'd have a cure – me abos would crush up a dingo's bollocks and mix it with spit but here I'm a bit cooffered. We'll have to get you back to your ship."

"We can catch a train..." said Mick.

"I wouldn't dream of it. Allie will drop you back."

The drive back to Chivvy proved to be far less traumatic than the frantic trip out with Margaret.

"Sorry about calling your mum mad," said Mick.

"No worries – she is anyway. She has this thing about Aborigines – runs a committee. She thinks she should spend time with them to get to know how they live. They feed her weird food and she stays out in the sun too long. She drives my dad to distraction but her heart's in the right place."

They disembarked in sight of the ship with many thanks to the departing young girl.

"S'aright," she said, with a twinkle in her eye. "Pity you couldn't stay – with all those girls coming tonight. Still, if you have the dog, what can you do?"

Jamie stood and watched as the little car pulled back into the traffic. "What did she mean, 'with all those girls'?"

"She's a tease, that one," said Micky. "She's pulling your pisser. Come on – let's see if we can find our way back to Mama's."

Plans for the evening changed when Mick insisted they call in at a café. He accepted a challenge to a drinking competition from a southern-Irish stoker called Kinsella. Jamie had to escort the loser back to the ship.

CHAPTER 12

PUNISHMENT

The following morning seemed as unremarkable as any other Sunday morning. As Jamie stood at the galley to collect breakfast Andy, still dressed in number ones, passed by. Wearing a wide smile and walking with an exaggerated swagger the National Serviceman disappeared into the messdeck.

Two things struck Jamie about that while he waited. One: Andy rarely smiled and two: what was he doing returning from shore at seven in the morning. Back in the mess Jamie found the answer to both questions.

"What happened to you, Taff? You missed a great night."

"I was sick."

"Oh, you poor bastard." Andy suppressed a laugh. "Perhaps I'd better not tell you then."

Mick, who had spent the night on the bench between the table and the lockers, surfaced, his face white on one side and red on the other where he had slept on the leatherette padding.

"Tell us what?" he asked, with a husky voice.

"Last night," replied Andy. "We had a party back at the Embassy. Girls and booze and booze and girls." Then in a quieter, self-satisfied voice, he said, "I stayed the night with one."

"Not the daughter? Not the Allie girl?"

"No. Mine was called Matty. Short for Mattilda I think."

"What do you mean, think?" said Mick, testily. "If you slept with her you should know her name."

"Well, what with all the dancing, the king prawns on a mountain of ice and the wine, we didn't have much time for talking. Especially later on."

The smug look on the swimmer's face began to irritate Jamie immensely. Mick started to irritate Jamie also as the full story unfolded.

"Wendell and I—"

"Wendell, who the fuck is Wendell?" exploded Mick.

"Wendell? Leading Writer Wendell Quick – he and I took these two girls – embassy staff they were – went back to their room and spent the night. They brought us back this morning."

"You mean that office writer bloke? Bloody Nora," said Mick, "they must have been desperate, and I went and got pissed with a stoker from Cork."

"Micky," said Jamie, matter of factly.

"What?"

"The next time you decide I'm sick don't bring me back. I'd rather take my chances with the crushed dingo bollocks."

At 0800 the Tannoy ordered turn to. It also ordered Jamie to report to the coxswain's office. Outside the closed door, in the office flat, a grumpy PO Grundy paced to and fro.

"Morning, PO," said a worried Jamie. "What's up?"

"You tell me," grunted Grundy.

"I've no idea," replied Jamie. "I haven't done anything wrong as far as I know. I left the jolly in Rome early yesterday but I was sick. P'raps it's that."

As he spoke, the coxswain's door opened smartly, releasing a puff of blue-white tobacco smoke into the passageway. PO Grundy darted into the office, closing the door firmly behind him, leaving Jamie nervously outside. Busy ratings hurried by, smirking or deliberately avoiding the criminal's eye, carefully watching that their haloes didn't slip.

"Inside, off caps," said an officious Grundy.

The coxswain, a patent naval figure with bushy eyebrows and a full, yellowy white set, could well have modelled the head on a packet of Senior Service. He smoked a pipe, which he usually stowed in the top pocket of his jacket. A charred area of the pocket witnessed the fact that the pipe often remained alight when stowed. It now glowed threateningly at Jamie like an extra disembodied eye.

"You were duty electrician last night," stated the coxswain from behind his desk.

"No, Chief. I had a sub."

"That was not a question, lad. You were duty EM last night. Your PO has confirmed. You failed, contrary to Queen's Regulations and Admiralty Instructions, to carry out your responsibility in that you failed to switch on the navigation lights at sunset."

"I had a sub, Chief."

"Save it for the Captain, lad. 1000 hrs, Wardroom flat, clean number 8s. Dismiss."

Outside, Jamie confronted Grundy. "What's going on, PO? I was ashore last night. Winkle should have switched on the lights at sunset."

"I know that – but it's your responsibility, my boy. Turn to."

"Bloody hell," swore Jamie. "This is not right. Wait till I see that bloody Winkle."

On his way aft just before 1000 Jamie convinced himself that any reasonable and intelligent person, and the Captain must be an intelligent person to be a Skipper, would see his point of view and dismiss the case.

'On the other hand I will have to shop Winkle' he thought, 'and that would not be right.'

Jamie had been wrestling with the dilemma all morning and had not caught up with Winkle yet for an explanation. As

Jamie joined the short queue in the wardroom flat, Lt Jollyman approached.

"Davis, you will be marched in to the Captain by the coxswain. I will be there as your divisional officer. Give your side of the story clearly and briefly."

"But I had sub…"

"I'll see you inside."

Nervously Jamie waited until the coxswain called his name. The tall Skipper stood behind a tall wooden reader like a preacher in his pulpit. He stared hard at Jamie.

"Halt, salute, off caps," ordered the coxswain. "Contrary to QRs and AIs did fail, on the dah dih dah …"

At that point Jamie lost concentration. He recalled Dusty's story of the horses and wondered if the Skipper was in a good mood.

"Lieutenant?" said the Skipper, loudly. Jamie focussed his mind again.

"All satisfactory, Sir."

"What have you to say, Davis?" said the Skipper to his desk.

"I had a sub, Sir, but I am not willing to disclose his name – although, as I wasn't even on board, Sir, I don't feel I should…"

"You failed in your duty. You should know when it's your duty. You *will* know when it's your duty. Guilty. Seven days number elevens."

"On caps," ordered the coxswain. "Report to my office, about turn, quick march."

'Bloody Hell,' thought Jamie, 'That was quick. I didn't have time to explain. I've been done. A green rub, a bloody green rub.'

"It was Winkle Ripley," shouted Jamie as he made his way forward to give up his station card and to receive his punishment timetable from the coxswain's office.

"How be," said Jamie to Winkle at the dinner table. "Did you enjoy your tot?"

"Yeah, thanks. How about you?"

"Nah, I'm going 'T' for a few days. No station card, see. No leave, either. All because some plonker, who is not a million miles from here, failed to switch on the Nav lights at sunset last night."

Jamie watched as Winkle's face changed – the realisation of his omission causing the man from Derby to choke on his pork chop.

"Oh, bloody hell. I forgot. I bloody forgot. Oh Taffy, mate. I bloody forgot."

"What's up, Welshy," interrupted Badger. "Number 11s, is it? What a shame – it couldn't have happened to a nicer bloke."

"Shit'n it, Badger."

"Sorry, Taffy," said Winkle. "When I get my tot tomorrow you can have sippers. How many days?"

"Seven."

"Seven days no leave and extra work," exclaimed Badger with glee. "Oh, what a pity – and we sail in less than a week. I should have said something, shouldn't I?"

"You knew that Winkle forgot?"

"Yeah, I knew, Sheepshagger. And he didn't forget. He was asleep."

"You rotten bastard." Jamie banged his knife and fork on the melamine table top in frustration. "You rotten sod. You deliberately made him miss sunset. One of these days I'll get you, Badger. I'll get my own back on you." Even as he said it he felt the naivety and futility of the words.

"That'll be the day," came the smug reply. "That'll be the day."

"Sorry, Taffy, mate," said Winkle, his quiet words breaking the silence that had descended on the mess, "make it gulpers, if you like."

As part of his punishment Jamie had been detailed to wait on the guests at the Captain's cocktail party.

"You'll be alright," reckoned Dusty. "I've done them before. You get to drink all the leftovers, and the food never gets eaten so don't fill up on too much supper before you go."

"Do you want to do this for me, then?" Jamie had asked.

"Nah, my nicks need ironing. Besides, you shouldn't be asking for subs," he giggled. "That gets you into trouble."

Dressed in a clean white-front, his No. 2 bells and with his hair washed and Brylcreemed, Jamie joined other miscreants and volunteers on the iron deck, ready to serve at the party.

"You," said a short and rotund leading officer's steward, "grab this tray, get in there and mingle."

"Mingle?" said Jamie, accepting a round drinks tray.

"Mingle, and stay out of sight. That's dry. That's the sweet."

"Sweet what?"

"Bloody 'ell. I'll be a doin' it meself in a minute. Sherry, that's what. Now piss off in there," then as an afterthought, "and come back 'ere when it's empty."

The beautifully-appointed timber-clad room must be the largest open space on the ship, thought Jamie. The long table normally fixed down the centre of the room had been removed. Chintz-covered easy chairs and coffee tables remained. Feeling out of place, Jamie wandered amongst the groups of monkey-suited officers, civilian men in smart suits and women in pretty dresses – including Mrs Margaret, the Australian Consul's wife.

"Hi there, youngster," hailed the good lady. "How's the dog?"

Both the Skipper and Joystick looked to see the source of the loud greeting.

"Er, fine, thank you. Sherry?"

"Nah, no worries. Here, Dahl." She touched the elbow of a tall gentleman in evening wear with a medal hanging around his neck. "This is one o' me young fellas on me tour, but he got took ill."

The tall man held out his hand, which Jamie shook with one hand while balancing the tray with the other.

"Are you better now, lad?"

"Yes, thanks. It was just a stomach upset." Jamie suddenly found the wardroom uncomfortably hot under the gaze of the Captain and the agitated Joystick. "Sherry, Sir?"

"Nah – your'right. Did my good lady give you the dingo bollocks line?"

Margaret's laugh almost stopped the room.

A few yards away the Captain, drinking pink gins with Civitavecchia's mayor, a dapper man dressed formally with chains and medals of office, called Joystick to his side. "One of yours, Christopher?"

"Er, who, Sir? Oh, you mean *him*, Sir. Yes, Sir. That's Davis."

"Did you invite him as a guest, Lieutenant?"

"No, Sir."

"Then I suggest you put a stop to his entertaining of my guests and get rid of him."

"Aye, Sir."

As Joystick approached, Margaret's daughter Allie appeared from nowhere and slid her arm through Jamie's, almost upsetting the tray of sherries.

"Well, well," she said, "lookee here. It's the boy with the tummy upset. How are you now?"

"Fine, thanks. Would you like a sherry?"

"In a minute, I have to finish this first." She downed the drink in her hand and exchanged the empty for a full glass. Something about the way she coyly looked under her lashes at Jamie and the support she was seeking on his arm told Jamie that this girl was getting tipsy.

"Davis," said the voice of authority from Joystick.

"Yes, Sir?"

"Oooh," Allie theatrically wiped her brow and almost spilled her drink, "it's hot in here."

Joystick, apprehensive of further attention from the Captain, relieved the girl of her drink. "Here, Miss, I'll take you out to the quarterdeck." Gallantly he offered his hand to the girl, then hissed to Jamie, "Get on with what you're here for before I..."

"No, it's alright, Captain," said Allie. "Davis can escort me. I'll be okay with some fresh air."

"Now, Allison, my girl, if we were in the bush me abos would know the cure for—"

"Margaret," warned the Australian Consul.

"No worries," beamed his good lady. "Take her outside and give her a glass of water, there's a good lad. Now, Lieutenant, what do you do on board this wonderful ship?"

Out on the wardroom flat Allie seemed to recover. Taking the lead, she pulled Jamie through the watertight door to the quarterdeck. She stopped behind the shelter of the three-barrelled Squid mounting, the anti-submarine mortar unit shielding them from the wardroom door.

"Thank Gawd you came along," she said with obvious relief. "I was just about to tell some twit in there to go stuff himself. Birds, the feathered kind, that's all he could talk about."

"Ah," said Jamie, "that would be the First Lieutenant. He's a bird person. Anyway, it seems you're okay now – I have to go."

"Oh, what a shame," teased Allie. "Can't you show me the engines or the steering wheel or something? I can't face going back in there."

Peeping around the Squid structure she spied the ladder leading to 'C' Gun deck and made for it. With a flash of golden limbs she nimbly climbed the vertical ladder into the darkness. Jamie followed, feeling justified in his neglect of duty as he was charged with taking care of the girl.

"Watch out for oil," he said. "Sometimes the mounting leaks oil."

Allie, leaning against the turret, ignored his advice.

"It's so beautiful here," she said, looking towards the darkness of the harbour. Jamie followed her gaze. Lights, twinkling along an invisible coast, reflected on the water. Brightly lit craft moved in and out of the ancient harbour – as they had done for thousands of years – the rhythmic sounds of their engines carried on a light wind. The breeze brought with it the smells of Italy and cooled the skin.

"Beautiful," said Jamie, but he referred to the white of her perfect teeth and the brightness of her eyes shining in the dim light.

"Would you like to kiss me?"

"How old are you?"

"Older than you think, which makes me old enough and most likely older than you."

"All right, then." Jamie took her into his arms, her small breasts firm against his chest. Her warm moist mouth tasted of sherry.

"Take me…"

"What?" Jamie released his grip on the girl.

"Take me, you know, out. Take me for a walkabout or something."

"Oh, you mean ashore. Sorry – not possible. I'm stuck here – on duty."

"Well, get someone else to do it, can't you?"

"Not an option – sorry. I'll see you back. Sorry Allie."

Jamie spent the remaining time that evening in the officers' galley, washing glasses and wishing terrible things would happen to Winkle. As some recompense he stuffed himself on fishy vol-au-vents and downed some untouched, unidentified drinks. At 11.30 he slipped a handful of fishy leftovers into the sleeping Winkle's hammock and turned in, feeling a little better.

CHAPTER 13

RETURN TO MALTA

Two days later *Demon* left Italy. Back in Grand Harbour, the ship tied up on the same buoy as before but this time the engines responded smartly, and no serious mishap occurred.

The following weeks passed quickly, taken up with exercises around Malta involving the considerable number of ships that came and went.

For the men of *Demon*, trips ashore usually meant a visit to the Lucky Horseshoe. Many would have preferred the Silver Dollar, mainly because of its reputation as the sleaziest bar in Malta, but the Silver Dollar continued to be colonised by superior numbers of *Dunness* ratings. Any *Demon* unfortunate who wandered in received a tirade of snide remarks on the ability of *Demon*'s Skipper.

One evening, as recompense over the 'Sub' affair, Winkle treated Jamie to a run ashore. As usual they made for the Horseshoe. After two Anchor lemon-tops Winkle became morose.

"Let me ask you something. Why don't the fellas like me do you think?"

Jamie felt no need for tact.

"Well, since you ask I'll tell you." He dismissed the thought that future lemon-tops could be at stake and carried on. "You don't talk to anyone, only about jazz. You read all the time and you insist on telling people that you come from 'Darby' and not 'Durby'. We all know it's 'Darby' but we say 'Durby' to annoy you."

Winkle thought about that for a while. Jamie downed some more lemon-top and waited.

"But I like reading," he said. "And it is Darby."

"You asked," stated Jamie.

"Yeah, thanks."

"Aand…"

"What?"

"Those bleedin' drumsticks. You play them all the time. You were even drummin' away to the hymn music last Sunday."

"Yeah, that was when that big bleedin' stoker told me he'd stuff my sticks up my arse – sideways."

"There you are then."

"Yeah, well, thanks – I think."

"Don't mention it." Jamie pushed his empty glass towards his benefactor and rolled a tickler.

"Anyway." Winkle lit up an evil-smelling Spanish cigarette that he had brought with him from Gibraltar. "How would you feel if you were getting there with a Signals WREN? I was getting there, you know. I was up past her stocking tops. Have you ever felt the skin above a girl's stocking tops? And the suspenders, they wear suspenders, you know, WRENS."

Jamie tapped his empty glass on the table, sensing that no reply was required. 'Que Sera Sera' sang out plaintively from the jukebox.

"And then, out of nowhere, I was whisked on board that tub just because some plonker decides to go visiting his girl. What about me and my girl?"

"He was no plonker. He was my mate – Latchbrook. Good mate, he was too. Anyway, how do you know he went visiting his girl? You weren't on board then."

"Badger told me."

"Bastard."

"Yeah," said Winkle. "He's a bit of a prick." Producing a ten bob note from his pocket he handed the money to Jamie. "Sorry. Get 'em in."

On his way back from the bar a group of noisy bootnecks barged their way in. In typical marine belligerence they upped the tempo of the music and changed the atmosphere.

"Do you like jazz?" shouted Winkle above the din.

"No."

"Good, drink up. I know a better place."

Jamie sighed, and thought, 'and that's another thing – you don't listen.' All the same he drank up and followed, considering that almost anything would be better than listening to a group of noisy, boy scout marines.

A half-hour walk brought them to a line of buildings on a sloping hill. Jamie could not have found his way there again. "How did you know where to go?" he asked.

"Floriana?" said Winkle. "Badger told me."

"Ah, Floriana," said Jamie. Looking around he spotted two pony-traps parked up under a group of trees at the end of the road. He smiled to himself, remembering Dusty's horse and buggy story.

"This must be it." Winkle led the way into a bar spewing light and piano music. Inside, the brightness dazzled and the smoky atmosphere caught in the throat.

"Hello boys." A deep voice boomed out from the murk.

Adjusting to the light they saw a tall figure dressed in a bright red ball gown, its tight bodice shining with sequins. With large, expressive hands – hands festooned with large rings – the woman ushered the two newcomers into the room. The blue of her shaven face, inexpertly covered by make up, and large feet straining bright red high-heeled shoes, gave away the fact that this was a Mr – not a Miss. With an exaggerated swirl, the hostess swung around and said, "Follow me."

"Winkle," Jamie tugged his companion's arm. "We're not going in there – it's a queer's place."

"Come on." Winkle followed the mincing red ball gown to a table near the door. "It must be good here. The place is full – and the music is real."

The music, tinkling out above the din of the bar, emanated from a piano in the centre of the room. Through the smoke Jamie made out the pianist, another large man in a turquoise-green ball gown sitting at the piano. A long cigarette holder containing a smoking cigarette bobbed in his smiling mouth. He wore a blonde wig.

"That's Fannie," said their host. "Isn't she great."

Winkle nodded; Jamie just sat, hoping to remain unnoticed in his seat.

"The bar's over there," continued the odd-looking figure, "the toilet's over there and if you want anything..." she paused, leaned back and looked them up and down, "anything... just call. I'm Terry. Welcome to Fannie's Piano Bar and enjoy."

She swept away to rejoin her table in front of the piano. Jamie recognised one of her companions immediately.

"That's Badger down there," said Jamie.

"So it is. What do you want?"

"I'm not stopping here." Jamie spoke just loud enough for Winkle to hear.

"Get stuffed. I'm thirsty. What do you want? Lemon top?"

Winkle left for the bar.

Jamie could not take his eyes off the back of Badger's thick neck and the thin ginger hair. He had never seen the old man so animated. He rocked with laughter at every Fannie innuendo and nodded knowingly with every Terry remark, whispered conspiratorially into his hairy ear. Jamie thought that Badger's ears were the most unattractive he had ever seen.

"There you go, Taff," said Winkle, delivering the beer.

"Not so loud," replied Jamie.

"What?" shouted Winkle.

"Shit'n it, for Christ's sake."

"Yeah, he... she can play that thing all right." Winkle slapped his thigh to the rhythm of the fast jazz number Fannie was thumping out on the ivories. The number ended to the shouts, clapping and stamping of the appreciative audience. Badger stood, announced his intention by fiddling with the buttons of his bell's flap, and headed towards the heads. Jamie ducked beneath the table but the three-badgeman, steadying himself for the trip, had trouble focussing and saw no one.

In the relative quiet between numbers Jamie pleaded with Winkle. "Let's go back to the Horseshoe, mate."

"We've only just got here," said Winkle, "'sides, I want to hear some more."

Returning from the heads, Badger shouted to the room, "'Sisters'?"

"Yeah, 'Sisters'," echoed some drinkers.

"Thank you," responded Fannie, "give us time fer a *drag* on a *fag*," the innuendo created the required response, "and we'll get at it."

Terry stood and took up a position in front of the piano. Fannie joined him and, with their brawny arms entwined and without the assistance of music they launched into the song.

"Sisters, Sisters, there were never such devoted Sisters."

The harmony surprised Jamie, who felt a pang of nostalgia for the shows at Chatham. Involuntarily he found himself singing along. Towards the end of the song Winkle agreed to leave.

"This isn't jazz," he said.

Glancing back as they left, Jamie caught sight of Badger standing between the two hosts, singing his heart out and ruining the harmony at the same time.

"Them'll be doing The Death of Nelson in a bit."

"What's the Death of Nelson?"

"You know, where they finish up with, 'Kiss me Hardy'."

"Do you think Badger's dodgy?"

"I don't know, Taff, but take a tip, don't drop your soap in the shower if 'ees in there."

They decided to walk back and Jamie told Winkle the story of the ponies dropping dead on the hill down to the harbour.

"That's a load of cobblers," said Winkle. "Who told you that?"

"I don't remember," said Jamie tiredly. Privately he thought, 'And that's another reason why people dislike you, Winkle. You have no sense of humour.'

CHAPTER 14

REGATTA PRACTICE

Colleagues and friends of Captain Norman De-Fotherinham knew him as a deep thinking man with an extremely well developed sense of pride. Only a very few of his closest friends had any idea that Norman hid, deep within himself, a drastic lack of self-confidence. He also nurtured great ambitions for his career and to this end, rather than any romantic motivation, he had married the First Sea Lord's daughter. Norman very quickly discovered that the First Sea Lord did not particularly like his own daughter so any advantage that the good Captain had hoped to gain from the coupling was less substantial than very thin air. On the contrary, the Captain quickly realised that the husband of the First Sea Lord's daughter would be expected to perform at a level exceeding everyone else. To this end, Norman saw that the salvation of his ambitions lay in gaining excellence in all things despite his marriage.

So far, on this commission, the ship had performed adequately, if one ignored the few mishaps that any highly technical unit suffers from time to time. Still, adequate was not excellent. No dispatches carried his name; no action had come his way, despite the rumblings in the Middle East. Privately he longed for some event which could provide Norman De-Fotherinham with the chance to shine.

And so it was that Captain De-Fotherinham welcomed the forthcoming Med Fleet Regatta, unusually large because of the build-up of forces in the region. Offering a unique level of competition, Norman saw the regatta as a chance for his command to triumph.

With a week to go before the regatta, *Demon* finished her latest set of exercises and headed back to Malta. Alone in his sea cabin, Norman daydreamed,

'De-Fotherinham. I knew he had what it takes, despite his choice of wife,' his father-in-law would be saying back at Admiralty House.

'Cock of the Fleet, Eh? Now that's an achievement,' the Admirals would remark over their pink gins.

'Won the Cock meself, before the war,' an impressed Vice Admiral would be heard to mention.

A tentative knock on the door broke into the Captain's reverie.

"Christopher, do come on in." The Skipper had asked to see Joystick in his day cabin. "I wanted a little word before we get in; confidentially, you know. I don't want to upset the others."

The Captain invited his visitor to sit down and leaned across his leather-tooled desk top, upon which stood a heavy-based photo frame containing the picture of a heavy based daughter of the First Sea Lord and two female children.

"I cannot emphasise how important the regatta is to the morale of everyone on board," he said quietly.

Joystick nodded sincerely.

The Captain continued, "I wanted to particularly speak to you because I believe your excellent team are likely to put a winning whaler crew together."

If Joystick could have seen the piece of paper in the Captain's hand he would have known that his name was last on a list of all the divisional officers on board and that each name had been ticked off.

"The secret," the Skipper glanced around the otherwise empty cabin, "the secret is to get volunteers. One volunteer is worth ten pressed men."

"I'll do my best, Sir." Christopher stood to salute. "Leave it to me."

Considerably heartened by the Captain's confidence, Lt Jollyman nevertheless wondered, as he made his way back to the wardroom, what on earth the Captain had seen in his men that he himself had not.

'That's leadership, for you,' he thought. 'Being able to recognise the potential in the men under you. Perhaps I too will learn that one day.'

In the days before the regatta Grand Harbour filled with warships keen to gain the benefit of calm water on which to train their sea-boat crews. Dghajsa men found life difficult weaving between whalers being pulled by sweating, straining men of all varieties.

"You'll be in charge of the Misc. mess crew," Joystick had said to Grundy. "You won't strictly be the Electrical Branch team but most of your fellas will be 'L' so do your best for the Greens. Get volunteers. A volunteer is worth ten pressed men."

Grundy visited the Misc. mess one evening and asked permission to address the members.

"I need volunteers for the whaler."

Almost before the sentence was out most of the men stood and looked toward the door.

"Sit," commanded Grundy, "if you please."

"Count me in." Andy flexed his pectorals. "I could do with some real exercise."

"Have you ever pulled a ton of wooden boat two miles before?" enquired Micky.

"No – but I've swam much further than two miles."

"Not quite the same."

"Good." Grundy hastily scribbled Andy's name on his notebook. "So that's one. Who else? Davis?"

"I've never rowed a boat in my life, PO – only the little ones on Poole Park Lake…"

"Good, that's two."

"Bloody hell," said Jamie, "I didn't say I would. I'll do it if you do, Dusty."

"I'll give it a go," he nodded.

"You won't dip out." Grundy touched the side of his ample nose in a very meaningful gesture.

"Umph," reckoned Dusty, after Grundy had left, "maybe we won't dip out but we certainly won't dip in."

Grundy called his team for their first training session at teatime next day. He had, by threatening or promising things individually, managed to fill the boat. Mustering on the fo'csle the portly PO electrician started to exercise his men.

"I thought we were supposed to be rowing," protested Winkle. The man from Derby, being small, had been press-ganged into the team as bow oar.

"We can't all use the boats," said Grundy, breathlessly. He felt obliged to jump up and down like PTIs do when taking PE. This didn't last long as he soon rationalised that the cox'n of a whaler did not really need to be fit, as he would be steering and shouting only. "Besides, you lot need to improve your fitness and stamina and, by the look of you, you have neither."

He was right. After five minutes of jumping up and down even Dusty's face ran with sweat.

"At least on the boat you get to sit down," gasped a pale and waning Pedlar. "I need a beer."

The session finished off with press-ups, 'to build up your biceps,' Grundy had said. Making himself comfortable on a deck wash hose locker, the PO puffed on a duty free and counted. Dusty managed twelve, Winkle and Jamie six, the rest three and Pedlar one. Pedlar reckoned two but his second didn't count, as his lower bits remained firmly adhered to the anti-slip deck. Andy, the swimmer, had to be stopped or he would have missed supper.

"That deck was bloody hot, don't you think, Dust?" Jamie examined his fingers for signs of blisters. "I could have managed a lot more if the deck was not so hot."

Later, in the Lucky Horseshoe, Jamie, Dusty and Pedlar undid all of Grundy's good work with many Anchor beers and a slap-up meal of steak, egg and chips. Pedlar reckoned he had benefited from Grundy's exercises, as he had not had such a good appetite for ages.

"It's Saturday tomorrow," said Jamie. "We'll go to the Lido, for some water-polo – swimming will be good training for the regatta."

That simple arrangement ensured the fateful meeting – the day that Jamie renewed his acquaintance with Eleanor Henderson – the day that he received a note inviting him for a beach picnic with his best friend's girl.

The days leading up to the regatta passed very quickly. Jamie welcomed the activity as it took his mind off the coming picnic, the prospect of which filled him with trepidation.

During the whole of the week, Grundy only managed to reserve a sea-boat on one occasion. Beneath the ramparts of Fort St Angelo, the Misc. crew attempted its first start. Almost without exception, each oar, dipped with great enthusiasm into the water, either refused to extricate itself or failed to enter in the first place, preferring to skim like a stone on a pond, resulting in a chaotic, uncoordinated rabble in the process. It was this defect in oar design that did for Dusty later. Once under way the stamina of Andy, the swimmer, and the great strength of Dusty Miller propelled the sea boat over the water at creditable speed.

Grundy reported back to Joystick. "No problem, Sir. Nobody can touch us."

"Well done, PO. We'll keep this crew as our secret weapon."

"You were right, Sir." Joystick reported to the Captain the day before the races. "We have a winner there. No one can touch them."

"Well done, Christopher," said the Skipper, wondering what he had been right about.

On the eve of the regatta, ships of the Royal Navy's Mediterranean Fleet and invited guests assembled at their allotted anchorages in Marsaxlokk Bay. Dozens of vessels lined up in two rows to provide a channel some two miles long for the races. Illegal betting below decks placed the New Zealanders as favourites along with the Royal Marines, because they were the biggest and fittest. The submariners were certainties for the wooden spoon, because they weren't.

Saturday dawned to a clear Mediterranean sky, but a breeze blowing from the south-east threatened to cut up the surface of the water in the bay. The ships on the easterly berths provided a windbreak and flattened the choppy sea on their leeward sides. As the day progressed it became evident that boats drawing the sheltered side of the course had a great advantage. With favourable draws both the *Dunness* and *Demon* crews avoided the choppy side and amassed enough points to qualify for the final.

By late afternoon the four qualifying ships prepared their crews for the final race. A detachment of Royal Marines from a British cruiser; a Kiwi boat; the best crew from *Dunness* and the as yet untried Misc. crew from *Demon*, manned their boats. Based on the intelligence supplied by Joystick, Captain De-Fotherinham had decided to save his secret weapon for the final. *Demon* had qualified by a combination of hard work from its other crews and the fortunate drawing of leeside positions in almost all of the heats. *Demon* drew a centre line for the last race but the sea had calmed considerably so position mattered little.

"Now, come on boys," urged Grundy. Alone amongst the cox'ns Grundy chose to wear his best white uniform. "We can beat this lot. Pace yourselves and remember all I've taught you."

This proved difficult as no one in the boat could put their finger on what he'd actually taught them but thinking about it took up the time as the pinnace towed them to the start. From the bridge of *HMS Demon*, the Captain and his officers followed their boat's progress with binoculars.

"Your crew appear to be a little uneven, Christopher," said the Captain. Nervously he compared *Demon*'s oddly-sized team with the uniformly large contents of each of the other whalers.

"A balance of strength and stamina, Sir, and Ripley, the little fellow in the bow, will keep the front out of the water."

"Umph," said the Skipper.

"Our stroke is Miller, Sir, part of our, er, Devonport's winning Field Gun Crew last year and we have a national swimmer too."

"Umph," said the Skipper.

Lining up with the bow of the cruiser on the start line, the towing vessels adjusted each competitor's position.

"Are you happy?" A lieutenant with a loud hailer called from the fo'csle of the cruiser. In response Grundy stood and waved, all the other cox'ns raised their arms in acknowledgment. The small saluting canon on the cruiser's superstructure puffed and banged. Unfortunately the start signal came before Grundy had properly settled to his seat. The tiller had swung away to his right so, as he grappled for the wooden handle, he missed the moment when Dusty, with a huge pull on his oar, skimmed the surface and fell with a sickening thud against the thwart behind. In fairness, the other crew members had started well and were concentrating wholly on their technique. Only Jamie realised that Dusty was in serious bother.

"Where's Miller?" asked Grundy.

"Down here, PO," said Jamie, pulling for his life, "unconscious."

Grundy stood, once more allowing the rudder to swing free. He clambered over the vacated strokes seat to view Dusty, lying prone on the duckboards.

"Keep going, keep going," ordered Gundy. Bending low, the PO struggled to lay the unconscious man across the boat, while trying to staunch the blood seeping from a gash in the large stoker's head.

"Lieutenant Jollyman?" said the Skipper, eyes glued to his binoculars.

"Yes, Sir?"

"Can you please explain why our boat is about to disappear between two ships? It is off the course and appears to have no coxswain."

"Disappear, Sir?"

At that moment Grundy resumed steering, bringing his straining crew back onto the course through the next gap in the anchored ships. Ahead he could see the sterns of the other three boats far ahead. The mass of spectators lining each guardrail cheered and hooted good-naturedly as the Misc. boat passed by – all except the *Demon*, whose spectators remained deafeningly silent. Grundy stood to salute his ship. Again, the tiller swung free.

"Lt Jollyman. Why is the stroke sleeping?" asked the Captain.

"Sleeping?"

"Do I have to repeat every question?"

"Er, no Sir. Miller seems to have fallen off his seat, Sir. Shall I recall them?"

"I don't think so," replied the Skipper as he left the bridge, "they seem to be enjoying themselves. Let them finish. Oh, yes, and I would like an explanation so perhaps you, Lieutenant, can join me later in my cabin."

The loudest cheers of the day came as *Demon*'s secret weapon passed the spectators lining the rails of the *Dunness* whose winning boat had crossed the finish line some minutes before.

CHAPTER 15

THE RENDEZVOUS

A call from the bus driver interrupted Jamie's thoughts.

"Your stop – please. You want here, no?"

Jamie thanked the driver and left the bus. He waited until the dust and exhaust fumes from the departing bus had settled before looking around him. Nothing stirred as the summer sun burned into Jamie's face – the extreme heat telling him to find some shade. He spotted a low tree some way up the road. Keeping the junction in view he found a little shade beneath the spindly bush and leaned on a rough limestone wall. He removed his cap, wiped the sweat from his eyes and settled to wait. Within minutes a car, followed by a dust cloud, appeared at the junction where the bus had stopped. Jamie removed his sunglasses to get a better view of the driver. With an inward sigh of relief he recognised Nelly – alone and waving as she approached. Reaching Jamie, she braked the car, allowing the dust cloud to catch up and drift past. Jamie stepped up to the passenger side door of the open-topped Citroen.

"Wow. Where did you get this?"

"It's mine – well, Daddy's really," laughed Nelly. "Jump in."

Almost before Jamie had settled into his seat Nelly had revved the engine, spun the wheels and shot off up the road. As the girl concentrated on her driving, Jamie looked her over, renewing his memory of her in every detail.

A few miles along the road the car crunched onto a small parking area overlooking the sea. Eleanor switched off the engine, allowing a silence to descend.

"I wasn't sure you would come," she said.

Jamie looked away from the blue eyes; eyes that he'd recalled so vividly whenever he had thought of this girl; eyes that now robbed him of coherent speech.

"I, um…"

"It's hot," said Nelly. "We'll talk later. Let's get down to the beach."

Vacating the car, Jamie walked to the edge of the hard standing and looked down to a small, secluded bay flanked on the left by a flat-topped rocky ridge and on the right by the cliff on which they were now standing. A steeply stepped path zigzagged between scrub and rock down to a white sandy beach. The blue, calm sea disappeared at the horizon into a hazy sky. A faint breeze, cooled by the water, wafted across Jamie's hot face as he stood on the edge of the cliff. Nelly threw Jamie the car keys.

"My bag is in the boot. Leave your things in the car if you like."

She disappeared down the path.

Jamie opened the boot and found a picnic basket. He removed his tight duck-suit top, folded it neatly and placed it with his cap onto the red leather seat. Shouldering the picnic basket he followed the girl down the crumbly path – a descent that proved awkward in smooth leather-soled shoes.

When Jamie reached the otherwise deserted beach Nelly had chosen a spot in the shade of a rock. She had slipped out of her dress to expose a pink one-piece bathing costume.

"Come on, slow coach," she chided with a smile that settled Jamie's nerves.

Self-consciously he stripped to the bathing trunks he had put on under his bells and settled on the towel Nelly had produced from the basket. After almost six months in the Med, the young man's body had matured and tanned to dark ochre. Nelly, in contrast, showed the reddening of early sun exposure.

"This," Jamie hesitantly opened, "is nice."

He indicated the expanse of white beach in an attempt to take his gaze away from the contours of the girl's body lying unbelievably only feet away.

The afternoon passed considerably quicker than a night watch. The pair chatted and laughed about the Pembroke shows, Scottish Dancing and the things each remembered about Chatham.

"It's so good to see you," said the boy, struggling to make conversation. "It was a bit of a shock, really. What are you doing in Malta?"

"I'm spending the summer with my father. He's here – attached to NATO Military Headquarters."

"Oh, I see," said Jamie, but he didn't really. Nelly could have said her father was attached to the Pope of Gozo for all he knew. "I, er, met him, actually – at the airport. We gave him a lift into town."

"Ah, so you were the Good Samaritan. Daddy told me a nice sailor had picked him up."

"Well, I had no choice, really. Not with your father."

"He also said he thought your face familiar. For a minute I thought it might have been Derek, until he described you as tall, dark and handsome."

Jamie blushed.

Nelly produced sun oil, which they used on themselves and on each other. They swam in the cool sea and ate the picnic. A bottle of Marsala, which they'd buried in the sand to keep cool, emptied at an alarming rate. Jamie found the courage to glance slyly at the girl's bathing suit and the unfamiliar shapes concealed within. At the top of her long legs he caught a glimpse of dark hairs peeping out of the material. He wondered why he was there, picnicking with the daughter of a naval officer of some rank attached to Mediterranean NATO headquarters. In truth he knew why he was there but he was determined not to be the one to open. He wondered also at the dreams and hopes of a girl like Nelly, privileged in all things including spending her summer in the Med. He knew that he was not a part of those dreams and waited for the inevitable.

"You've grown up, James," said Nelly. "Grown into quite the young man."

Jamie wriggled with embarrassment, acutely unable to answer the direct statement. Nelly saved him with her next words.

"Do you, er, hear from him at all?" she asked. Feigning disinterest she traced circles in the sand with her long index finger.

"I've had one or two letters. That's a lovely ring."

He reached out but didn't touch her hand.

"It was my mother's. This one is Derek's." She showed Jamie a thin, plain silver ring, which she wore on the middle finger of her left hand. "Is he alright, James?"

She used his full name just as his mother used to.

"He's fine, now that he's out of the..." he hesitated, not sure how much Nelly knew of the detention.

"...Detention Centre," she completed. "I know all about that. You know I tried to make him return to his ship that weekend. We had such a lovely time at first but he was so determined to stay with me – and so unhappy. He is so sensible with most things but nothing I said made any difference. I've not seen him since he left me that day to visit home."

Jamie listened, aware of her need to talk, sure now that he was there because of Derek. Perhaps this was her way of assuaging any feeling of guilt and responsibility she may be harbouring.

"He was kept at Portsmouth when he was released," she continued. "Working on recommissioning small ships or something like that. I made Daddy tell me." She smiled. "I'm surprised Daddy didn't have him sent to Hong Kong or some barbaric outpost."

169

"Like Wales," Jamie smiled too.

"Wales?"

"A joke. He tells me he's done a diving course – he wrote about it in one of his letters – just the sort of dodgy thing he would do…"

Nelly lowered her eyes. Jamie felt obliged to continue, to say something – however crass.

"He never talks about you, you know, like matelots do sometimes – he wouldn't talk about you – and God help anyone that did."

Jamie, sensing the emotion the girl must have been feeling, placed a tentative hand on her shoulder.

"I know," she nodded. "He told me."

"That's because you're too special…" Jamie left the sentence unfinished.

She lifted her face. Tears had appeared, transforming her eyes into pools of crystal clear liquid – dewdrops that spilled and rolled easily down her oiled cheeks. She lay back and said, very quietly, "Thank you."

Feeling foolish and embarrassed Jamie removed his hand. For a long while nothing was said.

To break the silence which threatened to become awkward Jamie said, "How did old Hoppalong…er, I mean your dad… how did he injure his leg?"

With a smile she replied. "In Scotland. My father was liaison or something, working with torpedo factories during the war. We all lived there, on Clydeside, near the docks. A bomb came."

Jamie wished he hadn't asked but Nelly continued in a steady voice.

"My mother and my brother were killed and my daddy's leg was crushed. I was lucky. I was asleep – the explosion lifted my bed – turned it upside down with me underneath." She chuckled but without mirth. "I was lucky I suppose."

Jamie said nothing, noting the 'my daddy' of a little girl. He felt ashamed to have used her father's nickname and even more ashamed of the little round patch of sand that had adhered to the front of his trunks.

With a slight shock Jamie realised that the sun had moved down from the sky to the horizon in front of them, meeting and slowly devouring its reflection. With the cool of the coming evening Nelly came to life, springing to her feet.

"Have you ever been midnight bathing, James?" She stared down into his face with the eyes Jamie remembered, daring and manipulating. Turning to face the sea she stripped off her bathing suit.

"B-But it's not midnight," was all that he could manage to say.

She skipped to the water. "Come on, get 'em off and come on in."

Jamie rose, took off his trunks and, bending awkwardly in an attempt to conceal his dignity, he ran into the water. Staying clear of the naked girl, Jamie played and swam, enjoying the coolness and freedom around his groin. Very swiftly the day turned to twilight. Occasionally Jamie looked across at the girl, wondering what would happen next. Then – a pang of fear grabbed him. The darkening surface of the sea remained oily flat where the splashing Nelly should have been. Spinning in a circle he checked the water in all directions then concentrated on the spot he had last seen her. A sound turned his eyes to the shore to see her white form padding back up the beach. Relieved, he followed, pressing his hot erection against the cool of his stomach to stop its uncontrolled swinging as he padded up the beach to her. She stood on her towel and extended her hand. He stopped.

"Come here," she said softly.

Reaching out their hands met and she pulled him, gently but firmly, to her. Jamie put his arms around her, the now familiar tingle of arousal shuddered through him at the feel of her soft, cool skin. He bent to kiss her, surprised at how far he needed to lower his head to find her lips. Her soft mouth opened, the salty wet warmth blending with his, moving and exploring and exciting. Holding his shaft she dropped to the towel. Opening her legs wide she pulled him down. He knelt, looking down at the dark triangle, knowing how good it would feel when he entered.

A memory of Mama, gentle little Eyetie Mama, and her hot moist envelope that he had slipped into so easily, flooded his mind.

'What the fuck am I doing?' he thought. 'This is not my girl. This is not a pro. This is the girl that my mate spent sixty days in jankers for.'

He stood and moved away.

"What is it?" she asked.

"Sorry, I'm sorry." Jamie searched for his trousers and pulled them on. "I have nothing... I could give you a baby... "

"I have..." Nelly reached for her bag.

"Stop – I have to go," said Jamie.

Nelly dropped Jamie off at the bus depot in Valletta. Without thinking, he allowed his feet to take him towards the main street instead of down the hill to the harbour. The balmy evening had ensured a full turn out of people along the main thoroughfare. Beret-clad old men with gnarled hands and leather tanned faces sat around café doorways, drinking hot tea from glass tumblers. Young girls, chaperoned by black-clad mothers and grandmothers, ambled along making safe eyes at groups of chattering youths as their paths crossed. Children, hand in hand and dressed in Sunday best, ate ice cream; their proud parents close behind, nodding and renewing acquaintance as they paraded. Almost every wall and hoarding carried fading YES/NO posters, relics of the months old referendum

172

campaigns waged by the island's political parties for or against integration with Britain.

Jamie noticed none of these things as he hobbled along – the ache in his testicles making each step painfully difficult. Leaving the crowded main street he headed for the Gut and into The Lucky Horseshoe.

"Taffy, boyo," called Dusty from a table near the bar.

Adjusting to the light and feeling immediately at home, Jamie joined his mates. Dusty, half-cut, seemed unaware that the bandage, which should have provided protection for the gash in his head, had slipped down around his neck. Pedlar, sitting next to a girl twice his age and size, acknowledged Jamie with difficulty being almost cross-eyed in ecstasy due to the girl's hand being agile inside the flap of his bells. Toffee and Scouser danced – or more correctly, held each other from falling – at the jukebox.

Finding a chair and making space on the cluttered table for his tickler tin and lighter Jamie sat. Immediately Carlotta appeared. Uncovering an ample breast she pushed its nipple hard into Jamie's ear.

"Jamie, my Dahleeng boyfriend, you buy me dreenk? Where you been? I mees you."

"Hi, Carlotta," said Jamie tiredly. "Anchors all round and get yourself some of that pink water you con us with."

"I'm on wine," slurred Dusty.

"Get your own then. That'll be two for me. I've got some catching up to do."

Delivering the drinks and the change, Carlotta squeezed into a chair next to Jamie and poured the beer expertly into a glass.

Jamie downed it like a camel at an oasis.

"You thirstee Taffy. Where you been all day?"

"With his fancy hofficer girlfriend." Dusty downed another glass of two shillings a bottle white plonk.

"Shit'n it Miller – it's none of your business," warned Jamie. In the silence that followed, Jamie rolled a tickler which Carlotta took over. With a delicate pointed tongue she licked the paper and lit it for him. Despite Dusty's size Jamie had never witnessed the big man take offence, except where Badger was concerned.

"Warra bout my dotter? I save her for you," pouted the bar girl. Jamie gasped in involuntary pain as Carlotta slid her hand inside the flap of his white bells. "Oh, my God," she exclaimed, "you in beeg trouble. You need me – now."

Standing, she whispered in his ear, "You follow me to toilet." With a tug she pulled Jamie to his feet, flounced away and disappeared through a door behind the bar.

Jamie followed and in the locked toilet Carlotta unbuttoned his flap. Carefully avoiding his painful testicles and to the rhythm of the muffled 'Hound Dog' being played on the jukebox, she expertly relieved him. This time it was right. With a few strokes from a friendly bar girl, in the toilet of a seedy bar, his ache disappeared. He felt no guilt, only gratitude, and, for the first time that day, he relaxed. Back in the bar he bought a bottle of Anisette. Carlotta provided four glasses and a jug of water.

"We were saying before you came in," said Dusty.

"What?" asked Jamie.

"We were sayin', weren't we Pedlar."

"Yes, we were," said Pedlar, making a face as the milky Anisette and water burned its way down his throat.

"What were you bleeding well saying?" said Jamie, preferring his neat and clear.

"All those ships yesterday, you know, at the regatta. We've never seen so many ships since the Review in '53."

"Before my time, that," said Jamie.

"Yeah, well, we were just saying."

While they pondered the number of ships that had attended in Marsaxlokk Bay they all got drunk.

Leaving the Lucky with expansive au-revoirs and goodbyes they managed to lose Scouser and Toffee; no one worried as the two friends preferred their own company and had probably popped into a greasy café for steak, egg and chips. With the unerring sense of direction drunks maintain, they made their way to the harbour. Across the main street, now almost empty, and down the long stepped hill, the trio progressed, sometimes forwards, often sideways and frequently backwards. Halfway down the steps, Pedlar started the singing:

"It was on the bridge at midnight,
Throwing snowballs at the moon,"

Jamie joined in,

"She said Jack I've never 'ad it,
But she spoke too fuckin' soon."

Dusty had difficulty in remembering the words so he just did the actions. The other two continued:

"She was on the bridge at midnight,
Picking blackheads from her crutch,
She said, Jack now I've 'ad it,
He said yes, not fuckin' much."

They eventually reached Customs House steps having waited for Dusty to spew up against a wall.

"No bloody boat," said Jamie.

"Kip 'ere," said Dusty. Carefully he placed his cap onto the dusty stone quayside, stretched out and closed his eyes.

"We'll get a Dghajsa," decided Pedlar. He spotted a group of the colourfully painted boats bobbing up and down in the water. "No drivers – we'll drive ourselves."

Selecting the nearest, Pedlar attempted to unfasten its rope.

"Eywa, Johnny." A boatman emerged from behind a half-painted boat, cradled at the end of the jetty.

"Aha," exclaimed Pedlar, "where's Spiro?"

"Spiro," declared the boatman. Swiftly the Dghajsa driver scuttled over to the cradled boat to tug a reluctant colleague out into the open.

"'s not Spiro," said Pedlar. Without arguing, the relieved colleague scampered back to cover.

"You'll have to do," said Pedlar. "Home James – four for the *Demon*, if you please."

Understanding only the ship's name the boatman shook a calloused forefinger. "Ey, Johnny, you drunk."

"Thash alright," said Pedlar, sympathetically. "So're we – we'll drive."

"Eywa, Deemon," sighed the boatman.

Getting Dusty aboard the small craft threatened to be difficult – until Jamie suggested holding the boat broadside on to the quay and rolling him aboard like a barrel of oil. With great skill the Maltese boatman avoided a capsize as the Dghajsa took the weight of the bulky stoker. Pedlar took up a precarious position in the bow, holding onto the high prow with one hand while howling a song into the night:

"Que Sera Sera,
Whatever will be, will be."

He repeated the same phrase over and over, renewing the gusto every now and then.

Jamie splashed water onto Dusty's face to wake him up; vaguely aware that it would be advantageous if Miller were conscious when they arrived at the ship, as they couldn't roll him up the ladder. At a point roughly halfway to the ship Pedlar, thrown off balance by a high 'Que', lost his footing and dropped up to his knees in the water. With grim determination he held on to the thwarts until Jamie pulled him in. The long-suffering boatman crossed himself and continued at an astonishing speed towards *Demon*.

When Pedlar's plaintive serenade was first heard by the gangway watch-keeper he'd called out the Officer of the Watch, who arrived on deck in time to witness three drunks scrambling from a Dghajsa onto the ladder. With supreme effort the trio negotiated the ladder and tried to appear sober, standing to attention as best they could, under the glare of the gangway light.

"You three are a disgrace," hissed the Officer of the Watch, who did not like being called out. He was right. Their white suits were filthy, especially Dusty's with black elbows and knees and spew covering his shoes and halfway up one leg. Pedlar dripped water onto the deck; the size of the puddle he had created surprised him greatly.

With undisguised disgust, the duty officer looked up into Dusty's dirty face. "Where's your cap?" he demanded.

"'Scused caps, Sir. He was severally injured," said Jamie.

Pedlar took up the narration, "Injured doin' 'is duty, Sir, in the whaler and that's why he is like he is. This 'ere's the bandage the 'ospital tied him up with. He suffered from a coma, Sir – and concotion, Sir."

"Concotion?"

"Yes, Sir. He keeps falling over and that's why we're all dirty."

"Show the offisher, Dust," said Jamie. His two supporters attempted to turn the bulky stoker to bring his stitches into view, but failed due to the inertia. A titter from the watch-

177

keeper who had heard some good ones before brought a withering glance from the Officer of the Watch.

"You get him for'ard," said the officer. "And just one peep out of any of you and you will all spend the night in the paint locker – concotion or not. Understood? Now move."

On the way forward they decided to give Dusty a shower, which they did, quietly and all fully clothed.

The following morning all three joined the queue at the water cooler then went in search of bits of uniform, which they eventually found in soggy bundles in the washroom.

Two days later Jamie received two letters. One, an impressive, long, crisp envelope dominated the one from Gwyneth. His sister's – a single page airmail letter/envelope – related in unintentional understatement that Dad was home now: not too bad, but on oxygen. He sleeps downstairs on the bed John had put in for him. Not to worry and we love you.

'Not to worry?'

Somehow, from the stiff, crisp quality of the larger envelope Jamie knew that the letter would be from Nelly. Addressed to 'EM Jamie, *HMS Demon*,' it carried no stamp so Jamie figured that she must have delivered it by hand to the BFPO Office. Leaning with his back to his locker, Jamie opened and read the letter.

Sunday.
'My dear James,
If I leave this for another time I will probably never gather the necessary courage – and that would leave you with an impression of me that I would hate.
First let me apologise for today. I tried to explain to you all the way back in the car, but the words wouldn't come. What I did was inexcusable and I would understand if you

hated me, but you are so like Derek. I know he and I are storing up problems for ourselves, but he consumes me. I felt close to him when I was with you. Please forgive me.'

'So I was right,' he thought. 'She didn't want me – not really."

As he read he detected in himself a doubt; the emotion in the words surprised him – somewhat shattering his vision of a confident, mature and privileged woman – but the words seemed to lack sincerity.

'She's a weird one – that one,' he thought, not knowing whether to hate her or not.

The letter concluded with:

'I hope our paths cross again, soon.
Yours, in anguish,
Eleanor.'

Always comfortable with his own company, Jamie left the mess and wandered out on deck. Climbing the ladder to the fo'csle he sat with his legs dangling over the ship's side. The colourful ferry boats plied their trade back and forth across the harbour disturbing the liquid reflections of the ramparts and buildings all around. Shamefully, his thoughts dwelled more on the letter from Nelly than of the plight of his family.

'Perhaps I should have carried on and made love to her. She wanted it and by God – I did too. I'll never see her again, probably, so what was the harm?'

Before receiving the letter Jamie had not questioned his motives; had not felt confused. He reached to his shirt pocket, removed the letter, screwed it into a tight ball and dropped it into the water.

"Well, that's that." He watched as the good quality paper mingled with the putrefying gash floating against the ship's side.

179

For a long while Jamie sat and thought; thought of the girl; thought of his friend Latch and thought of his dad. Only the metal edges of the scupper cutting into the underside of his thighs roused him. Rising he rubbed the feeling back into his legs, and with a last look down to where the letter floated he turned aft.

'Bloody fool,' he mused as he retraced his steps back to the mess, 'it would only have been a fuck. I've fantasised about it often enough and when it's presented to me on a plate I get all noble and turn it down. Bloody fool.'

CHAPTER 16

BLIGHTY

Later that week most of the ships that had gathered for the regatta had left Grand Harbour. *Demon* followed and headed south-east – the ship settling into passage routine with no hint of an exercise or involvement with other ships – and with no hint of the problem that would see the ship turn and retrace her course back to Malta.

Taking advantage of an afternoon off, Jamie collected his towel and went in search of the sun.

"What's the buzz," Jamie asked Carl the Signalman. Carl often joined Jamie on the catwalk above the after torpedo mounting to sunbathe during off duty hours.

"No idea. Our heading is taking us east – towards Egypt would be my guess."

"Why Egypt?" Jamie removed his shirt and sat with his back to the sun.

Carl, a National Serviceman with an exceptional interest in politics, could be relied upon to know what going on in the world – a knowledge drawn from the newspapers his father sent him in the mail.

"Colonel Nasser – some army fella – was elected President of Egypt a couple of months ago. He's been trying to get finance out of Britain and the US to build a dam. He got fed up waiting, so he nationalised the Suez Canal to raise the money."

"What's that to us?"

"It depends on how you look at it."

Carl loved an audience – an event all too rare from what he considered to be a backward lot on the Lower Deck.

"There's a great deal of British money invested in the canal, and whoever controls that shipping route controls the supply of oil from the Gulf. France is miffed as well."

"My uncle was in Egypt, during the war. Alexandria."

"Well, he wouldn't be there now. Nasser has thrown our army out. But who can blame him – it's his country."

"Well, it wouldn't be his country if Monty hadn't stopped Rommel."

"This is peace time, Taffy." Carl adjusted the white floppy hat he always wore while sunbathing, and closed his eyes. "Anyway, shit'n it, I need some kip."

After a while, the afternoon heat became too much for Jamie. Gathering his gear he climbed down to the battery shop, the small space situated beneath the for'ard end of the catwalk, to check the batteries that he had put on charge when the motorboats were lifted from the water that morning. Inside the tiny workshop Jamie checked the thermometer; the mercury registered a worryingly high temperature. Conscious that too much gassing from lead-acid batteries created an explosive hazard Jamie checked the charge rates and adjusted the rheostats. Reaching above his head, he checked the suction from the extraction duct. Satisfied that nothing more could be done, he started to dip the cells on the largest of the batteries when the explosion, logged by the officer of the watch at 1422 hrs, thumped into Jamie's back, the force of the blast knocking Jamie off his feet. Instinctively he released the syringe to save himself as he crumpled onto the duck boards. Acid from the syringe sprayed across his right thigh and down his shin.

As his mind cleared from the ringing of the blast, Jamie gathered himself and looked around. Above his head a number of jagged holes had appeared in the after bulkhead, allowing new shafts of sunlight to cut through the dust produced by the explosion.

"Hell's bells, what was that?" he shouted. Struggling to his feet he made to dash outside but the severe burning on his shin changed his mind. He lifted his leg into the lead-lined sink and turned on the water tap. Furiously he splashed and directed the flow over the stinging spots.

A petty officer appeared in the doorway. "Are you all right lad?"

"Yes, PO A few acid burns, that's all. I'm okay."

"What's the damage?"

Jamie indicated the holes.

"No pipes or cables damaged? Right, nothing serious. Get yourself down to sickbay."

"Damage Control Party to the After Torpedo Deck," sang out the Tannoy. Jamie stepped out onto the Iron Deck, and into a rush of passing bodies.

"What happened?" he tried to ask a seaman running by. "Not a torpedo?"

"I don't know, but something's gone up."

Jamie joined the throng but stopped in his tracks when the catwalk came into view. The for'ard end of what was once the catwalk had been lifted and broken apart, leaving jagged, twisted wreckage above the torpedo tubes.

'Christ. That's just where I was sitting,' thought Jamie, 'but where's Carl? He was there before...'

The gunnery officer appeared from aft at the rush and climbed onto the tubes.

"Sir," shouted Jamie, "there was someone up there on that..."

"Just the one?"

"Aye, Sir. A signalman..."

"He's okay. They've taken him to sickbay. Now clear the area."

Jamie arrived at the sickbay to find Carl sitting in the surgery clutching his white floppy hat, now red with blood, to

183

his right upper arm. The doctor appeared with a bowl and cleaned the nasty gash before swiftly stitching the ends of the flesh like darning a sock.

"Are you okay?" enquired Jamie. "What happened?"

Carl ignored him and winced when the Doc pierced the skin again and again with a curved needle.

"What went up?" Again Jamie received no reply.

"No good speaking to him, lad," said the doctor. "He's lost his hearing. Sit there."

Jamie sat and an SBA cut up some yellow, waxy gauze and taped them to the burns on his leg.

"That shouldn't be a problem to you," said the Doc. "The water you applied did more than we can. Take two paracetamol if it stings."

"A compressed air bottle exploded," said the SBA. "Matey there was thrown away from the blast onto the after structure. Very lucky, I'd say."

"Not as lucky as me. I was sat over it a few minutes before," said Jamie. "1422 hrs. I'll always look on that time as lucky – somebody must be looking out for me up there."

Eight hours later *Demon* arrived at Malta Dockyard for emergency repairs.

At 0910 the following day Jamie received a telegram.

'Regret Dad passed away yesterday afternoon. Please come. Gwyneth.'

He had been called to Joystick's cabin, a small space aft with two bunks and a desk.

"Are you alright, Davis?" asked the officer. "Leg's better?"

"Yes Sir – thank you Sir."

"Has your father… I mean, was your father ill?"

"He's been ill for ages – his lungs – from the coal pits."

"I'm sorry, son. Would you like to sit here for a while?"

The offer took Jamie off guard – his mind, racing and confused, had not yet registered grief.

"Thank you, no, Sir. I'll be okay."

"Right – well, if you need anything let me know, or speak to Petty Officer Grundy."

Jamie turned to leave.

"Before you go, let me ask you something. Sometimes compassionate leave is granted in cases like this. If we can hitch you a lift from an RAF Flight – they're fairly regular from Malta, particularly now and the damage to the tubes is a dockyard job and sure to take a few weeks – would you like to go home for a few days?"

Jamie thought of Gwyneth, alone and dealing with the business of burying his Dad.

"I should be there if it's possible. Thank you – yes, I would like to get home."

"Do you have any civilian clothes? Money?"

"No civvies and only a little money."

"I'll try to get an advance on your next fortnight's pay and get you ashore to buy some clothes. Anything else?"

"No Sir."

"Right, listen out for the Tannoy. I'll be in touch."

Twenty-four hours later, Jamie strapped himself into a noisy RAF transport heading for RAF Lyneham in Wiltshire. He wore borrowed slacks and short-sleeved shirt, donated by the wardroom. The speed of the arrangements had so far taken thoughts of his loss from his mind. The hectic planning and this, his first flight, left him with no inclination to ponder.

The RAF, swiftly and with great efficiency, deposited Jamie at Bath railway station with a travel warrant and instructions for the return trip. A young trainee nurse returning from leave shared his carriage. In the short period of their acquaintance the two had exchanged addresses and promised to write. The depth of his suntan created the opener, but the ease with which he managed the encounter indicated to him how mature he now imagined himself to be. The girl left the train at Bristol on her way back to hospital.

At Cardiff General Station he crossed to the Valleys branch line and caught the last train to Trebarry. Alone in the rattling, smoke-smelling carriage, he watched as the familiar landscape, blending into the darkness, came and went. At Trebarry station Jamie left the carriage and slammed the heavy door shut.

"Aye, aye, young Jamie," greeted the Station Master as he waited to clip his ticket. "Home for the funeral then?"

Jamie nodded. "Hello, Mr Jenkins."

"Aye, sorry about your dad. That dust is a terrible thing."

"Yeah. Thanks."

"Compensation, don't forget the compensation."

"Aye, thanks, Mr Jenkins."

Jamie walked up the cinder path, the crunch of the coke reminding Jamie that he still carried a blue scar on his knee where he'd fallen on that very path coming home from school. He stopped on the old stone bridge that he and his sister had used on countless mornings to cross the railway line. Summer, winter, rain or snow, they had taken the short cut from the Coal Board houses up on the side of the mountain to the village in the valley below.

Looking over the bridge he remembered the many times he had stood on that platform waiting for the train with his Mam to go to Bournemouth on holidays. The chill of the night made him shiver.

"I was here when he came home, y'know."

Jamie hadn't noticed Mr Jenkins' approach.

186

"1945. I was here when he went off to war too. Almost five years, it was."

Jamie had no need for an explanation – he knew what the Station Master meant.

"Like a stick, he was – skin and bones. I carried his bag for him. He said no – but I insisted. Carried it all the way to your house, I did."

"I'm sure he appreciated it."

"Deserved it," said Mr Jenkins.

The Station Master, in a move he had made a thousand times, removed his fob watch from the pocket of his GWR waistcoat, flicked open the cover, read the time, closed the cover and replaced the watch. Without another word he continued across the bridge, up the path and out of sight.

Jamie followed; then turned left into the Crusher – a disused rail access to the quarry. Ignoring the darkness and the overhanging growth Jamie confidently walked the stony cutting – as he had walked it many times before. He had once kicked a tin can the whole mile of its length, receiving a severe clip from Mam for the scuffed toecaps of his school boots. He also recalled, with a smile, soiling his trousers within minutes of home because Gwyneth would not let him do it outside.

Leaving the Crusher, Jamie easily found the broken wire fence, squeezed through and scrambled up the grassy slope into the end of his street. From the road one could look down into the front rooms of the houses on the lower side of the street. By now someone would have noted his arrival. By tomorrow the whole of Heol Isaf would know he was home. A single lonely street light illuminated the pavement outside his house. He stopped for a while, remembering the evenings spent playing games beneath that light; running indoors to listen, spellbound, to *Dick Barton, Special Agent* on the radio. Looking up at the house he could see that the front room light was on but the curtains were drawn at every window. Climbing the steps he took the path around to the back door, unable to avoid the overgrown bushes spilling from the untended garden. He unlatched the back door without surprise that it was not locked.

"Hello," he called from the scullery. Nothing had changed. The huge copper boiler still sat in the corner. He had once put wood in that boiler, set it alight and lit the gasses coming from the vent at the top. The school had been doing a project on charcoal making. Mam made him scrub it out before she used it to boil the clothes.

Jamie placed his small case onto the huge wooden table that took up most of the kitchen.

"Jamie?" Gwyneth emerged from the front room. "Jamie, you've come."

Grasping her younger brother to her, she burst into racking, heaving sobs. Jamie hugged her in silence, feeling the tension in her flowing through him until her crying ceased and she too became silent.

"Sorry, I haven't done that up to now."

Jamie's chest tightened and his throat ached but he managed to hold back the tears that wanted to come.

"My God, you've changed. Look at you."

"You're the same," he said, feeling absurdly shy under the gaze of his sister.

"How did you get here? My, you're brown; where's your uniform? Do you want something to eat? When do you have to go back…?"

"Hold on Gwyn. I've only just arrived." They both laughed, relieving the pent-up emotion.

Very late that night, Jamie climbed the familiar stairs to his room. Exhausted, he fell into his old saggy single bed. Despite his tiredness he knew sleep would not have come if he had not learned all there was to know. As his sister had related his dad's last hours, a realisation had grown in Jamie's mind. Feeling stupid, Jamie forced himself to ask.

"Gwyn. What time did our dad die?"

"Time? Two something, I believe. Yes, Twenty past two -- in the afternoon…"

Suppressing a shiver, Jamie said, "Fourteen twenty two."

The next day Gwyneth took Jamie to see his dad at the Chapel of Rest. In the cold room his father, dressed as if for church, lay silent in a box. He looked healthier than Jamie could ever remember, with rosy cheeks and blood red lips – but small, oh so small and bony.

"Dad," said Gwyneth. "Jamie's come."

Jamie touched the crossed hands and kissed the parchment skin of his father's cold cheek.

"Sorry, Dad," he said. "Sorry I was not here." Tears welled and ran down his face.

"Don't be silly," admonished Gwyneth. "He knew you couldn't come. Anyway, he knows you're here now. Say goodbye."

"Hang on, Gwyn," said Jamie, impatiently. His sister's attitude disturbed him. "So long, Dad – I love you."

"I love you too, you old bugger."

The shortness in the words shocked Jamie. He was unsure, from her face, what to think. With a last look at his dead father, he followed Gwyneth outside.

"What was that about?" said Jamie as they walked away.

"You don't want to know," said Gwyneth.

"Try me."

"Oh, it's to do with John, that's all. Our Dad wouldn't let us get married."

"Who's John, anyway?"

"Don't you start," threatened Gwyneth. "John is my fiancé. He works with me."

"Why, didn't Dad like him then?"

"It wasn't a case of like. Dad didn't want me to marry anyone. He wanted me to live with him all the time: to look after him. We could have done that together, John and me, but that old bugger made my life a misery unless I gave *him* all my attention."

Old feelings of guilt returned to Jamie. "I'm sorry, Gwyn. I should have helped..."

Gwyneth stopped and turned to her brother. "Don't be silly. It's me really." She took Jamie's hand. "I feel terrible – I miss him – more than I thought I would. And... and I can't forgive myself for fighting with him. I..."

Jamie stopped her and hugged her as people passed by in the street. The subject would never be spoken of again.

The next few days were busy but not too busy to learn of the goings on in the Middle East. Every day, the radio news bulletins carried items on the actions of Archbishop Makarios and the Cyprus riots. Israel, threatened and threatening in return, argued and flexed. The entire area from Turkey to Egypt seemed to be in turmoil. For the second time he heard the name of Colonel Nasser.

John, who visited often, took Jamie to the local pub one evening.

"You're in the thick of it there, then," he had said on the walk to Trebarry.

"Seems so, but you wouldn't know it. We don't get to hear any news. You know more than we do."

"Well, take care," said John. "I asked you out because I wanted to see how you felt about Gwyn and me."

"Whatever she does is up to her, not me."

"Yes, but you're the man of the house now. I want to marry her. I would have left this until after the funeral but you'll be going back then. I have a good job; secure and good pay..."

Jamie had taken a liking to John – a neat, clean-looking man. Flattered at the responsibility, Jamie played along.

"Well, all that's okay – but I'll not stand for any nonsense."

"Nonsense?" queried John.

"Nonsense, like bashing her or keeping her short."

"Bashing her? What, your sister?" The two nodded agreement on the unlikelihood of that.

"Alright then," said Jamie, "you have my permission. Mine's a pint of lemon top."

"Lemon top?"

"Okay, make it a mild."

The day of the funeral, paid for by the Co-op insurance, dawned bright and clear. As Jamie finished dressing in his father's black suit, shirt and black tie, he looked out from his bedroom window. At the pithead across the valley, white smoke from the stack next to the winding platform stood straight up. Jamie had often watched that smoke; watched its colours change; watched its movement – sometimes swirling in light airs, sometimes whipping away at right angles in high winds. It had been Jamie's reliable weather vane for all of his growing life.

Below him on the street a crowd had gathered – waiting for the hearse to arrive. On the journey to the Methodist chapel, two streets above, the cortège grew, trailing behind like the tail of a lizard.

From his position behind the hearse Jamie looked back.

"There's hundreds of them," he said to Gwyneth. "I didn't know Dad had so many friends."

"He probably didn't know half of them – but they love a good funeral around here."

Two days later, Jamie left Trebarry. Sitting in the train he removed his father's watch from his pocket, wound it and slipped it onto his wrist. It was his first watch and the only thing he'd wanted from his father's things. Relief at being away from the draining tension of the past days caused him to slump, tiredly in his seat. Family members had appeared from all over; some he knew; others he had not heard of – the faces a blur of condolences and pitying words. Confusingly, Jamie felt apart from the family – a stranger in what used to be his own world. Only his sister remained as a soulmate, but even Gwyneth, caught up in her own life, seemed different to the girl he had grown up with.

Guilt at feeling relief caused him to worry and fidget. He knew, somehow, that a part of his life was over; that he might well not be back here again. Since joining up he had felt still attached to home, like being on the end of infinitely stretching elastic. Now there were no ties remaining, the future in time and in place remained his alone. Gwyneth would get married soon, leave the house and live in Caerphilly.

"There will always be a bed for you," John had said.

"There will always be a home for you," Gwyneth had corrected, but to Jamie the words, though sincere, seemed meaningless – the elastic had been broken. More than ever, his home would be among his friends, back in *Demon*. He couldn't wait to get down the Gut with Pedlar and Mick and Dusty and to tell them of the time he got a bit off a nurse on the train to Bristol.

Jamie arrived back on board late in the afternoon. He had squeezed into a very uncomfortable canvas seat, along with other service personnel, on a fully loaded and very noisy air-freight carrier. The plane had landed at the RAF field at Luqa amongst a hive of activity. Huge jet bombers and other military aircraft parked in considerable numbers at the edges of the runway. A shining new Bedford bus belonging to the RAF dropped him at the dockyard gates.

Jamie had been away ten days.

"How's Blighty?" was a question he was soon fed up with being asked.

"Still there," he replied.

"What's been happening, Dust?" asked Jamie at supper.

"Not much. The yard's been working round the clock to fix us up. We should be leaving the day after tomorrow – for Cyprus."

"Great."

"Not so great. We're patrolling the island – a boring job by all accounts – steaming round and round to intercept gun runners."

"Yeah, I read about it back home. Some of our lads were blown up last week by a mine – in a truck. A couple were killed – up in the mountains."

"Bastards. Fancy a run ashore? It'll be our last chance for a while – there'll be no shore leave where we're going."

"We'll go local." Dusty led the way through the dockyard gates and out into the street. "It's not as sleazy as the Gut but you can't have everything – and the beer's cheaper. Besides, it takes an age to cross to Valletta in a Dghajsa. More drinking time."

The sun, dropping behind the skyline of Hamrun, blackened the distinctive silhouette of the spires and domes of the higher ground above them. The two enjoyed the walk through narrow streets and passages, cooler after the heat of the day. Women, sitting on chairs outside their front doors, ignored the passing sailors and chatted animatedly. Children played children's games; kicked a ball and made noise like children everywhere.

"Have you been down the Lucky?" asked Jamie.

"Once. Carlotta wanted to know where you were. She had a lovely young girl there. She said it was her eldest daughter – the one she was saving for you."

"You what?"

"Yup. Gorgeous, she was. Sixteen years old and ripe as a peach. Tits like water melons, eyes like black cherries…"

"Christ, she sounds like a fruit salad. Anyway, Carlotta promised her to me so get lost, berk," said Jamie, unsure as always when Dusty was throwing a line.

"No, true. I told her you wouldn't be back so she let me have first go. She said I looked like a nice boy and as I was a friend of her Darleeng Jamie, I could have first go."

"You lying bastard," said Jamie, punching his large companion on the upper arm.

Taking a narrow cut in a row of buildings, Dusty led Jamie down a set of stone steps and onto a wharf lined with bars and cafes. Dirty workboats and paint-stressed fishing craft rested against the quayside. Unlike the Gut, the doorways of the few modest bars lacked girls but the tinny sound of jukebox music issuing from each drinking place reassured the two.

"This is us." Dusty pushed open a rattley door and ducked into the brassy interior of a well lit bar.

Inside the narrow bar gingham-covered tables lined each side of the room like a transport café back home. The only decoration, a faded picture of the Queen, hung slightly skewed on one wall next to a pristine image of Dom Mintoff. Mick and Ginger waved at them from a table next to the bar.

"Grab a pew," invited Mick.

Jamie bought four lemon tops.

"How's Blighty?" asked Ginger.

"Still the same," said Jamie.

"Taffy, I'm glad you're back. We need you to do us a favour."

"Name it," said Jamie, feeling magnanimous. "S'long as it's not dhobying Dusty's nicks."

"What's wrong with my nicks?"

"No, it's nothing that bad," said Mick. "We have a little problem. We were just talking about it, weren't we Ging?"

Ginger nodded and continued the explanation. "What do you think of Badger?"

"Not much. He's a bastard."

"Have either of you lost any money?" asked Ginger, quietly. As he spoke he furtively looked around at the other tables that were fast filling with *Demon* liberty men.

"Not that I know of," said Jamie.

"What about you, Dust?"

Dusty thought, giving himself the time needed by refilling his glass from the bottle of anchor. "We-ell, now you mention it…"

"Yes?" said Mick, expectantly.

"No, I haven't."

"Ignore him," said Jamie. "He's in a funny mood. What's it about?"

Mick and Ginger leaned forward. Micky whispered, "A few lads; more'n one, are after coming to me saying they've lost money."

"Where from?"

"From the mess, you… just be quiet and listen for a minute. We all know that the worse thing – well, apart from fartin' in your 'mick – the worse thing a man can do is steal from his mates. You were home so you are the only person that's in the clear – no offence, Dust."

"None taken," said Dusty.

"As far as I know the amounts have not been great but stealing is stealing. Any money, mostly change left on top of lockers, goes – it disappears."

"I can't imagine Badger pinching change," said Jamie.

195

"I can," said Dusty.

"We've narrowed it down and he's the prime suspect," said Ginger.

"Turn 'im in," said Dusty.

"I can't – there's no proof," said Mick. "This is where you come in, Taff. By the way, how is Blighty?"

"Still there."

"Oh, good. What we would like you to do is set a trap. Tonight is our last chance. We're sailing tomorrow for God knows how long."

"Leave some money out – on top of your locker," continued Ginger. "We'll take turns to watch it."

"What, all night?"

"All night. It has to be done, so don't get too pissed."

Assuming his fiercest frown Micky looked at each man in turn, "and that goes for you all."

"I knew he was a bastard." Dusty looked longingly at his half-empty glass. "A tea leaf. That explains why he was demoted. This time he'll be out, you wait and see."

"I thought it was because he was an arse bandit," said Jamie.

"Who, Badger?" said Ginger. "No way. You can't stay in if you're a brown hatter. He would have been thrown out. I heard he struck an officer."

"I heard he sank the Ark up in Scappa Flow," said Micky. "You lot are like a shower of women. You don't even know that he was a senior rate in the first place."

"Shit'n it," warned Ginger. "He's just come in."

The four conspirators stopped talking, each finding the need to take a drink.

"Talking about me, then?" asked Badger, accurately. Without waiting for a reply he passed to the bar, bought two anchors and returned to a table by the door to join Taps the Sailmaker.

"That was close," said Jamie.

"Guilty," said Dusty. "Guilty as hell."

The four returned to the ship well before midnight, having planned the duty roster for staying awake. Jamie, more determined than ever to catch his hated adversary in something illegal, took the first two hours, keeping himself awake by reading a Mickey Spillane by the light of a torch under his sheet. From his hammock he could see the loose change that each had contributed to and placed strategically on top of Jamie's locker.

Just before 0100, Badger and Taps, obviously the worse for wear, stumbled in and in no time were turned in and away. Neither of the two older men had shown any interest in the money – it remained untouched.

'No point waking anyone,' thought Jamie, 'he'll be asleep for hours.'

Exhausted from the long day and the long trip Jamie fell into a deep sleep until Reveille sounded at 0600. Dragging himself awake he looked to where he had put the money – it still sat invitingly on his locker.

The duty PO swept through the mess like a tornado, hitting the undersides of the hammocks in his path with a short, wooden patrol stave. "Come on, you little sleepy heads, up and at 'em. Harbour Stations at 0800, hands off cocks..."

"Yeah. Yeah, we know," came the weary response of a thousand mornings.

After his visit to the heads Jamie began lashing his hammock. As he worked he looked to his locker fully expecting to see his money – but the money had gone. Badger, laying the top table for breakfast, averted his eyes as Jamie spun around.

"Who's had my money?" said Jamie loudly.

"Are you talking to me?" asked Badger. Then, as an afterthought, he added. "Sheepshagger."

197

"Shit'n it, Badger. Have you had my money? It was there, on my locker."

"Are you accusing me of stealing your money?" said Badger, menacingly.

"I'm not accusing you of anything, I'm asking you. My money was there ten minutes ago and now it's gone."

"Well, I think you'll find the Killick has it, Welshy. You're lucky. I usually put any loose change I find into the mess fund." Badger reached into his locker and rattled a 50 Senior Service cigarette tin in Jamie's face.

"Righto, then," said a shame-faced Jamie.

"You should be more careful," said Taps.

"Yeah, you should," said Ginger and Dusty.

"Yeah, you should." Mick, returning from the washroom with a towel round his neck, handed Jamie a fist full of loose change.

"Thank you, LEM," said Jamie with as much sarcasm as he dared without making Badger suspicious.

Later Mick caught up with Jamie on his way to the fo'csle for leaving harbour. "Would you believe that bastard? He's only been saving any bits of change left lying around to buy things for the mess. The man's an angel."

"Humph," said Jamie, still annoyed at being left to carry the can, "some bloody angel. He must have done something very bad to get stripped of his rate – and I intend to find out what."

CHAPTER 17

EAST TO CYPRUS

The trip from Malta to Cyprus passed without incident. Daytime temperatures from the early-September sun remained scorchingly high and Jamie kept well away from the torpedo mounts during his off-duty time. Each day the Captain stopped the ship to allow the bravest of the crew to swim over the side. Landfall off Cyprus caused no excitement save a rendezvous with an RAF Air Sea Rescue launch carrying bags of mail and a pile of diving kit. Along with the scuba equipment the launch also carried three fit-looking young men – including one Derek Latchbrook.

During the afternoon prior to arriving off Cyprus the First Lieutenant and Lt Jollyman had been called to the Captain's sea cabin.

"I thought we should discuss this." The Captain frowned at the short message in his hands. "It seems we are to receive an addition to our diving complement – three more hands – which is sound given the intelligence coming our way about activity this end of the Med."

Both officers leaned forward in expectation.

"Apparently one of our predecessors on this, er, exciting duty, intercepted some kit that we should worry about – limpet mines and the like, which could well have been used against us – but that's not what I want to talk about right now." The Skipper laid the message on his desk. "The reason I asked you here is this name; D. Latchbrook, one of your electricians, Jollyman."

The Captain had not used 'Christopher' when addressing his electrical officer since the regatta.

"Latchbrook, Sir? EM Latchbrook – the rating that went AWOL?"

"Yes, the same. Someone has cocked up it seems. He should not be coming back to the ship in which he offended. What do you think?"

"Yes, that's unusual, to say the least. Do you mean he's a diver now?"

"Attached."

"Attached?"

"Don't be so dim, Jollyman. He is still a tradesman but a qualified diver also – modern stuff."

"Oh, yes, Sir."

"What do you think, Jonathan?" The Skipper emphasised the First Lieutenant's Christian name. "Trouble, do you think? Mixing in? Morale problem?"

"No, I don't think so, Sir. As long as he does his job – that's all the divers care about. He could be Jack the Ripper for all they care."

"And he's a confident sort of chap," interjected Joystick. "He'll take any jibes and return them with interest."

"Right, then. All agreed, he stays, but you watch him, Jollyman, and if he steps out of line I will personally crucify him."

Work kept Jamie below decks, preventing him from observing the newcomers as they boarded the ship. He learned of Derek's arrival when he went along to the mess for his stand-easy cup of tea.

"Your mate's back, then, Welshy," said Badger.

"What are you on about now?" said Jamie.

"The deserter – your mate – he's back."

Jamie took a quick look around the mess but saw no sign of Derek.

"You won't find him here – he's been given a nice bunk – down with the other pampered lot. Specialist personnel my arse – seems to me you have to be a bloody criminal to get special treatment in this mob."

Jamie felt his temper rise, as always when exchanging words with the older man, but he suppressed a response.

"So the bugger's made it," he said to himself.

"He's right – it's Latchbrook." Mick slumped onto the bench and reached for his tea. "He's one of the new divers. Grunds has just been telling me to prepare some portable floodlights – it seems we are at risk from frogmen."

"Bloody hell," exclaimed Jamie.

"Scared?" sneered Badger.

"Why don't you give your mouth a rest?" Dusty reached across the table and grabbed a cup with one large and very dirty hand.

"Listen to this." Pedlar entered the mess with a bundle of mail and dumped it onto the table. He had obviously opened one on his way from the mail office. As the others scrambled to retrieve their letters he read:

'I think I have made a terrible mistake. Rodney, the man I thought I could love and trust turns out to be a rotter, so we will not be getting engaged after all.'

"Did you hear that?" said Pedlar, "the rotten bastard."

'He is married and has three kids. I cannot love and trust a man that is married and has three kids so I will give you a second chance.

All my love,

Wendy.

P.S. I hope you haven't been sowing your wild oats like Rodney.'

"Ah-haa," said Pedlar triumphantly. Carefully he sniffed the pink sheets and slipped them into their pink envelope, unaware that a similar missive had found its way to the seaman's mess for'ard and was being read at this precise moment by a two-badge able seaman called Raymond.

Jamie found two letters addressed to him – one from Gwyneth and another, a small white envelope addressed in a neat hand. The second letter puzzled him – he couldn't identify the handwriting. Laying aside the new letter, he opened Gwyneth's.

'I will be marrying John Llewellyn, the draughtsman from Caerphilly. We have no date as yet – we have to save up first.'

'Short, sharp and to the point,' thought Jamie. He turned his attention to the white envelope.

"Unless you're blessed with X-ray eyes," said Dusty, "you'll have to open it."

"It's from Jennifer." Jamie spread out the folded sheets. "The nurse I met on the train – when I went home."

"Did you get a bit?" asked Pedlar.

"Private information," said Jamie. "Now leave me to read my mail."

'… you can call me Jenny and I have moved to the hospital at South Molton. That's in Devon,' wrote Jenny. *'I hope you won't mind, but I told my friends I had met this handsome sailor on the train and that you had kissed me in the corridor. When you reply just say you enjoyed our kiss as they don't believe me.'*

'The little liar,' thought Jamie, pleased at being thought of as handsome.

"Well?" said Dusty as Jamie folded the pages back into the envelope.

"Well what?"

"What does she say?"

"Private information."

Later that day Jamie found reason to pass the diver's caboose on the port waist. Through the open door of the small workspace Jamie spotted the familiar figure of Derek kneeling on the deck, the blonde quiff re-grown and falling across his forehead as he worked.

"Latch, you old sod," called Jamie from the open doorway. "What a surprise. How are you?"

Derek, one of four men working on breathing gear and rubber suits strewn about the deck, glanced up briefly, "okay," he replied.

Jamie expected his old friend to stand and come over but instead Derek addressed himself to one of his colleagues.

"This is the wrong size, Jacko. What's that other one, over there?"

Jamie waited, unsure and confused. The other divers looked his way but said nothing.

"Call round for sippers," said Jamie, "or a can. You know where I live…"

Receiving no reply Jamie moved away, almost freezing with embarrassment when, after a few steps, loud guffaws emanated from the open door. Puzzled and hurt, Jamie returned to his work.

CHAPTER 18

CYPRUS PATROL

Detecting and chasing the men trying to supply EOKA terrorists with arms seemed an exciting prospect. In reality, Cyprus patrol proved anything but exciting. Every small ship or fishing boat that *Demon* encountered turned out to be engaged in legal business and met all the requirements of registration and cargo. The heat of late summer plus a lack of activity created a listless ship's company – a slow patrol speed and an oil flat sea did little to improve the mood. On a Sunday evening, two weeks into the patrol, Jamie bought his allowance of two cans of beer from the NAAFI cubicle and settled for a quiet evening. Puzzled and hurt at the snub from Derek, Jamie held on to the hope that one evening his old mate would be back to his cheerful self. Dusty Miller joined Jamie in the half empty mess – many of the mess members had crowded into the for'ard seaman's mess to watch 'Mutiny on the Bounty'. Jamie, one of the ship's film projector operators, had shown the film so many times he'd started calling people 'Mr Christian'.

Jamie cracked open a Watneys. "D'you have any kids, Dust?"

The giant stoker talked very little of his family. Jamie knew him to be married but Dusty received very few letters. Never one to speak without thought, Dusty opened his tickler tin and rolled a delicate cigarette with his large Field Gun Crew scarred fingers before answering.

"Nope," he said, "and I don't want none, either."

"Sorry, mate, I didn't mean to pry."

Dusty accurately wetted the edge of the paper with his tongue and sealed the tube. "That's okay. Kids are alright. I like kids. It's the missus I don't like. She only married me for the allotment."

"Why do you stay with her then?"

"I dunno. It's somewhere to go when I'm home, I suppose. And it's quite nice, sometimes – for a while. I get to sleep in a warm bed; nice nookie – till she gets fed up. Then she can't wait for me to go. Not very motherly, my Bev, and she likes her nights out."

The length of Dusty's reply surprised Jamie. Dusty rarely talked of his private life.

"I wouldn't have kids, not with her, anyway. I'm happy the way things are." He brightened up. "I must be to sign on for the twelve."

"You were seven and five, then?"

"Yup – up until I joined this rust-bucket."

"You puckin' lot must be puckin' mad," interjected Andy. The National Service REM closed the book he had been pretending to read at the end of the table. Andy had so far resisted 'fucking' as an expletive but there was no doubt that he appreciated its value as he often resorted to 'puckin'' when he needed to emphasise a point.

"Twelve years? In this mob? What a sentence. You get less for robbing a bank."

"What are you doing here, then?" Jamie mentally kicked himself, as he knew the answer.

"What the puck do you think? I'm here at Her Majesty's pleasure. I am conscripted, that's what I am. I thought I would see the world, get some experience. Instead I'm stuck in this overheated tub, going round and round a God forsaken puckin' island, seeing nothing."

"Seeing nothing?" exclaimed Jamie. "Did you not see the sunset tonight? You'll go a long way to see a sunset like that. Anyway, you've seen Rome. 'See Naples and die'. Well Rome's close enough."

"I've come a long way alright, but not to see a puckin' sunset. I want to do a useful job."

"We're doing a useful job," said Jamie lamely, "deterring arms smuggling."

"Useful? I don't know how many millions of tax payers money this tub cost and all they do with it is go round and round a—"

"God forsaken puckin' island," interrupted Dusty. "That's a beautiful island, that is. I've been there and those arms we stop could be used to blow up our fellas."

"We shouldn't be in the place anyway." Carl the signalman, busy massaging his scalp with a round plastic spiky pad, screwed the top back onto a bottle of Vaseline Hair Tonic and continued. "We've no right to be in other people's countries."

"If they ask us, we have," retorted Jamie.

"Ask us? Do you really think that all these countries coloured red on the globe have invited us in. 'Please come in and pillage all our resources, Mr Bull, and while your at it take a few of our people for slaves.' I should coco."

"We haven't taken slaves from Cyprus, have we?" said Jamie to Dusty. "Only waiters."

"Bloody hell." Carl's face had turned red. "You regulars don't know your arse from your elbow. If it's still, paint it. If it moves, shag it – that's you."

"Who pulled your chain?" Dusty rose to his full height. "Nobody asked you so keep your nose out."

Jamie readied himself to intervene but Carl turned his back and returned to massaging his scalp.

"He's right, though," said Andy, as Dusty sat down. "You regulars just go along with anything you're told. Obey orders, keep your puckin' heads down and believe everything your officers tell you."

"They never tell us anything," snorted Jamie. "And anyway, I don't see any of you lot refusing orders."

"Maybe not," smirked Carl. "I have to get through two years, but at least I keep abreast of what's going on in the world. I know enough to reason why we do something. When was the last time you read a newspaper?"

Jamie glanced at Dusty. He knew it took a lot of provocation for the big man to lose his temper. He also knew that Dusty cared little for National Servicemen.

"Do you know why we're here?" continued Carl. "Do you know why those people are struggling on Cyprus? Do you know who Makarios is; what EOKA stands for?"

"Piss off," said Dusty. "It's got nothing to do with us. We just do our jobs."

"You should start smoking," said Jamie. "A tickler calms you down in moments of stress."

Carl ignored the comment and continued to address his comments at Dusty. "Do you have any inkling of the tensions building in the Middle East? Everyone has the right to self determination, at least in my book they do."

"Where's the Middle East?" asked Jamie, getting bored with Carl, "and what's the use of knowing anything like that? It would only worry us. Let that lot in the wardroom do the worrying, we'll do the shagging."

"My God," said Carl in exasperation. "That's just the attitude that allowed Hitler to get away with his atrocities – the greatest crime against humanity…"

"That is it." Dusty crushed his empty beer can with one hand and pushed himself up with the other. In two steps he reached Carl and yanked the signalman to his feet.

"What the hell are you doing," said Carl, struggling to free his airway.

Dusty dropped Carl to his seat but continued to wag his large finger in the signalman's face.

"A lot of blokes on this ship were in the war and they wouldn't stand for you talking like that so shit'n it."

"Okay, okay. I'm sorry, but that film in there," he thumbed in the direction of the for'ard mess, "that mutiny came about because the crew of the Bounty were left in the dark. Bligh was a brilliant navigator but he expected people to obey without question."

"The Navy's always been like that," said Jamie.

"Maybe so – but that was the cause of that little lot – autocratic intolerance…"

"I don't know about that, Mr Christian," said Jamie. "All I know is that it's a bloody good film and you get to see some half-naked girls."

"I give up." Carl turned away to recommence, with vigour, the massage of his barren scalp.

Dusty leaned over to whisper conspiratorially in Jamie's ear. "'Ees been doing that for six months and I haven't seen a hair yet, have you?"

"No, but what do they know. There wasn't even a sunset tonight."

As day followed each long day the crew became fidgety. Each morning the sun rose into a clear blue sky from a flat sea and heated the ship to uncomfortable levels. On the bridge each new Officer of the Watch scanned the chart to determine the extent of his allotted navigation box and settled to his private thoughts. The unlucky ones lost the tall chair to the Skipper, who spent hours scanning the horizon, hoping against hopeless hope that a runner would appear. Each afternoon the Skipper stopped the ship, lowered the sea boat to act as guard boat and ordered 'Off duty hands to bathe, starboard side.' At first most of the off-dutymen took the plunge including Andy, the swimmer, who performed wonderfully graceful swallow dives off the STAAG platform. An unsubstantiated sighting of a shark

208

cut the numbers down – then someone said that there were no sharks in the Med, only barracudas. This cut the numbers down even further. The sight of a rifle barrel protruding from the bridge did little to help. Often, after the swimmers had cleared the water, the diving team practised scouring the ship's bottom for mines. Jamie watched with interest as the gunnery officer dropped stun grenades a safe distance from the divers to *Demon*strate to them the effect of underwater detonation. Despite Derek's unwillingness to re-establish contact with Jamie, Jamie took pride in the competence that his old friend *Demon*strated as he carried out his tasks.

"Divers are a snooty lot," reckoned Dusty. "We were the same on the gun crew. Like us they think they're above everyone else so don't worry about it. Look at me now, shovelling shit out of blocked heads. He'll come down to earth with a bang in a while, mark my words."

CHAPTER 19

EARTHQUAKE

On a Tuesday morning, four weeks into the ship's Cyprus duties, Jamie awoke to feel *Demon*'s engines throbbing at high revolutions. Since Jamie had turned in after the middle watch some event had obviously occurred to interrupt the patrol routine.

"What's the Buzz?" Jamie forced his tired head above the rim of his hammock. A breeze, lacking for the past four weeks, blew refreshingly in through the open scuttles.

"Dunno," said Pedlar, returning from the heads. "We've been steaming like this for two hours."

"P'raps we're intercepting a runner," said Jamie as he swung himself down to the deck.

"Train smash again." Andy eyed the breakfast tray waiting on the mess table. "Rubber eggs – and why does that chef pour the tomatoes over the bacon?"

"It hides the green bits," said Jamie.

"I like my bacon crispy," continued Andy. "Damn…" A sudden change of direction heeled the ship over, catching Andy pouring the tea.

The Tannoy blasted out a pipe.

"This is the Captain speaking." The note of undisguised excitement in the clipped voice silenced the chatter in the mess. "You will have noticed our high revolutions. We have been ordered to make ourselves available to the Turkish Government. An earthquake has occurred on the coast north of here – not too far from our present position. Information is scant but we are proceeding at speed. Stand by – I will update you later. That is all for now."

No one spoke for a long minute; then Ginger said, "What's to the north?"

"Turkey, you plonker," said Mick.

Demon continued at high speed all morning. By tot time the wind had increased from the south-west bringing with it a muggy heat. The sea, running from the port quarter, produced an uncomfortable, bumpy yaw. The 'further information' promised by the Captain had not materialised. Rumours started to multiply.

"Earthquakes only occur in the north of the country," Andy paused in his meticulous task of sharing out the Toad in the Hole, "which means we'll have to go through to the Black Sea."

"Wrong heading," informed Carl. "From our position we would have to go north-west. We're heading north-east. 015 degrees to be exact."

"What will we have to do?" asked Andy.

"Probably provide technical assistance," offered Mick. "Medical and stuff. Connect electricity and water pipes, things like that. Leastways, that's what we did in the West Indies – now that was a bastard."

"Earthquake?" asked Jamie.

"Hurricane," stated Mick, simply.

"Are we friends with Turkey?" asked Jamie.

"Of course we are," said Mick. "I've been there on a visit. You have to watch yerself, though. Lots of holding hands goes on and that's just the fellas. They wear baggy trousers – just in case."

"Just in case what?" said Andy.

"Just in case they get caught short givin' birth. 'Man born of Man will live forever,' that's what they say, so watch yerself."

"Bugger me," said Jamie.

"Exactly," said Micky.

"This is the Captain speaking." Again the Tannoy silenced the mess. "We now know a little more of the situation. An earthquake, approximately 6 to 7 on the Richter scale, has occurred in the hilly region some miles inland from the town of Mersin. The authorities have requested international assistance and we are at their disposal. We have reduced speed for an ETA of 0600 tomorrow, local time, which is one hour ahead of us. Clocks will go forward at midnight. That is all."

"Mersin," repeated Jamie. "Have you been there Mick?"

"Never heard of it, mate, but there must be casualties to ask for help."

The afternoon passed quickly with the ship preparing for any contingency they may find ashore. Joystick and Grundy supervised the gathering of electrical equipment that could be required including a heavy toolbox and two fully charged and tested portable spotlights. By 2100 a stack of equipment had been gathered on deck, collected by an assorted group of ratings.

"Right," said Joystick, "gather round. Things are not clear but past experience has shown that in these circumstances we can be most effective by providing communications, some technical help with water and electricity supplies and perhaps early medical help. Davis and Latchbrook will accompany me with the first relief party ashore. You two – turn in and be back here at 0500. Wear number 8s, boots and overalls and bring a jersey. It can get cold at night in these places. Petty Officer Grundy will remain aboard to organise a follow up party if required."

At 0500 Jamie stumbled out onto the iron deck to join the first relief shore party gathered beside the forward torpedo tubes. Jamie had slept badly after digging out his creased and musty No.8s trousers that had been stowed in his kit bag since Gib.

212

"I think my feet have grown," said a large figure that had followed Jamie out on deck.

"Dusty," said Jamie. "What are you doing here?"

"I thought I'd got away with it – but some bright spark made a last minute decision. Presumably I've been selected because of my experience with shithouse pipes."

Secretly very pleased to know that the big stoker would be with them, Jamie watched his large friend adjust the laces of his size 13 boots.

"Wearing sandals all the time must make your plates flatter and more spread out I expect," reckoned Jamie, uncomfortable himself in unfamiliar socks and boots.

As they waited, Jamie looked about at the assembled shore party. Tom Lightly, the PO medic, fussed with the straps of a heavy-looking white canvas bag. A red cross had been roughly painted on its side. Paul Smitte, the multi-lingual coder, chatted to a signals rating as they both fiddled with the knobs of a portable radio. A half-dozen other ratings sat or squatted amongst the equipment; some whispered amongst themselves but most remained silent and looked to the shore.

Jamie tried to see the contours of the land and was able to make out a group of lights that twinkled off the starboard bow. As he leaned on the guardrail the clipped voice of Lt Cdr Worthing interrupted his thoughts.

"Lt Jollyman is in charge of this party." He indicated the white-overalled Joystick by his side. "The coxswain will be his number one. We don't know a great deal of what will be required of us. You, as experts, will be first ashore and there will be transport to take you to the affected area. We will be alongside in the port of Icel at 0630 so move into the canteen flat. Stay there – the galley will get your breakfast. Listen for the pipe."

"Experts – what do you think of that then?" said Jamie, scoffing his sausage sandwich.

"The only thing you're expert at is filling your face," said Dusty through a mouthful of sandwich. While they ate and drank tea, the ship came to life. The order to close up at Harbour Stations brought people hurrying past. Cooped up in the canteen flat the shore party could only listen to the noises of manoeuvre as the ship tied up alongside.

The call to the shore party came as the sound of main engines died. Jamie took up his position beside his equipment, shielded his eyes against the early morning sun and took in the new surrounds. Encircled by scrubby hills, the town, an untidy collection of white and sandstone dwellings, stretched away to the right from the port where *Demon* now berthed. To the left, past the stone jetty, an uneven line of sun bleached Gullets strained against their stern lines, their bowsprits pointing like fingers to the open sea. On the otherwise deserted quayside a small group of men, some uniformed, waited and watched a gangway being manhandled into position. A road width away from the jetty a line of old stone buildings sat hard against a stone block wall seeming to hold the hills from tumbling onto the dock.

"Fall out," ordered the coxswain, who wore his working jacket with the pipe scorches over No.8s, "and don't go away."

Jamie, Derek and Dusty sat on their bundles of overalls and jumpers in the shade of the torpedo tubes.

"It looks okay – I can't see any damage." Dusty scanned the buildings scattered on the foothills above the docks.

"Twenty or thirty miles inland the Skipper said," offered Jamie. "That's further than that lot of mountains in the distance, I reckon."

"Well, they'd better get a move on. People could be trapped and waiting to be rescued and we're sat here getting numb bums; doing sod all."

"We're not here to *rescue* people, are we?" said Jamie, nervously. "We're experts, that's all."

"Experts, my arse," snorted Derek. "You just make sure you take a handkerchief. They'll use us to dig graves more'n likely – by now. You wait and see."

Jamie shaded his eyes against the glare and followed the walled road, a white scar against the darker scrub, until it disappeared over the first hill. He wondered what was waiting for them at its end.

The arrival of two vehicles took Jamie's attention. The first, an open Jeep type with a wide wheelbase led the way. A covered truck with a snub-nosed bonnet followed close behind. The military transports, each driven by a young khaki-clad soldier, approached the ship and stopped some yards from the gangway.

"Right, you lot," shouted the coxswain. "Get this gear into the truck."

"Those Turkey Pongos could have parked a bit closer," grumbled Derek as he struggled down the gangway with a portable lamp and his bundle of clothing. Deck hands hurriedly loaded the lorry with plastic water containers and cardboard boxes. Some of the Chef's bread crates had been packed up like picnic baskets.

"In you go," ordered the coxswain, "and if you haven't made a will it's too late now."

"Ha, ha," said a few, trying to fit legs where legs would not go.

"I hope this 'ere's a short trip." Dusty found space for one large leg between a water container and a canvas stretcher. The other he rested on top of a crate.

With a jerk that rearranged the load, the lorry noisily moved off. Jamie and Derek, who had boarded last, waved farewell to the seamen on the jetty with a two-fingered salute.

"Try and stow some of this gear under the seats." The leading telegraphist protectively hugged the radio. "Or we won't get very far."

215

Eventually, despite the heat and the unpredictable bounce of the truck, the shore party managed to organise themselves without injury and settled for the journey. As the truck ground its way up the relatively smooth hill from the dock the vista of the harbour and the coast spread out behind; the ship, huge on the small quayside, stood out, sharp and bright and clean and somehow bizarre.

"How did we manage to get into there?" shouted Derek above the whine of the truck.

"The Skipper must be learning," said Jamie. Very quickly the view changed as the truck descended a slight slope on the other side of the hill to join a highway. Running parallel to the coast, the highway took the vehicles east, affording infrequent sightings of the sea shimmering in the mid-morning sunshine. Occasionally a noisy lorry or an overloaded pick-up truck passed, hurtling by at a speed that made Jamie cringe. After an hour the truck slowed and turned off the main carriageway onto a side road.

Jamie caught a glimpse of a road sign. "Tarsus," he shouted to Derek. "That's something in the Bible, isn't it?"

Derek ignored the question, leaving Jamie to vaguely recall the name from one of the Rev Tucker's bible readings.

Very soon the surface of the road deteriorated as it wound itself upwards into the hills. Making painfully slow progress, the truck negotiated the rough road; its verges vague, and often only identified by dry stone walls – walls that served as boundaries for small buildings and yards holding chickens and goats. Jamie strained to detect damage to the structures in view but failed, and people working in the fields and yards appeared to be uninjured. Many stopped their chores and curiously watched the passing vehicles. Happy children chased the slow-moving convoy and waved and shouted after them. The ten occupants in the rear of the truck, concentrating on tactics to avoid bruised bums, spoke very little.

Many of the slopes adjoining the road held olive groves that reminded Jamie of the apple orchards seen from the train at home, but less green. As time passed, the landscape changed. Scrubby bush and short trees gave way to straggly pines. In parts, large spiny cactus grew like impressionist sculptures along the roadside.

Shortly after 1100 the truck pulled off the road and stopped. Joystick appeared: a white floppy hat perched precariously on the top of his head.

"Bale out, lads. Break out a water container and some cups – there's some in there somewhere – but only one cup each. We don't know what we'll find up ahead."

"My aching arse," complained Derek.

"My aching legs," complained Dusty.

"Tango Lima Lima." Sparks twiddled the knobs on his radio and listening intently inside his earphones. "Come in, Tango Lima Lima. This is Alpha Bravo One. Signal strength check please, over."

Jamie took his water and sat with the others in the shade of a group of conifers overhanging from the hillside above the road. Jamie watched with amusement as Smithy searched among his seven languages to engage the driver in conversation on the cab step. Each seemed to be struggling for understanding, which eventually came with some exaggerated back patting and nodded smiles.

"We can get by with Greek, Sir," reported Smithy to Joystick.

"Good, ask him how far."

Much jabbering and shoulder lifting resulted as the two settled into their communication. The equally young driver of the Jeep wandered over to join the conversation, but not before he had indicated his desire for a cigarette, which Joystick satisfied. Jamie rolled a tickler and asked Derek for a light.

217

"Put your brown end to my red end," he said out of habit, "and suck back."

"Don't say that too loud. This is the land where man born of man…"

"Yeah, I know," interrupted Derek.

Smithy reported to Joystick. "They don't know much. Apparently they've been given a destination about an hour away. Reports coming out are confused but there is a group of villages and outlying farms which the Turkish army and the Civil Services have not got to yet. They've been told to take us to what they think is the worst area."

Smithy had slipped into forgetting to say 'Sir'.

"Communications are poor so they don't exactly know what to expect. There should be a gendarme post there, but only Allah knows if they are still alive…"

Suddenly the ground beneath them moved followed by a low rumble – like the hunger pangs of the earth. Each man froze.

Joystick sprang to his feet, the first to react.

"Get away from that hill," he shouted as he ran into the road. Pebbles and dust showered down onto the sheltering group, galvanising the men into action. As one they sprang to their feet and followed their officer to gain the protection of the truck. Another growling movement shook the vehicle and dislodged stones and earth from above. In a cloud of dust the rubble came crashing through the pines to pile up where they had sat. Some debris landed in the Jeep, which had parked further along and closer under the hill. The coxswain, enjoying a pipe in the Jeep, disappeared from view as a cloud of dust enveloped the vehicle. Slowly, the chief emerged into sight, his navy jacket covered in white dust. Unhurried and using deliberate moves – as if not wanting to cause another quake – he slipped out, to crouch behind the low Jeep. For a long few seconds silence ruled until Joystick spoke up.

"Okay, it seems to have passed. Load up and we'll move from this hill."

Very quickly both drivers started their transports and drove along to stop further down the road, away from the threat of landslide.

"Bloody hell," said Jamie, his voice shaking from the experience. Unnerved by the sudden loss of firm soil beneath his feet Jamie thought to himself that ground was not supposed to move; only ships' decks did that.

"Joystick did well," said Derek.

"Yeah," said everyone else.

"Anyone hurt?" asked 'Doc' Lightly. The medic, keen to use the kit he had brought in the large pack with a red cross painted on the outside, stood up in the Jeep and waited for a response. Getting no answer he returned to his seat in the leading vehicle.

With everyone settled again, the convoy moved off. Derek chose to sit further forward allowing Dusty more legroom at the rear. The rough road continued to take them higher into the hills, the pine trees larger and more numerous in the rocky terrain. Since leaving the outskirts of Tarsus two hours or more back, the signs of civilisation petered out.

"Where do you think they're taking us?" asked Jamie.

"Too bloody far." Dusty moved his large, aching legs to dangle them over the tailboard.

"There's something." Dusty pointed across a deep valley. A group of small buildings, appearing intact, clung to the hillside opposite. Well spread out and with the usual stone walled yards, the area formed a sizeable village cut out from the pine forest all around. As the view receded they passed a junction with a smaller road leading down and across the valley, winding through fields of crops, to the settlement.

"Opozanti," read out Jamie from a sign.

"Opozanti – sounds like it means opposite," reckoned Dusty.

"Opposite what?"

"Opposite here, you twat," said Derek.

"But there's nothing here to be opposite to," said Jamie.

"Shit'n it, Taffy," said Derek.

"Well, opposite or not, we're not going there, so shut it – the both of you," said the Leading Radio Operator.

"I'm hungry," said Dusty.

Reaching a relatively level plateau the vehicles pulled onto some scrubby land and stopped.

"All out," ordered Joystick. "We'll eat here. It may be a while before we get the chance again. Go easy on the water. As you can see, there's not much around."

"Bugger all, as far as I can see," grumbled Derek.

"Cheer up, mate," said Jamie, "it may not happen."

"It's already happened. I should be diving in cool, clear water not sat here on a mountain with you lot."

Derek turned away pointedly to end the conversation.

"Please yourself," said Jamie quietly.

"Listen up," said Joystick as they ate sandwiches and stretched aching limbs. "First of all watch out for aftershocks. They could go on for days. Stay away from hazards as much as you can, we don't want to give the sailmaker unnecessary work, do we?"

"Very droll," said Derek.

"To be serious, we can't be far from the village of Okeraysali, I think that's how to say it. Ramazan, that's our driver, knows the place. By the way, the truck driver is Demitri. He has family there."

Joystick took a bite from his sandwich. A cool mountain breeze, a relief from the coastal oppression, threatened to lift the white floppy hat from his head.

"Stay together; obey orders and you'll be okay. That's all."

Resuming their positions on the truck the convoy re-started. Jamie regretted the noise from the old vehicle that prevented conversation – he had resolved, at the first opportunity, to tackle Derek about the obvious change of heart that had created a barrier between them since the Londoner had rejoined the ship. Despite the jolting from the rock hard suspension Jamie gave in to the effect of warm sunshine and a full stomach and dropped into a light doze – but not for long. Within minutes of him closing his eyes the truck braked and slewed to a halt, throwing men and equipment forward. Untangling themselves the occupants checked each other for injuries and found none.

"It's an ambulance trying to pass." Doc Lightly had appeared at the tailgate. "Stay where you are, we're backing up a way."

The truck reversed gingerly into the trees at the roadside allowing the ambulance to pass. Its driver paused briefly to converse loudly with Demitri.

"Jandarma," shouted Demitri above the din of his engine, waving acknowledgement to the ambulance as it accelerated away.

Continuing very slowly the small convoy negotiated the road that had become rougher and bumpier. After some minutes the driver shouted again, "Okayraysli, Okayraysli," and leaned eagerly forwards. The object of his enthusiasm, a farm building to the right of the road, seemed to be more or less intact. A group of people sitting well away from the house gestured to the Jeep and shouted response to the driver's question. Passing further small farm-like buildings the two vehicles rounded a bend to be confronted with the remains of a village. The first building, a single story house at the beginning of the street, seemed to be intact. Further along, the more substantial structures had collapsed, spilling stone, wood and tile into the road, blocking vehicle progress. Slowly the convoy progressed into the village and stopped.

"Out, all out," ordered the coxswain. "And stay with the truck."

Jamie dropped to the ground, almost collapsing from the stiffness in his legs. Straightening up he surveyed the desolate scene before him. The village lay in a dip under an escarpment of white rock, the face partly covered with green growth. The road, running straight through the small town, lifted at the far end to disappear through a cutting in the rocky ridge. A few yards down the road rubble from one of the collapsed buildings formed a barrier, beyond which a wider, open area, apparently the centre of the village, could be seen. To the right a solid, well-kept square building remained almost unscathed. Like a sleek rocket ship in a Dan Dare comic a towering minaret rose from it, reaching high into the sky. Here and there a few people worked silently amongst the debris, their faces masked with scraps of material, their clothes dirty and torn. Some sat on rocks and debris, hopelessness written in their slumped bodies.

Demitri clambered over the mound, shouting to attract attention. Joystick and Smithy followed. The people working on the buildings looked up briefly. Some waved tiredly, some didn't. Three of the men working on the rubble gathered to talk to the visitors. Within minutes two men in light khaki emerged from a small intact office block beyond the mosque and joined the group. Joystick's white-overalled figure with the incongruous hat stood out like a beacon.

"Fuck me," said Derek, the first to speak. "What a bloody mess."

"You can say that again," said Dusty.

"Fuck me, what a bloody…"

"All right, shit'n it," said the cox'n, but without his usual rancour. "You save it for later, lad. You're going to need a sense of humour by the look of this place."

Demitri, Smithy and Joystick started back – Demitri the quickest. As the Turkish soldier approached he started saying something and pointing to the rubble in the street. Smithy calmed him with a few words.

"He's worried," Smitte explained. "Demitri has family that lives in a farm further up the valley. No one here has news of them and he wants to get up there but the Jeep can't pass."

"Right, hold on a sec. Listen up you lot," said Joystick. "There's been considerable damage, as you can see. Seven or eight houses and shops this side of the road and half a dozen to the left there."

"Any casualties, Sir?" asked Doc.

"There are people still missing – and unfortunately there are some dead." He pointed to a line of trees at the side of the road. In the shade a number of body-sized shapes lay neatly lined up and wrapped in black shrouds. "The seriously wounded have been shipped out. SBA?"

"Yes, Sir?"

"Grab your box of tricks and see if you can help the walking wounded. Some of those poor souls digging over there need help. Radio Operator; wind up your portable and establish contact with control – let me know when you've done that. Now, all of you – there's a stream down behind the mosque but don't be tempted to drink from it – stay away from it. We have enough water of our own."

Lengthening shadows from the trees signalled the advancing day. Jamie shivered but not from cold.

"Latchbrook; take Davis and Miller and clear a path for the Jeep. Then the three of you go with the driver chappie for a recce and report back. Understood?"

"Aye, Sir," said Derek.

"Listen to me, Latchbrook." The coxswain handed Latch three pairs of canvas gloves. "You go careful. Do as the officer says. Do nothing, just look and report back, right?"

"Yes, Chief, you know me," said Derek hurrying to help clear the road.

"Aye, I do," said the cox'n. "That's the trouble. Now get going."

As if on cue, just as Jamie lifted the first lump of masonry from the road, the earth again registered its anger, grumbling deeply and shaking. The figures working on the buildings around the square leapt up and scrambled for open space. A half demolished building to the left of the street caved in on itself with a crash dispersing dust in a cloud that spread outwards like a small atomic mushroom. From somewhere in the chaos a scream rent the air. No one moved. The scream turned to cries, long, wailing, pain-filled cries – cries that shook the Doc into action. Bent low, as if to avoid enemy fire, and clutching his bag to his stomach, he darted towards the newly-collapsed building. Seconds after he disappeared the cries stopped. Time passed with all eyes on the point where the Doc had entered the rubble. Minutes later he reappeared, shook his head, and returned slowly to the exact position he had just vacated. The world had lost another soul.

"Right," said Joystick, "there shouldn't be another aftershock for a while. Gather timber where you can and shore up any dangerous buildings – take your lead from the locals. There's only a couple of hours of light left so move it."

The main party, including the telegraphist with his radio, clambered over the barrier and dispersed to the site where most of the activity seemed to be. In a very short time, with the Turkish driver Demitri working feverishly with his bare hands, the road was made passable. The Jeep, hurriedly loaded with water, sandwiches and one of the portable lamps, took off: its deep cut tyres throwing up debris and dust as they spun and dug into the loose road surface.

At nerve-jangling pace the little vehicle raced down the road and through the cutting. Beyond the escarpment the road dipped steeply then rose into a steep climb. Looking back, Jamie could see the remaining roofs of the village but he quickly lost sight as the road curved around a thickly wooded hill.

"Where the fuck is he taking us?" said Derek over his shoulder to the other two sat in the back.

"Pardon," said Demitri.

"Never mind 'Pardon' mate. You keep your eyes on the road," said Derek, hanging on as the bouncing vehicle negotiated yet another corner. With the engine complaining at the low gear the Jeep slewed around hairpin bends and up and down steep inclines. For a while the rough, rutted, path followed the watercourse serving the village but soon the stream was lost to view. After some miles the vehicle rocketed through a tree-lined opening, levelled off and slewed to a stop. Demitri switched off the engine and all four sat still. The silence rang in their ears after the noise and rush of the trip. Farm paraphernalia littered a compound around them. Directly ahead a stone-walled house, complete with door and windows stood apparently intact. Vacating the vehicle, Derek pushed open the reluctant door.

"There's bugger all behind here," he reported.

Like a Hollywood set the front wall hid a lack of substance behind. The roof held some remnants of aged tiles but most had fallen into the house. The door, standing ajar, revealed the collapsed structure behind.

"Nobody'd stand much chance in there." Dusty, standing at the right hand window pushed at a shutter, which swung open revealing a lean-to formed by the collapsed beams of the upper floor. Demitri became frantic, running to and fro, looking for a way in and making dramatic noises and gestures.

"I wish he spoke English," said Derek.

"He probably wishes we spoke Turkey," said Dusty.

"What do you reckon, Dust?"

"Dunno." Dusty looked from Demitri back to the collapsed roof of the farmhouse. "It seems he wants us to go in. The only place possible as far as I can see is through this window and under that lot there."

"Report what we find—" Jamie started but found himself being pushed out of the way by Derek.

"We haven't found any thing to report yet, have we, you twit."

"Who are you calling a twit," responded Jamie.

"Shit'n it – the both of you," said Dusty. "The pongo seems to think we should go in – so we go in – though God knows what we're looking for."

Followed closely by Jamie, Derek led the way into the building. Cursing and spitting dirt, he crawled under the ceiling, passing obstructions back to Dusty at the rear.

In the confined space every movement of rubble created clouds of choking dust. The men found some cotton material for masks that restricted breathing but also helped to quell the smell that was becoming apparent as they progressed.

After a while Derek called back. "I'm through, there's pots and pans and things, I think it's a kitchen. Pass the lamp. God, the stink."

The smell, pungent and offensive in the extreme, reached Dusty who was glad to take a walk to the Jeep for the portable lamp. The daylight had almost gone, the wide sky darkening rapidly with little twilight, as is the way in these latitudes.

"It's getting dark out here," he called, passing the portable.

"Not as dark as in here... God, what was that?" Crawling forward Derek's right hand had pressed on something hairy and cold, something soft and malleable. Recoiling he called, "Where's that bloody lamp? There's something here. It's bloody 'orrible – and it smells."

Jamie switched on the portable. Bright in the confined space, the lamp created thick shafts of light in the suspended

226

dust. Shadows danced as he pushed the heavy battery box past Derek's legs.

"Okay, leave it there," said Derek as the light fell onto the obstacle.

"Oh, my God."

"What?" said Jamie.

"It's a…"

"What?"

"It's a body. A dog or something – yes, definitely a dog. It's got a bashed in head. We have to get this out – it's making me puke."

Reaching past Derek, Jamie gripped the dog's rear legs and tugged. The body refused to move.

"Pull, for Christ sake," shouted Derek.

"You'll have to free it. It's stuck."

"It's caught – there's a bloody great stone across its neck. Pull."

With another tug the animal suddenly became free. Jamie fell backwards, the dead dog catapulting onto his chest. Jamie's shoulder crashed into a beam causing the roof to move. Debris showered down. The two men froze, silently waiting for the worst.

"What's happening?" shouted Dusty from outside.

"Come on out, Del. It's not safe," said Jamie.

"Hush," said Derek.

"Get out here, you silly sod," called Dusty.

"Shit'n it, there's a noise."

A knock, hollow and erratic, but definitely not caused by random falling objects, sounded somewhere in the wreckage.

"I hear it," said Jamie holding his nose against the sickening smell of the carcass lying alongside him. "Where's it coming from?"

"Further in – there's a door. I can just about see it. Back out a minute."

"With pleasure," said Jamie. "And bring your pet with you. It stinks."

CHAPTER 20

RESCUE

Filthy and tired, the men gathered around the Jeep gulping drinking water. Jamie spat out his first mouthful to rid his mouth of the taste of the dead dog. Demitri extracted a rolled-up mat from under the driver's seat. Without a word he laid it out. Kneeling he started a ritual praying. Derek poured a little of his water over his bloodied and dirty wrists where falling material had caught the exposed skin above the protection of the gloves.

"Are you okay?" Dusty examined Derek's wrists. "Can't I get in to help?"

"No. You're too big – you're better off out here getting the bits clear. Now listen up, I think the knocking is coming from a door in the far wall. A section of the ceiling has fallen and wedged it closed. We'll continue digging and see if we can open it."

"Right." Dusty, despite his seniority, appeared to have no trouble in accepting the leadership that Derek had naturally taken on.

"Jamie, take a look around the back," said Derek.

"I already did. The rear wall of the building is that rock there. There's no back entrance."

For the next hour the four worked like miners. At some point the knocking stopped and Demitri could get no response from his calling. In what had once been the kitchen Derek cleared a space large enough for a man to kneel but the ceiling section remained wedged against the door.

"Get Dusty in here," said Derek, "and bring some timber – we need a strong length of timber for leverage."

Dusty just managed to squeeze through, pushing a length of four-by-two before him. His bulk filled the space that Derek had cleared. Between them, the two arranged a fulcrum point for the timber. Dusty attempted to lever the ceiling section upwards away from the door but the immense weight above defeated his efforts.

"We'll have to break the smaller bits from the beams. I can't lift the whole fucking ceiling," said Dusty in frustration. "And Latch – be bloody-well careful, there's a lot of weight up there."

"Tell me something I don't know."

Firmly but slowly, Dusty and Derek broke away the loose plaster and lathes beneath the beams and passed the debris back to the other two. Mud formed on the hard stone floor as water from a leaking pipe mixed with the dirt dropping constantly from above. Inches above the heads of the two sweating workers heavy, rough hewn timbers held up the floorboards of the upper rooms.

"I can't free up these bloody logs," complained Dusty.

"Hold on," said Derek. "Stop a second. If we can't move the stuff to open the door, we'll just have to push it in."

"Fuck off," said Dusty. "That door has a beam wedged against it. If we push the door in the whole fuckin' lot will descend at a rate of knots onto my head."

"No, Dust, look. The wall will take the weight of the ceiling."

"It had better or we'll be flat pancakes."

"Well, let's see if we can shore up the biggies."

"No chance, we don't have enough bits of the right size – no tools and no time."

"Okay, Dusty, it's up to you. I say we ram it with the four by two. Jamie," shouted Derek, "shine that bloody lamp onto that door and get yourself and Demitri out."

Jamie focussed the emergency lamp's beam into the gap. He could see the vertical planks of a sturdy door but only the bottom half of two were accessible.

"Shit. No room for a swing," said Dusty. "I'll use my size twelves."

"Be careful."

Sitting with his back against a toppled ceramic sink the large man placed his large boots firmly against the bottom of the door and pushed. The extreme effort produced sweat that ran in rivulets down the dirty face of the ex-Field Gun Crew man.

"I can feel it giving a little," he gasped, pushing and easing in turns.

"What's going on?" called Jamie from back in the tunnel.

"Shit'n it. I told you to get yourself and Demitri outside. I'll call you."

"Piss off," said Jamie.

"It's no good; I'll have to give it some welly. Out you go as well, Latch," said Dusty. "There's no point in both of us getting an early bath."

"Get stuffed and get wellying," said Derek.

"Okay, mate. It's your funeral. Here we go."

Bracing himself against the sink, Dusty drew back his right leg and slammed his boot into the bottom of the door. With a mighty crash the left plank cracked and broke, flying into the void behind, leaving a gap two feet high. The ceiling dropped a little and stopped with a jolt. Dust and debris filled the air. As soon as the dust had settled Derek grabbed the lamp and pushed past Dusty. Wriggling on his belly he found enough space to push his head through the opening to peer into the void. A stone staircase dropped away and the light illuminated a face at the bottom, shining like a moon in a starless sky.

"Demitri," called Derek over his shoulder.

"Hold on. Keep Demitri with you for a minute, Taff," interrupted Dusty. "Let's get this other plank out first."

"Get back." Derek shouted into the cellar. The head disappeared into the darkness. Derek pulled himself and the portable out of the way. With another huge kick the second plank broke away and flew into the cellar. The door panel, carrying the weight of the ceiling spars, caved in easily. One of the spars dropped, catching Dusty high on the ankle. With supreme effort he held back the scream in his throat. Taking a gulp of breath he wrenched his leg free. When the mist of pain had cleared his mind he dragged himself aside to allow Derek to slither through the gap and down the stairs.

"Get Demitri," he called back. "And shine that light down here. There's two, a man and a lady. The lady's out of it. Where's Demitri?"

The lined and leathery face of an old man appeared in the opening. Dusty, wincing in pain, reached into the hole, grabbed the man by his arms and pulled. Jamie took over and passed the wiry-framed old man back to Demitri who helped him negotiate the wreckage to the outside. Out in the fresh air the Turks hugged each other, gabbling and crying in turns until Demitri assisted the old man into the Jeep and fed him a mug of water.

"Give us a hand with this lady, Dust," called Derek.

"'Fraid I won't be much help," said Dusty. "My leg's had it a bit."

Jamie, waiting in the tunnel, crawled forward and grabbed the woman under her arms and pulled her through the opening. Derek climbed back out of the hole and between then they passed the old lady out to Demitri where the driver succeeded in trickling a few drops of water into the unconscious woman's parched lips. Gently he lifted her into the Jeep where he rested her head in her husband's lap on the back seat. The old man seemed oblivious of all except for the small body in his lap. Bemused and lost he stared into his wife's parchment face: a yellow, lined face framed absurdly in a brightly-coloured headscarf. Demitri, showing some knowledge of first aid, checked the pulse at her throat. Nodding vigorously and saying something incomprehensible the Turkish soldier heaved the water canister and food basket out onto the ground, started the Jeep and swung out onto the road. Within moments the sound of the Jeep had gone. Jamie looked about him, peering into the darkness of the tunnel they had excavated.

"Where's Dusty?"

"Here." The large stoker dragged himself from the tunnel. "I think I've got a bit of a problem."

"What happened," said Derek. Leaping over the sill he pulled the heavy body of the stoker into the clear.

"That second kick; the poxy beam dropped and caught my ankle."

"Caught?" said Derek. "More like smashed it good. Jame, get that lamp out here. Let's have a look."

Using the lamp Derek inspected Dusty's injury. From a bloody lower leg the foot lay flat on the ground when it should have been pointing somewhere in the air. Derek touched it – Dusty screamed.

"Why didn't you say?" said Derek. "The bloody Jeep has gone. You should have been on it, you idiot."

"Idiot, is it? You're only saying that 'cos I can't get up. Anyway, nobody asked me."

At precisely 2145 the First Lieutenant knocked on the Captain's door,

"Signal, Sir, from Christopher."

"Christopher?"

"Er, Lt Jollyman, Sir. He wants to know if he should return or stay, only…"

"Only what?"

"Well, it seems that he has lost three of his chaps."

233

The Skipper stared, his temper not too good after weeks of sitting on the Cyprus station and now after a full day sitting at a jetty waiting for what? After dispatching a small recce group twelve hours earlier, no further request had been received. Expectations of some recognition from this job seemed to be edging towards the negative. He glanced malevolently at the photo of his wife.

With a feeling in the pit of his stomach that bordered on despair, the Captain held out a shaky hand for the signal. "Lost? You mean – lost?"

"Well more like mislaid really, Sir. They went off in one of the Turkish transports to—"

"Mislaid?"

"Yes, Sir," continued the Jimmy. "They went off in the—"

"When?"

"Earlier today, Sir – about 1700."

"And he asks if he should come back?" The Captain rose to glare down at Lt Cdr Worthing. "Now you go back to your radio and you tell Lt Jollyman that he stays to find those men – if it takes all night."

"Yes, Sir."

The Jimmy turned to leave.

"By the way, who did he lose?" asked the Captain. Involuntarily he reached to the picture of his wife and placed it face down on the polished surface of his desk. An icy hand gripped the Captain's heart as Worthing read out the names.

'A confirmed runaway,' thought the Captain, 'a boy and a shit-house cleaner – all three wandering unsupervised around the politically-sensitive Turkish countryside.'

Carefully the Captain slipped the photograph into the top drawer of his desk and turned the key.

Misc. Mess remained unusually quiet through the long evening of the day that two of its members went missing.

Rumours spread around the ship that at least six of the men sent ashore had died.

"Ours will be okay," reckoned Ginger. "Dusty will look after them."

"Probably getting pissed on local wine," reckoned Mick.

"Probably fucking the arses off the local peasant girls," said Pedlar.

"Probably scarpered." Badger paused for a moment from ironing his nicks. The comment silenced the others. "Good riddance, I say – to both of them, and that AWOL bloke too. Good riddance."

"Bollocks," said Pedlar. "You are an insensitive cunt if ever I saw one. They're probably working their guts out. Better them than me... and I take that back. A cunt's useful."

"Up yours." Badger carefully folded his ironing. "And you're right, a cunt's more useful than a prick."

After the Jeep left, confidence amongst the three remained high. Demitri would deliver his relatives to some hospital and return. But, as minutes turned into hours, doubts crept in. Jamie had ripped the sleeve from his No. 8s shirt to bandage up Dusty's smashed ankle. Somehow, between them, they had managed to pull the heavy man through the window. Thankfully the stoker, propped against a tree, had fallen asleep. To take his mind off their predicament, Jamie decided to speak to Derek.

"Are you okay?"

"It's bloody cold; I could murder a cuppa."

"Yeah me too. What I meant was, are you okay – with me now?"

"With you?"

"You haven't exactly been the friend I joined up with – and got pissed with in Devonport – not to speak of taking on Teds in—"

"Okay, okay," said Derek, then he fell silent. In the pale light from a star-studded sky Jamie peered towards his companion, hoping to gauge the reaction. What came was unexpected.

"You saw Nelly…" then a long pause. "In Malta."

Guilt flooded Jamie's tired mind.

"Yes. I did, but…"

Derek continued. "What sort of friend takes his mate's girl out when he's miles away – and doesn't bother to tell him. What's a man supposed to think about that?"

"I couldn't tell you; you haven't been exactly approachable. Anyway…" Jamie was about to say that nothing had happened but caution stopped his words.

"What's wrong with writing?" continued Derek. "Makes me think you've something to hide."

"Rubbish," retorted Jamie. "How did you know, anyway?"

"She's my girl, you prick. We write to each other. You spent the afternoon with her on the beach."

Jamie could not mistake the accusing tone. The possibility that Nelly would tell Derek about the picnic had not entered his mind. How much did she reveal? Would she have told about the naked bathing and – and the rest?

"What did she say," ventured Jamie.

"Why?"

"Nothing. I hope she told you the truth, that's all."

"What truth?"

Jamie felt he was digging a hole for himself; the full truth was the last thing he wanted Derek to know.

"The truth – that we talked – nothing else. We talked about you the whole of the time."

"That's what she said," said Derek. "So why did you not tell me you had seen her?"

236

"I meant to write but things happened. I lost my Dad and I went home for the funeral. Then before I knew it you were on board."

"I didn't know – about your Dad, I mean. So you went home? When was that?"

The tension seemed to ease.

"The last weekend in August, the RAF flew me to some place called Lyneham. I got a bit off a nurse in the train."

"You little liar."

"I know."

"The last weekend in August," repeated Derek. "I was lifted out of Lyneham that same weekend – to Malta. We must have passed somewhere."

"Did you see Nelly?"

"In Malta? No. She was back home by then. Anyway I transferred to Cyprus straight away. I've been practising with the diving team in Limassol waiting for you lot. The last time I saw Nelly was during my diving course at Pompey. She got away from her Aunty when old Hoppalong left for Malta. We managed a weekend together."

The memory of meeting Nelly's Father at Luqa brought a wry smile to Jamie's face. With a jolt, he remembered Nelly telling him that she had not seen Derek since the infamous weekend he went AWOL. He decided not to complicate things by querying it, or by relating the Luqa story. The conversation ceased. Derek scratched the dirt with a stick. Jamie waited for the verdict.

"What would you have thought – if it had been the other way around?"

Self-righteous indignation welled in Jamie's Welsh heart.

"I would have trusted you completely."

"Would you? No shit? A beautiful party like Nell – with me?"

"Well – maybe not."

In the semi-darkness, Jamie thought he detected a smile.

"How've you been, you long Welsh twit?" said Derek. Self-consciously he patted Jamie's shoulder. "I've missed you."

"Shit'n it." Jamie hoped that the night was dark enough for his friend not see the relief on his face.

The cold creeping from the stony earth kept the two fidgety and sleepless. Dusty slept on and off, his breathing shallow and laboured.

"He's hot," said Jamie. I reckon the poor bastard's got a temperature. Do you think Demitri is coming back?"

"God knows." Derek sorted out two cigarettes from a squashed pack in his top pocket and passed one to Jamie. "But I do know we need a fire. You were a boy scout, get some wood together."

"Dib, dib, dib," said Jamie.

"Dob, dob, dob," said Derek.

Building a stone circle they lit a fire with the plentiful supply of timber from the house. Jamie piled on the fuel, glad of the heat as the night air became colder.

"Wot – no tea?" Dusty groaned as he pulled his bulky frame nearer the fire.

"Indian or Chinese?" asked Jamie. "You'll have to settle for Aqua Pura – and supper tonight is hard-tack."

Dusty refused the hard-tack biscuits. "What's it like, Taff? The leg, I mean." He leaned forward and winced as the foot moved.

Jamie gently uncovered the ankle. "It's a bit of a mess, I'm afraid. Does it hurt much?"

"Comes and goes. Sometimes it's numb, like my head," he tried to smile, "but mostly it aches like shit."

"Your boot should come off – it looks swollen."

"Leave well alone, lad," said Dusty.

"Demitri shouldn't be long now. You try to sleep."

"Look," said Dusty with a grimace. "You and I know he would be here by now if he was coming. You're a mate, and a good one as it happens, so don't shit a shitter."

"You're the best shitter I know, Dust. Just hang on. Try to sleep."

Jamie lit a cigarette for the big man and moved back to Derek. The moon rose from behind the yard wall: a huge orb, full and red. Gradually it turned to silver as it lifted into the clear sky, becoming bright enough to cast a pale shadow.

"I never did tell you about that weekend, did I, Taff?" Derek pulled deeply on his cigarette. The flaring tobacco briefly lit his brooding face. Feeling no need to ask which weekend, Jamie stoked the spluttering fire and listened as his friend related the events that had so altered his life.

CHAPTER 21

THE WEEKEND

With little money and no ticket Derek had managed to remain undetected on the non-corridor train from Weymouth. At Romsey he'd mingled with a noisy group of matelots, boarded the London-bound train and, using skills honed through adolescent years of travelling free around London, he'd avoided the guard and arrived at Waterloo. Mixing with a loud group of excited, leave-bound sailors he'd slipped through the ticket barrier and headed for a telephone kiosk at the station entrance.

"I knew you would come." Nelly leaned heavily on Derek's arm as they walked a lakeside path through Regent's Park. She wore a light-coloured wool coat with a large fur collar turned up against the chill of a London January evening.

"I shouldn't be here."

"Will they miss you?"

"The firing squad? They never miss."

"Silly," she laughed. "Will they miss you on your ship?"

"Not until Monday morning, with luck," he said with a Derek smile. "I arranged for my station card to get itself lost."

"Where will you go tonight? Are you hungry?"

"'Home' and 'yes' in that order." He realised that his last meal had been hours ago in a different world, afloat somewhere on the English Channel.

"Come home with me. I have a room away from my aunt. We can get in at the side door. I'll get us some food and no one will know you're there. It's a large house."

"Where's your father?"

"He works here; in London; at Whitehall."

Derek blanched.

"No, no. He's at Portsmouth, for something or other, for the next week. Don't worry."

Nelly tugged at Derek's sleeve, leading him to a bench facing the blackness of the softly lapping lake. Their vaporised breath caught the light from a building across the water. Some disturbed ducks squawked and splashed and fell silent. Derek removed his cap, turned to Nelly and kissed her, a long deep transfer of weeks of missing and longing and waiting. No stirring of loins or swellings or tinglings. This kiss was a joining, a testing, a giving more intense than any sex, more reassuring and more satisfying.

"I've missed you," said Nelly.

Derek said nothing. He kissed her again. This time their touching lips passed pulsing, urgent signals to strange and secret parts of their bodies, moistening and stirring and hardening.

"Come on, you must be starving," said Nelly, her voice light and happy. Skipping away she pulled Derek after her, oblivious to the cold that threatened to freeze the lake that night.

"What about your Aunty? Aren't you supposed to be home by now?"

"Don't worry about Aunt Letty. She's a treasure. She thinks I'm staying with a friend."

"Girlfriend, I hope."

"Silly. Anyway she'll be asleep by now. Gin you know. She takes a few with dinner. Come on."

Half running through the park gates they turned towards the bright lights of St Johns Wood and crossed a wide road into the high street. Almost immediately they arrived at the side door of a quietly impressive square brick house. The girl unlocked the door and ushered Derek inside. On tiptoe she led him up two flights of stairs and into a large bedroom. Quietly she moved to the tall, small-paned window and pulled a draw cord that shut out the street light and shut out the world.

Fragrance and softness conspired to drown Derek's senses as he awoke on Sunday morning. The unfamiliar feel of the fine cotton against his own nakedness and the deepness of the downy pillow told him he was with Nelly; in her bedroom; in her bed. Panic briefly invaded his consciousness, retreating when her golden head, inches from his own, came into focus. Reaching out with his leg he encountered hers, smooth and firm, which he pulled towards him. The deep sleep after the loving of the night had relit his desire.

The waking girl groaned and stirred, turning until her round buttocks fitted snugly into his lap. His erect member had nowhere to go except between her legs. With the ease of female instinct she wriggled and moved, compelling the intruder to slip into her moist vagina. He remembered then that this was how they had slept, with his spent force still inserted and his arms holding her close.

"Ooh," she said, "again?"

"Again?"

"Yes please," she whispered softly. So he did.

Two hours later the pair stirred. Nelly brought tea and toast to the room.

"What about your Aunt?"

"She stays in bed Sunday mornings. We'll go out, just in case, but she rarely comes to my room."

A light covering of snow met them as they left the house. Arm in arm, they walked the wide pavements of London – uncaring of time or destination – concerned only with each other. At Marble Arch they crossed the wide thoroughfare into Hyde Park. The snow and frost, unnoticed on the streets, created a wonderland on the greenery. Low winter sunrays sparkled through the branches of leafless trees and turned the

242

grass to diamonds. A pair of squabbling robins disturbed the peace and caused a shower of glistening stardust to fall in their path.

"You'll be going back then," said Nelly in a half question.

"'Fraid so. I'll have to get going. They'll miss me."

"You know I might have a baby – after last night."

"Yes, I know. Do you want one?"

"I would – if we were married."

"I can't marry you. Not right now."

"You could if you didn't go back."

Derek stopped. He kicked an imaginary blade of grass from the path. "I have to. They'd catch me and put me away."

A young couple jogged by, their smiling faces looking flushed from the cold and the effort. White plumes of breath swirled in their wake. Nelly re-engaged Derek's arm and they continued walking.

"It is possible. Daddy tells me that quite a few sailors go missing and they never see them again. Somehow they manage to change their identities or something."

Wandering out at Hyde Park Corner they listened for a few minutes to the ranting of a communist speaker who tried to rile Derek as a servant of the capitalist government. Conscious of his lack of a leave pass he pulled Nelly away and started up Piccadilly. At the Circus they found a coffee shop and entered. The steamy warmth inside the small café and the heady aroma of fresh coffee was welcome after the cold walk.

"We wouldn't have anything. We'd have to work."

"I have some money and I can type. I can work in an office."

They watched each other over the rims of their cups, the girl looking for confirmation that her plans could be reality and the boy searching for re-assurance that what he was about to do was going to be alright.

"I'll have to go home and change. I have twenty-five pounds in my bank book."

"You mean you'll stay?" She almost spilled her cup in excitement.

"Stay? We can't stay here. We'll go up north, away from here; away from the Navy – Manchester or somewhere like that. Do you know Manchester?"

"No."

"Nor I."

Inured from the weather by their exhilaration, the two wandered around London all day, planning the future, each dismissing the doubts and fears that had the temerity to invade their minds.

Separating at Charing Cross they promised to meet at Euston at 1100 the following day.

Nelly kept the appointment. For hours after the agreed time, she waited at the freezing entrance to the station. For hours she refused to accept that Derek would not come. Darkness compelled her to return home; to sit with her Aunt at dinner; to pretend that the cold had caused the red rims around her lovely blue eyes.

Derek, despite a heavy doubt sitting unwelcome in the pit of his stomach when he had left Eleanor, fully intended to join her the next day. He had arrived home cold and hungry, gaining no warmth from the kitchen of his mother's semi-detached. The lino that had covered the floor for as long as Derek could remember had long since lost its pattern. He filled the kettle and lit a ring on the gas hob with matches from the box always kept on top of the grill.

"Ma," he called, knowing she would not respond. "It's me."

Removing his great coat, he hung it on the hook at the back of the door and made his way through the hall to the front room.

244

With difficulty he negotiated the books, newspapers and magazines piled high in the ill-lit passageway.

"Hi, Ma," he said as he opened the door. For a moment he failed to see his mother, her figure, seemingly smaller, lost against the backdrop of more books filling every area of space. A low coal fire burned in the grate making the room only marginally warmer than the rest of the house. Mrs Latchbrook looked up and over her spectacles. Seeing Derek, she reached into a gap in the books and turned down the volume of the muffled hymn playing on the radio.

"Derek? I didn't cook dear."

"'S alright, Ma. I'll make us some toast."

"Good boy." Mrs Latchbrook turned up the radio and returned to the large book in her lap.

Ivy Latchbrook had always preferred her own company. Even when she married Harry she rarely saw her husband. He worked long hours at the photographic labs at Park Royal developing new film materials. She adopted Derek, an East End waif found wandering amongst the rubble of the blitz. He was delivered to the Latchbrook's semi a week or so before his seventh birthday. She'd agreed to adopt the boy in an attempt to change her life, but she soon became bored with child rearing and returned to her only love – books. Harry left his wife less than two years later for a lab assistant who shared his enthusiasm for science and his lack of enthusiasm for children. Derek loved the woman he called Ma – loved her as the only anchor in his life: someone who could be relied upon to always be there. To Derek, Ma was home. To Derek, Dad was just someone who had given him a new surname.

At 0915 Monday morning Derek answered the front door to a naval shore patrolman and a policeman.

"EM1 Latchbrook?"

245

"Hang on – I'll get him." Derek, dressed in civvies, moved back through the book-lined hall to the kitchen. At the back door he grabbed his greatcoat from its hook. Quietly, he lifted the latch and opened it. A second shore patrolman stood there grinning.

"And where are we off to, sunshine?"

"Hang about, I'll get my brother for you." Lowering his head, Derek attempted to push past the bulky regulator.

"I think not, son." The regulator grabbed Derek and spun him back into the kitchen. Caught unawares, Derek stumbled into the corner used to store boots and wellies. An old cricket bat, untouched for years, offered itself. Derek grabbed it and came up swinging. It took three of them to subdue him and to bundle him into the police car waiting in the road.

At 1100 Derek, instead of being at Euston with Nelly, found himself sitting in a holding cell at Paddington police station waiting to be escorted to Portsmouth.

"That's one tough bastard." Derek stoked the fire: raising sparks and re-igniting charred wood.

"He's a great bloke, old Dusty. We could have done with him at Gillingham. D'you remember – those Teds?"

"We did okay."

"D'you think that Turkey pongo has the sense to take his relatives to the village? He must have known we had a medic there – do you think?"

"He'd be back ages ago if he had. He's probably gone to a hospital somewhere. Don't forget – he didn't know Dusty was hurt."

"We have to do something." Jamie lowered his voice and looked to the prone figure. "He's suffering more than he lets on. He's sweating like a good 'un."

"Look around. We need a cart or some wheels."

246

"I already did. If there was anything it's under that lot there."

"How far did we come?"

"It's hard to say – perhaps three or four miles – but it could be more. Demitri was giving it some welly."

"We'll walk. It'll be mostly down hill. I'll splint his leg and support him best we can. He's too bloody heavy to carry."

Doing their best to avoid moving the foot, Derek secured two short planks to the leg with strips of material Jamie foraged from the debris. He extended the splints beyond the foot for some protection but just lifting Dusty caused the heavyweight stoker to cry out.

"We can't do this," said Jamie.

"Alright, I'm alright," gasped Dusty. "Stop fucking about and get going. I'll manage."

Filling pockets with the remaining food and carrying the water, the three set off through the gap and down the road. With every step Dusty moaned, until he became used to the movement and adjusted his leg to avoid the worst jarring. Derek and Jamie took turns supporting him.

"If my recollection of navigation is right then we won't go far wrong if we keep the moon behind us," said Derek.

The moon, almost full, provided good light except when the time passed under trees and gullies. Dusty progressed with no complaint but for involuntary gasps when the rough road caused him to stumble. His great weight and height proved to be more of a strain to the much shorter Derek.

"Okay rest a while," said Derek after half an hour. "Any sign of lights ahead, Taff?"

"Nope, but I'm sure we're on the right track."

"Well, there's a fork up ahead. What do you reckon?"

"Shit," said Jamie. "I vote for the left one."

"I vote for the right one," said Dusty. "But stop a minute – I need a rest."

247

Lowering the big man onto a rock the two others moved away a few yards.

"Shallow breathing; high temperature – he's in shock. We've got to get him to a doctor soon." Derek moved back to pour water over Dusty's parched lips.

"This is stupid – trying to walk him. He won't make it."

"I am here, you know." Dusty shook his head to clear it. "And I haven't given up yet."

"Shit'n it," said Jamie. "I'm going to go ahead. You two stay here."

"I'll go," said Derek.

"For once in your life you can shit'n it too. I'm going. I can run faster and farther than you. I," he declared proudly, "have just been trained for the regatta by no other than Petty Officer Gordon Grundy. I have stamina. Anyway, you can do best by staying put – you know more about first aid."

"Well, you'd best get going Jimmy boy. This one's out of it."

Dusty had slumped unconscious to the ground.

Jamie removed his woollen jersey and handed it to Derek. "Keep him warm. I won't need this. I'll see you mate, I'm off."

"Take care – and Taff."

Jamie looked back.

"We'll miss you. Don't forget to write."

At the junction Jamie scoured his memory for some clue that would give him the right road, but nothing emerged. Relying on his instinct, he took the left fork, which dropped through a tree-lined cutting. Resisting the urge to move swiftly he settled into a steady jog, unsure of how long he might be doing this. In clear stretches of road the moonlight threw his shadow before him, which he tried to catch but failed. Time deserted him as he plodded on – forcing the worry of being on the wrong track to the back of his mind. Imaginary creatures scattered from his path and once or twice real creatures fluttered through the roadside trees. To lessen the fears he concentrated on the road ahead, but no matter how hard he tried the 'what ifs' encroached.

'What if this is the wrong road?'

'What if I'm heading into the interior, never to be heard of again?'

'What if Dusty doesn't make it?'

Sweating profusely and with pain shooting up his legs from both feet he realised his progress had slowed. With every jarring step he felt more tired; felt his eyes closing – enticing him to sleep. He remembered his father telling him that it was possible to sleep on the march: to doze and, at the same time, to move one foot after the other. His dad had marched; from Belgium to Poland; miles and miles, through night and day. And when they arrived they put him to work in the mines near Auschwitz. He rarely spoke of the war but in a melancholy moment he had told Jamie that every day, as he marched from his prison to the mines, he could see the concentration camps. Jamie recalled his father's face, grim and grey as the gravely ill man told of the smoke stacks spilling black smoke. For years he and his fellow prisoners watched as truck loads of anonymous figures drove past. Blessedly no one in his Stalag knew the fate of the poor souls until the winter of 1944 when rumour and guesswork turned to fact; when the purpose of those hideous chimneys became known. Racked with guilt and fear; fear that he may never see his family again, Maldwyn determined to escape. For weeks before his dash, the camp information network filled with talk of a Russian advance. His chance came when the Germans ordered an evacuation of the whole area: work camps and concentration camps. For many, the long march back into Germany resulted in death. For Maldwyn, the march offered an opportunity to escape. Before the end of the first day, Jamie's father had taken advantage of the confusion and the scant guard cover to dive into a snow drift. For hours he waited until the last of the marchers had passed. Knowing that the only way to remain free was to walk back through Russian lines, he headed east. Eventually, half-dead with cold and hunger, the Russians picked him up. But that was not the end for Maldwyn. A long trek south faced the malnourished and sick man. After weeks of walking and talking his way onto transports, he arrived at Odessa on the Black Sea.

'Odessa', thought Jamie. 'That wasn't too far away, was it? Somewhere to the north, across the Black Sea...'

A twist in the road put the moon on Jamie's left. He recognised nothing. With confidence fast deserting him, Jamie, with supreme effort, blanked everything out – aware only of the slap of one foot after the other; each step eating up the yards to the assistance he had no way of knowing was there.

At the limit of his endurance, with the dark darker, and the pain deeper, he stopped. He dropped to his knees; the impossibility of what he was doing flooded his mind. His whole upper body heaved, his chest sucking in great gasps of air into his searing lungs. Stones on the rough road indented his knees but he had too much other pain to feel them.

'The wrong way. I'm going the wrong way.' Desperately he tried to pierce the dark ahead. Then a light flashed, in the sky – not a flash, more a beam, out of which a face appeared, somehow not for real but still in front of him.

"I'm proud of you," his father said. "Breathe steady, my son. Not far, not far..."

Through the elusive face another light, this time like lightning in a far storm, arced through the sky. The boy's heart leapt. To his right a stream captured the moonlight as it cascaded down its rocky course. He remembered a stream, just after leaving the village: not far from the escarpment. He struggled to his feet and started them moving again, stupidly singing over and over a line to a song he remembered from long ago:

"Onward Christian soldiers,
Marching as to war,
With the cross of Jesus
Going on before…"

Then below him the terrain had some form that he recognised: roofs and buildings – a rocket-ship spire – then a gap, a familiar gap. With each step the opening took shape in the dark ahead. Elation quickened his pace, each lead foot slamming and echoing as he passed through the cutting into the village beyond.

The First Lieutenant knocked confidently on the Captain's door at 0220. With his sleeping mind tuned to any noise, the Skipper sat up, struggling to open puffy eyes.

"Yes? Come in."

"I've just spoken to Jollyman on the radio, Sir. His missing three have been found. I'm afraid one has been injured."

"Thank God for that," said the Captain, as he swung to the floor from his bunk.

"Sir?"

"Not for the injury," he tutted impatiently. "Thank goodness that they're found."

"Yes, Sir."

The Jimmy averted his eyes as his CO pulled on his trousers over striped pyjama bottoms.

"Well," he barked. The Captain was never good on waking. "Read it out, man."

"From Lt Jollyman. 'Three ratings found alive. ME Miller serious leg injury. One needing treatment for blisters on feet and one OK SBA recommends airlift. AM if possible'."

"Umph. Air Sea Rescue? To where? Cyprus I suppose. They have a lorry, don't they? Bring him back here."

"The casualty is too badly hurt for us to treat, Sir. It appears they saved the lives of some locals. Miller got hurt in the process. Quite the heroes, apparently."

"Umph." said the Captain, thoughtfully, "take a signal. To Admiralty, London. Request a helo lift. Let them sort out from whence and any diplomatic clearances required – and explain that our casualties are the result of rescue work in conjunction with our Turkish friends. That's all."

After the First Lieutenant left, Norman retrieved the photograph of his wife and carefully placed it back on his desk.

The RAF helicopter landed at first light on the near flat bed of the stream at the back of the village. Very little water flowed at this late summer time, but enough liquid remained to throw spray and muck very efficiently over the waiting ratings detailed to guide the helicopter in. A young man in a khaki flying suit emerged from the open passenger deck. Quickly he crossed the stony ground to the waiting party gathered about the stretchered Dusty. After a brief word with Doc Lightly the RAF medic decided to leave the casualty in the ship's stretcher for the trip to Cyprus. With Jamie hobbling along behind, the stretcher party bundled Dusty into the helicopter where the doctor set up a drip and detailed Jamie to watch the bottle. With a surge of noise the Whirlwind heaved itself into the air, its viciously-cutting blades clipping the tips of the surrounding trees. Through the open door of the passenger compartment, Jamie looked across at the minaret. Close to the top a gallery came into view – a white clad figure, robes flowing in the wind from the helicopter, stared solemnly at Jamie. For a second their eyes met – the white clad figure waved – then he was gone. Tipping alarmingly forwards, the aircraft accelerated, gained height and very quickly left the broken village behind.

At the army field hospital set up on Limassol's airfield, a businesslike crowd of RAF people whipped Dusty away, without ceremony, to a makeshift operating room. Jamie, with the help of an orderly, hobbled into a large tent to a welcome cup of tea, his first hot drink since the previous day.

"My name's Tam," said a white-coated orderly. "What's your name?"

"Davis," said Jamie. "Royal Navy."

"Well, Davis – Royal Navy, what the Sam Hill have you two been up to? I've never seen anyone so dirty."

Tam pushed a thermometer into Jamie's mouth. With undisguised distaste the orderly lifted Jamie's filthy wrist and counted his pulse.

"Finish that tea – let's get you into the bath – you stink."

Jamie's blistered and bleeding feet stung in the water, which smelled of disinfectant, but he wallowed in the luxury, scrubbing the dirt and grime embedded in his hands and face until the water turned a murky grey.

Fighting his need for sleep, Jamie heaved himself out of the bath, dried himself and returned to the ward.

"How's my mate?" Jamie followed Tam to one of a dozen bunks lined up neatly down both sides of the tent.

"We have a makeshift theatre – he's down there at the moment. He'll be all right. Now jump into bed, the doc will be along to check you out as soon as he's free. Meanwhile we'll have these rags down to the laundry – they smell of sewage."

Lying back in the cool comfort of the bunk Jamie thought back over the previous day – unable to believe that so much had happened over such a short period of time. He felt again the relief that had flooded his exhausted mind as he emerged from the escarpment to find his shipmates asleep in and around the lorry. He smiled to himself – remembering the shock on Joystick's face to be woken by a babbling, filthy idiot unable to string two words together. Joystick had lost no time in setting out with the SBA and four others to recover Dusty with a stretcher – refusing Jamie's request to accompany them.

As Jamie dropped into that well between consciousness and deep sleep, he recalled the light that had flashed in the sky as he knelt, exhausted, on the road. He would never tell anyone about the voice; about the face of his dad – who would believe? That he himself believed was enough – despite being told by the coxswain that no light had been used at the village that night – and no one had seen lightning either. As he fell asleep he tried to recall his father's face but failed.

Jamie awoke feeling ravenous and bursting for a pee. Leaving his bunk he passed a bed with the unmistakably large frame of the stoker filling it to capacity and asleep. A cage under the sheet covered one leg.

"They think the foot can be saved, which is lucky for that poor sod," said Tam from behind Jamie. "The state of that dressing someone had put on…"

"Poor sod," agreed Jamie.

"He's off back to Blighty. The doc cleaned it and straightened it but it needs more work. The ankle joint was dislocated and fragmented. Ligaments and bones got damaged. Pretty well shattered it was…"

"Yeah, well, it catches up with you. You can't go around humping dirty great field guns around and not get hurt. Um, any chance of some dinner?" asked Jamie, "and do you serve grog here?"

As Jamie waited for food a smartly uniformed young RAMC officer visited Dusty and checked him over. He also stopped at Jamie's bed and drew up a chair.

"How are you feeling?" The doctor offered Jamie an extra-long American cigarette.

"Much better now, thank you, Sir."

254

"Good, good. We treated your feet while you slept. They'll be okay given time."

The doctor looked at Jamie long and hard, making him feel uncomfortable. "I hear that you and your friend have been involved in some operation in Turkey. Is that right?"

"Well, yes Sir, but…"

"That's okay. If it's classified, please don't think you have to divulge." He edged closer. "But, er, it was Turkey, was it?"

"Yes, Sir, but…"

"Up near the Russian border, were you?"

"No, Sir, we were nowhere near…"

"Greece, then. Up near Greece? The field gun – you're part of some sort of Special Forces unit?"

"No, Sir. The field gun; I was only joking. It doesn't exist…"

The officer stood and nodded gravely. "Okay, okay, I understand you can't divulge anything, er, clandestine… It's just that something is going on and no one seems to be letting on. I just wish I knew why the bloody hell we're here."

Through the rest of the day and evening Jamie sat with Dusty, fed him some food and tried to talk but conversation proved difficult as the big stoker closed his heavy eyes before one or two words had been spoken. Two airmen with red crosses on their arms arrived and fussed with a wheeled stretcher. Jamie stood back as Tam prepared Dusty for the airlift.

"Oy, Rip Van Winkle," said Jamie. "You're off home you lucky bugger."

"This one's a big, lucky bugger," said one of the airmen. "What do they feed you on in your mob?"

"He'll have one of you for his tea if you're not careful with him," said Jamie.

"Gear. Has he got any gear?"

"I'll look after his clothes." Jamie handed the airman Dusty's cigarettes and wallet, which they tucked into his blanket. Jamie watched as the group started down the ward; sorrow gripped his heart.

"Hold on, will ya. Hold on a sec. Bloodywell stop." The airmen halted the trolley. Dusty struggled to raise his head to focus on Jamie. "Give me a minute."

Jamie caught up and looked down on his friend. The unshaven face looked dirtier than ever but Jamie saw only the eyes – the intensity in the brown, staring eyes shook him. There was something he had never seen before in those eyes, something pleading, something fearful. Jamie had never known Dusty to be afraid of anything.

"Aren't you goin' to say goodbye?" said Dusty.

"'Course I am, silly bugger. Anyway, it won't be long before I see you again – when you come back."

"There's no coming back for me, Taff. This is it. Civvy Street for sure. Fucked myself up this time, good. I wonder what my Bev'll say..."

"Get stuffed, I'll be watching you knacker the other leg when you win the Royal Tournament..."

"'Urry it up, I've got a plane to catch," said one of the airman.

"Tell that Brylcreem boy to shit'n it." Dusty pushed his hand out of the blanket and clutched Jamie's with his huge Field Gun Crew-scarred fingers.

"I didn't get the chance to thank you; you and that mate of yours, for what you done. I wouldn't have made it, you know."

"Get stuffed. You are one tough bastard, but thanks anyway, Dust. I'll miss you. Who's going to clear the shithouse pipes now?" Jamie's attempt at jollity failed to produce a reaction. "And watch they don't stick that foot on back to front. You'll be walking round in circles for the rest of your life."

This time Dusty's big face attempted a twisted smile, his eyes closed and his grubby sausage fingers tightened their grip. Tears welled and ran down his temple to drip from his ear and to stain the white pillow. Jamie slipped his free arm beneath the stoker's head and hugged him until an airman separated the two with a tug on Jamie's sleeve.

Pulling Jamie away, the airmen resumed their journey. With pain returning to his feet, Jamie hobbled after the stretcher party. He caught up with the group as they reached the entrance.

"One thing, Dust," he called. "You haven't told me and I need to know; Carlotta's daughter, at the Lucky. Did you really have her?"

The mobile stretcher swung outside into the fragrant Cyprus evening, but not before Jamie caught sight of the enigmatic smile playing on the lips of his departing friend.

"Bastard," said Jamie, then the big stoker was gone and out of his life forever.

CHAPTER 22

ULTIMATUM

Three days later *Demon* broke into her resumed Cyprus patrol duties to pick up Jamie at Limassol.

"Latchbrook has written a report." Joystick caught up with Jamie on his first morning back. "From what he says it appears you did well."

"Thank you, Sir."

"Don't thank me too much, Davis. The Captain came very close to charging you and your compatriots with ignoring orders."

"But…"

"But nothing – you were told to take a look and report back."

"Yes, Sir."

Jamie waited, fully expecting another green rub.

"You were – are – lucky. The Turkish driver should have reported back to me but he didn't – if he had, we would have known your whereabouts. That small detail saved your skin – just."

"Yes, Sir. Demitri was a bit… well, it's over now. Can I ask, Sir? The old gent and his lady – were they alright?"

"Who knows, Davis? Maybe – maybe not. All we know is that the earthquake left 156 dead. Your lady in the cellar could have been one of them."

Jamie hoped, more for Dusty's sake than for any other, that she had survived.

Grundy grabbed Jamie after Joystick had dismissed him and asked what had happened to the portable lamp and did he realise how much paper work had to be filled out to requisition another.

Badger made unnecessary comments about how much sweeter was the air now that Dusty was gone.

Derek still passed his time with the divers but he visited Jamie's mess often and picked the bones out of all that had happened in Turkey.

Jamie volunteered to pack up Dusty's gear and placed a simple note inside the top of his kit bag that said 'Bastard, I hope she gave you a dose' in large letters. He found the valve spanner that Dusty always carried in his overalls pocket and stowed it in his locker – wrapped up safely with his father's watch.

Dusty's billet remained empty.

September moved into October bringing clouds and occasional rain to the waters around Cyprus. The first heavy downpours carried yellow sand particles that left the ship off-colour and gave the crew plenty to do keeping her clean. Later, cooler air and more persistent rain washed away the summer heat but did nothing to alleviate the boredom of the endless wallowing patrol.

Scouser and Toffee acquired a dog each and walked them dutifully morning and evening. During the watches the dogs behaved immaculately, making no noise and lying asleep at their masters' feet.

Unexpectedly Toffee's dog became pregnant, which surprised everybody as it was called Butch. Toffee blamed Scouser's dog Rover, but there were dogs in the stokers' mess too, so it could well have been one of those. Jamie put his name down for one of the puppies but lost it very soon after taking delivery.

In a reshuffle Jamie moved to Weapons Control, which meant assisting the Chief EA. Initially he missed the freedom of deciding his own tasks. He thought that fetching and carrying tools and holding a torch for the artificer lacked challenge, but, by questioning the chief constantly, he learned new things daily.

Misc. mess continued to socialise in two groups. The older members gathered at the forward table playing crib most evenings. A particularly noisy Uckers game being played on the after table brought an edgy response from the oldies.

"Shit'n it." Badger, losing to Taps, shouted out in irritation. "How can I think with the racket you lot are making?"

"Yeah, keep it down a bit," said Mick, asserting his authority as killick of the mess.

"You don't have to think to play that game." Jamie had lately found himself less willing to take denigrating remarks from the three-badgeman.

"And you can shut up too, Welshy," replied Badger. "You don't have that shithouse cleaner to help you now."

The mess silenced, exaggerating the pinging of an unbalanced blade from the fan on the port bulkhead. Jamie, after a long pause, stood, placed the dice thrower back on the board and moved towards the crib players.

"I take it you are referring to my mate, Dusty?" Jamie stood above the older man. A shadow of uncertainty passed over the round, freckled face, which seemed a shade paler than usual. Jamie prepared himself for the punch to his stomach, determined to give as good as he expected to get. Heady with his own daring he carried on. "You obviously haven't heard then, Three Badger." Jamie exaggerated the full title deliberately. "My mate Dusty is to get a medal." He paused for effect. "Turkey is giving him a substantial settlement. How's that for a shithouse cleaner?"

"That's enough." Mick sprung to his feet to stand in front of Jamie. Badger surprised Jamie by saying nothing. With a snort of derision, the younger man turned away. As he returned to his place Jamie hoped that his little lie had gone unnoticed –

perhaps he alone knew that the only recognition Dusty Miller had received for his sacrifice was a 'mentioned in dispatches'. Jamie hoped that someone, somewhere, had 'mentioned' it to Dusty.

By the middle of October the ever-present roots of *Demon*'s rumour grapevine spread as the ship's company sensed a change ahead. Instructions to write letters home and to have them with Postie by 23.59 reinforced the expectation. *Demon* headed south-east at a pace not experienced for the past six weeks.

Early the next morning the reason for the haste appeared in the shape of an RFA, high and grey in the water and full of good things. In an exercise that lasted most of the day, the RFA replenished *Demon*'s diminished fuel and supplies. Large bags of mail left and even larger bags arrived. By late afternoon the supply ship, considerably lighter, disconnected her loops of black fuel pipes allowing the destroyer to peel off. Pointing her bow to the east *Demon* sped away, crushing the hopes of those that dreamed of sampling anchor lemon tops in the exotic bars of Malta.

With no word from the bridge rumours fed off the smallest of clues.

"What's the buzz?"

"I don't know."

"What's our heading?"

"South East."

"What's south-east?"

"Lebanon, Israel – the Middle East."

"Are we arguing with Lebanon?"

"I don't know – ask Carl."

Jamie, Pedlar and Ginger cornered Carl after supper one evening.

261

"You handle the signals, Carl – what's going on?" asked Pedlar.

"Don't ask me," retorted Carl. "You know as much as me."

"Come off it," said Ginger. "You haven't stopped telling us that we know nothing. Now – why should a British warship creep around this part of the Med?"

Carl sighed a deep sigh and thought for a moment. "We have a treaty obligation to protect Jordan from Israel. The Israelis have been making noises lately."

"Why? Is Israel fighting Jordan?"

"No, but the Arab nations – Syria, Jordan and Egypt in particular – want Israel out of it."

"So we are on the side of the Arabs against Israel," said Jamie.

"No. Only Jordan. Egypt wants to control the canal so the British, French and Israelis have a common interest to keep the canal open. Nasser has other ideas. To complicate matters he is also courting the Kremlin. There's evidence that the Russians are supplying the Egyptians with jets."

"So if there was a war we would be allies to Jordan against Israel and allies with Israel against Egypt," said Jamie with devastating logic.

Carl thought about the statement and responded, "No, well, yes. Oh, shit'n it. You lot don't understand."

"You are not wrong, there, mate," said Pedlar.

During the next few days *Demon* altered her speed and direction so often that even the plotters in the Ops Room lost any idea of her whereabouts. Buzzes continued, fed by snippets of conversation gleaned from the wardroom by stewards or from glimpses of signals decoded, stamped 'secret' and passed to the Skipper. A week before the end of October, tensions on board increased dramatically. The Captain ordered the ship to close up at defence stations, a condition of watchfulness, in a two watch system, eating and sleeping while off watch, sitting and waiting while on, ready to revert very quickly to action stations – and at night no lights were shown. Below decks the uncertainty created an atmosphere, each man withdrawn into himself. Banter stopped. That the ship had entered some undefined threatening situation was the only certainty. The first call to 'Action Stations' turned out to be a false alarm. Many more followed, interrupting what little sleep the crew managed to get. The Captain ate and slept in his cabin on the bridge, rushing to the bridge or Ops Room in response to a radar or sonar contact.

With little respite, the hours and days passed slowly, the grinding routine made worse by the heat and confinement of closed compartment doors. Every man on board received anti-flash gear, the close-knit, white-cotton helmet and gloves designed to keep flame out. Worn by everyone during action stations the hated gear was also very effective in keeping heat and sweat in.

Smithy the Coder spent long hours glued to his chair in the radio shack, listening and interpreting communications that filled the radio waves in the area. Attempts to wheedle information from him failed, and being 'T' even promises of sippers and gulpers were brushed aside.

As the days passed the weather deteriorated becoming steadily windier making long hours confined at defence stations uncomfortable and tedious. Tempers flared and the demand for information, for a solid reason for the vigilance, grew on the messdecks.

At last, on the 30th of October as the afternoon gave way to the first dogwatch, the clipped speech of the Captain spoke up on the Tannoy. "This is the Captain speaking. I am aware that you are impatient to learn the reasons for our current state of readiness."

Derek and Jamie, washing their hands ready for tea, stopped and listened.

"You could say that again," said Derek.

"Shut it," said Jamie, straining to hear the rest.

"I can now tell you that hostile action between Israel and Egypt over the control of the Suez Canal started yesterday. We have issued an ultimatum to both parties to stop fighting and to withdraw troops ten miles from the canal. British and French units, in the interests of maintaining this essential route, will then provide the means to safeguard the waterway. The ultimatum expires in twelve hours. Be aware that reactions are not always predictable. Be alert and ready for immediate action. That is all."

"What the bloody hell does that mean?" said Jamie.

"It means what he says," said Derek. "We'll be piggy in the middle while Israel and Egypt fight it out for the canal."

In the mess the conversation buzzed as the bread was sliced and the jam spread.

CHAPTER 23

INVASION

The sights and sounds of the war against Colonel Nasser's Egypt were, in the main, hidden from the majority of the men closed up below decks. From the rejection of the terms of the ultimatum issued by France and the UK, *Demon* joined a fleet of British and French warships heading for the Egyptian coast. From before dawn on the 1st November she escorted aircraft carriers launching sortie after sortie of bomb-heavy aircraft. Keeping constant watch on sonar and on radar for any sign of retaliation *Demon* kept station close to her aircraft carrier, ready to peel off to rescue any unfortunate pilot who could not stay airborne. From somewhere a rumour started that the U.S. were not too happy with the actions of the Allies against Egypt. Tension on board increased as reports that the 6th Fleet had massed just over the horizon ready to intervene, a situation made all the more credible when a US submarine, stupidly or very bravely, tried to infiltrate the allied fleet. The overwhelming threat from British and French anti-submarine units convinced her to surface. Flying the Stars and Stripes, and under the watchful eyes of a frightening array surface vessels, she left the area.

"This is stupid." Carl, the signalman, joined the off duty half of the mess members to eat a quick lunch. "What the bloody hell does he think he's doing?"

"Who – and doing what?" Jamie continued to eat as he talked, in case another call to action stations effectively cancelled his meal.

"The Skipper."

"What's the Skipper to do with anything? He's following orders just like everybody else."

"He could protest."

"Protest?" said Taps. "He's doing what he joined up to do, you idiot. Why should he protest?"

"Those aircraft," retorted Carl. "Hundreds have passed overhead from those carriers out there. Have you seen the smoke from ashore? They're probably killing civilians and God knows who else – women and children most likely – and all for a bloody canal."

"You idiot." Badger banged the table and stood. The intensity of the older man's outburst surprised even Jamie. He watched as Badger stared menacingly across the divide to the midship's mess table. "They're knocking out their airfields and planes. If this ship were on the end of an attack from aircraft you wouldn't be talking like that. If you knew what just one bomb could do to this million pound technical wonder you'd applaud every one of those carrier planes taking off over there. Knocking out their airfields, that's what they're doing, not killing civilians, you plonker."

"Yeah? Don't tell me there are no civilians on their airports."

"I didn't expect to be forced to puckin' well beat up some third rate country either," joined in Andy the swimmer.

"Forced?" Taps placed a placating hand on Badger's arm. "Nobody forced Nasser into taking the canal, did they? All he had to do was pull his army out. This war is his fault entirely."

"What about the Yanks? What if they decide to have a go at us?"

"They won't do nothing, they're our friends…"

"Bloody hell," said Carl. "What about the Soviets? Are they our 'friends' as you say? I'm living with a bunch of morons. Frightening, frightening…"

A timely announcement from the Skipper took the sting out of the argument that threatened to get out of hand, "...following a sustained effort to nullify the Egyptian Air Force a ceasefire has been agreed. The ship will assume a more relaxed state, but be ready to close up at any time."

"Bloody hell," said Taps. "That was the shortest war I've ever been in. There you go, Carly boy," he shouted to the midship's mess, "that's what happens when you bomb the shit out of yer enemy's airfields."

For the next few days *Demon* wallowed within sight of the sandy coastal ridge a mile or two west of Port Said. The Captain ordered a stand-down. For the first time since arriving off Port Said the crew moved freely about the upper deck. The numbers of other ships supporting the action surprised Jamie. Despite poor visibility he watched as destroyers and smaller escort vessels moved about, finding clear positions. To seaward, Jamie counted three aircraft carriers and a cruiser. Heavy weather persisted, creating a lumpy sea that produced an uncomfortable movement in the coastal swell. With the ship in a more relaxed state, those off duty found time to catch up on dhobying, cleaning and sleeping, but not for Jamie. He was required to assist the CEA with a problem in 'B' Turret.

Late on the evening of the 5th November, Captain De-Fotherinham called his Heads of Department together.

"I'm afraid the so called ceasefire is off," he said, "which means that the assault is on." He waited for the news to sink in. "We are to support the marines with 4.5 gun fire on our section of the beach at dawn tomorrow. Any questions?"

The gunnery officer spoke up. "B gun is playing up, Sir."

"What's the problem?"

"An electronic fault. The Chief EA is attending to it now."

"That gun must be perfect by the morning. Work all night if necessary."

"Sir."

"I will call action stations at 0200. I want the men fed and the decks cleared away by then. Turn them in and good luck."

By midnight CEA Ben Harding had corrected the problem.

"Keep your fingers crossed, Taffy, lad."

Jamie, exhausted from hours spent running between the bridge and the gun, fetching and carrying and testing systems, looked forward to a rest. In the cramped space of the equipment filled gun turret the CEA crouched in the gun captain's seat. Intensely he watched for signs of hunting from the direction indicator.

"But what caused the fault?" asked Jamie.

"At this moment I don't really care what caused it, son. It works so we leave it."

"But..."

"Piss off and get some sleep. You'll need it."

For the short time left, Jamie crashed on the mess bench until the ship came to life again an hour later. The chefs had prepared an unusual meal of kidneys swimming in brown gravy, boiled potatoes and plenty of bread.

"Condemned men," said Pedlar, dolefully.

At 0200 on the 6th of November, a starless night cloaked the stealthy advance of darkened British destroyers as they moved to prearranged positions along the shoreline west of Port Said. *Demon* prepared her guns to lay down a barrage of gunfire in advance of the Royal Marines' landing craft and helicopters being readied and loaded with assault troops. Like huge bug eyes, the gun director above the bridge trained the main armaments to the allotted target area. In the crowded forward switchboard compartment the telephone rang.

"Davis," said the Chief EA. "Grab the tools and meet me up top. That bloody 'B' gun is hunting again."

Jamie followed the Chief up top, glad to be doing something. As he stepped out into the cold and near darkness of the upper deck, Jamie heard the rhythmic, repeating whine of 'B' gun. The mounting rapidly moved back and fore in short, sharp oscillations. Looking aft he could just make out the silhouette of 'C' gun, its twin barrels aimed steadily and menacingly toward the shore. 'A' gun also pointed at the low coastline, ready to deposit violent destruction onto anything that would dare oppose the army at present embarking in landing craft all around. Only 'B' gun misbehaved.

Inside the turret the gun captain, Leading Seaman Beresford looked down from his seat at the sleek H/E shells lined up in the ammunition hoist. He vented his frustration into his anti-flash gear.

"Fuckin' thing won't stay still. I get trained all my fuckin' life for this and when I get the chance to shoot something for real the fuckin' thing won't stay still."

CEA Harding politely asked him to isolate the power to the turret; to unplug his communication line and to step outside to provide room to work.

"Davis. Get that cover off," the chief ordered.

Jamie squeezed into the impossibly small space between the huge metal breach blocks and the left bulkhead of the turret. Rapidly, he removed the servo panel cover.

"It's the feedback generator – it's got to be." With a shaky hand the chief unscrewed and slipped out the hand-sized generator. Jamie spun the gear wheel while the chief held the meter probes across its terminals.

"No output. Bloody duff gen," cursed the chief.

Caught up in the tension, and sweating profusely inside his cotton anti-flash covers, Jamie focussed the beam of his torch onto the offending item. Spinning the gear wheel again he spotted that the shaft remained still.

"The pin's broken," he said. "The gear wheel is turning on its own."

"You're bloody well right," said the chief. "The pin's broken. All we need now is a bloody pin. Have you got a pin, Taff?"

Jamie redirected his torch to his toolbox. A frantic search revealed nothing remotely like a pin.

On the bridge, the Skipper watched the sky to the east. He imagined the orange hue at the horizon brightening to yellow. Pacing to and fro he checked his watch; only minutes to go; mentally he reallocated targets for his two serviceable weapons.

"Guns?" The gunnery officer understood immediately the unspoken query.

"No report yet, Sir."

In the turret the CEA wiped the sweat from his brow. "The workshop – get yourself down to the workshop, lad. Find something that'll fit…"

With a sinking feeling, Jamie pictured the numerous watertight doors he would have to open and close to reach the electrical workshop. Then, from somewhere an idea entered his mind. 'My belt – the buckle pin could just about be the right size.' With shaking hands, Jamie undid the buckle of his belt and presented the pin to the hole in the gear. It went in. With a whoop the chief cut the soft metal with his pliers, bent the ends over and replaced the generator and covers.

"Be gentle with her," he said to the gun captain as they changed places. Magically the turret moved smoothly and positively.

The percussion hit them a split second before the noise as the 4.5s opened up. The first salvo caught the CEA and Jamie as they climbed down the vertical ladder off the gun deck.

270

Unprepared and hampered by his heavy toolbox Jamie hung on with one hand as the ship recoiled under the combined firings of all her heavy weapons. Missing out the last two rungs, he dropped to the deck, crouched low and headed for the fo'csle ladder. Another blast slammed Jamie in the back, robbing him of his senses and filling his eyes and lungs with stinging cordite smoke. Instinctively he followed the CEA to the door into the canteen flat. Impatiently he waited as his boss forced the clips off the heavy metal door. With his whole being crying out for cover, Jamie found himself screwing up in anticipation of the next percussion, the expectation worse than the actual bang. With regular crashing explosions each gun barrel sent its heavy, 56-pound shells screaming away to wreak havoc on the foreign shore. The breeze, blowing west to east, carried sulphurous smoke from each discharge across the ship. Inside the canteen flat the noise from the guns, amplified in the constricted space, vibrated the very air about them. Through the messdeck door Jamie could just make out the unmistakable figure of Badger. The lone figure sat ghostlike on the mess bench; hands clamped firmly to his ears. Dust filled the air, choking and stinging the eyes. With every salvo, fluorescent light covers crashed down to lie on the tables and the deck. Yellow fibreglass insulation, loosened from overhead, hung in ribbons like Christmas decorations, shaking with each firing from the guns above. Returning to his action station, Jamie felt intense relief to be away from the incessant crump of the guns.

After what seemed an age, the firing stopped – but not for long. Vibrations from the straining engines indicated that the ship had speeded up. Jamie, feeling the ship heeling in a sharp turn, could only guess at the action above. Then the guns opened up again, the recoil of the combined salvoes shuddering through the very structure of the vessel. Repeated spells of firing continued throughout the night. In the confined space of the switchboard compartment only the remote sounds and feeling of ship movement gave the occupants any idea of the action taking place up top.

At 0930 the First Lieutenant ordered the ship to revert to Defence Stations. Like rats vacating the bilges, men poured out onto the upper deck. In awed silence they took in the scene ashore. Black smoke rising from a large installation – carried from west to east on a light wind – formed a dense background to figures moving along the coastal ridge. The throaty sound of revving diesels reached the watching sailors as landing craft jockeyed for position on the shore. Helicopters buzzed busily above the activity. From high in the west, a jet aircraft dropped from the sky to scream along the length of the beach. Instinctively Jamie and his shipmates ducked until its RAF markings identified the aircraft as friendly. With a twitch of its wings, the jet lifted to the sky before swinging away seaward.

Unknown to those on board, the UN, responding to US pressure and Soviet threats, in furious political exchanges, persuaded the Allies to stop the action. A ceasefire, agreed by all parties, came into force from midnight on November 8th. By that time most of Port Said and the canal had been secured, the French occupying the eastern side and the British the west.

Jamie joined his colleagues to repair the damage suffered in the compartments and spaces adjacent to the guns. Tedium returned with a relaxed state of readiness. *Demon* anchored up close inshore with the fringes of the town in view, the smoke diminishing as the fires died down.

After breakfast, on an overcast Suez morning, Derek caught up with Jamie in the Amplifier Room.

"I hear mail is on its way."

Jamie carefully removed the probes of his meter from an open amplifier and looked across at Derek. To bring news of mail was not like his friend. Derek sat on the metal sill of the doorway and reached into his breast pocket for a pack of Duty Frees. He lit two and handed one to Jamie. "I, um, I'll be leaving in an hour or so."

"Yeah, I heard you're off. Lucky bastard."

"I'll be diving at last; with some Frenchies."

"What a great chance," laughed Jamie. "You'll be able to call them frogs without getting your head kicked in."

Derek half smiled. "The Gypos sank some ships in the canal – we have to clear them."

Jamie studied his friend. "Are you alright, Del?"

"'Course I am. It's what I've been waiting for."

"Yes, but are you scared?"

"Scared? What, me? Get stuffed."

"Well, I would be. It's dangerous, blowing up things."

"I'll be supporting the demolition team; with electrical stuff; lighting, cables, that sort of thing. Routine."

"Well, you be careful."

"Yeah, thanks." Derek blew smoke rings into the air. "I... I wanted to ask you something, you know, just in case..."

"Just in case what? You'll be back here in no time."

"Well, like you say, blowing up things can be dangerous. And I have to tell you something."

"What?" Jamie eased the Amplifier back into its slot and sat back against the bulkhead. The small room lacked ventilation so he stubbed out the cigarette on the sole of his boot.

"I'm going to be a dad." Derek watched the face opposite for the reaction.

Jamie stared back. "A dad?"

Derek nodded. A familiar smile played at the corners of his mouth; his high cheeks glowed red against his light complexion. "Nelly. She wrote to me when we got back from the earthquake thing in Turkey. February – it'll be born in February – maybe the 14th. St Valentine's – a love baby."

"You've known all this time and you didn't…"

"Didn't say? I know. I've been busy thinking, but I've decided – I want it. I wasn't sure before but I've decided – and now we'll have to get married, won't we?"

Jamie nodded, his mind working overtime. With great effort he managed to restrain his reaction. He reasoned that Nelly must have been pregnant when they picnicked. He wanted to scream out, 'She was pregnant, so what was she doing offering herself to me? She must have known that she was in that condition.' Rapidly he calculated back from February to August. 'Three months – she would have been three months pregnant.' Jamie buried his head in his hands to avoid any possibility that Derek could read the words buzzing in his brain.

"The only thing is, mate. The only thing is…"

"Spit it out, Del. The bloody canal will be open before you get there at this rate."

"Well, the only thing is – Old Hoppalong. Nell told him about the baby when she was in Malta. She's home now, back at college. He went ape. He told her that either she got rid of the baby, or if she had it she should have nothing to do with me."

"What did she decide?"

"She's having it. She played along with her father and agreed not to see me. Hoppalong thinks I don't know. Anyway, now this has come up and I wanted to ask you a favour – probably the biggest favour I've ever asked you."

Jamie nodded, foreboding settling on him like a black shroud.

"I…" Derek hesitated, searching for the words. "If anything happens to me I want you to make sure Nelly and the baby are okay. Nothing heavy, just keep in touch; make sure they're okay, yeah?"

Derek stood up. The two friends faced each other. Derek offered his hand. Jamie had never shaken his friend's hand before but he took it.

"That's a bloody stupid thing to say," complained Jamie. "Nothing's going to happen to you. You're too slippery for that."

"Say you will, Taff," said Derek. Jamie was taken aback by the note of pleading in the voice, uncharacteristic of the usually brash Londoner.

"'Course I will, daft bastard," said Jamie.

Derek pulled the younger man toward him and put his left arm around his shoulders. Jamie tentatively gripped the back of Derek's shirt and waited. Embarrassment separated the two. Derek turned and left.

Later, Jamie, standing on the port AA gun platform, watched as Derek and two other divers loaded gear into a landing craft. With a growl from its powerful diesels the small vessel lifted its bow and roared away. Derek looked back. He caught sight of Jamie and lifted one hand. Jamie lifted an arm in response, but a deep apprehension rooted him to the spot. He watched until the little craft merged with the land at the entrance to the Suez Canal. He then forced his feet to move: to return to his work.

The helicopter delivering mail caused a stir later that day. Hovering above the quarterdeck the line holding the first two canvas bags fouled the guardrail when the ship unexpectedly lifted in a swell. Only the presence of mind of a seaman who darted forward to untangle the line saved the helicopter from embarrassment.

Jamie found four letters waiting for him when he returned to the mess at teatime. He opened the two from his sister first. The first told of Gwyneth's plans for her marriage. She sounded happy and optimistic but sad that Jamie would not be able to come. The second told of the marriage and 'the family sends their love, especially Uncle Delwyn who says stay away from the belly dancers in Alex. Ha, ha. Oh, and don't forget the new name and address when you write.'

Next he opened the letter from Jenny. As he slipped the folded notepaper out of its envelope, two small photographs fell to the table. Pedlar, waving a pink letter in his hand, swooped like a shitehawk and retrieved one of the pictures. With exaggerated wide eyes he studied the image, protecting it from the grasping hands of the embarrassed Jamie.

"Don't snatch, Taffy boy. Wow, and who's this?"

"How do I know, I haven't seen it myself yet, plonker."

Pedlar handed it back. For a moment the smiling face in the snap evaded Jamie's memory; it took a while to recognise the features that he had only seen for a brief time on the train.

"Looker, ain't she?" He proudly stared at the pretty face; a face framed by dark hair contrasting with a pristine white nurse's headgear.

"A nurse, eh," said Pedlar. "They're the best. They know all about things, nurses do. She'll look after all your needs, she will, Taffy boyo."

"Dirty bastard. She's a pen friend, that's all."

"You said you got a bit on the train."

"I lied."

"Yeah, we knew." With a grin Pedlar turned his attention to the pink pages in his hands.

The second picture showed a group of happy, smiling girls on a beach. Catching the mood of the snap, Jamie smiled too. Dressed in a one-piece bathing costume with no evidence of straps, Jenny showed off a creditable cleavage

"How does she keep that up?" Winkle sneaked a look from over Jamie's shoulder.

"Piss off." Jamie, chuffed at the attention, continued to smile as he read.

'I'm the one in the middle,' Jenny wrote, *'if you can bear to look. Perhaps you can send me a picture too. There is news*

276

here of fighting in Egypt. I hope you are not involved. We have fighting here, every Saturday night. People get hurt and it can be very frightening.

Love, Jenny.'

He picked up the last of his letters. The smile on his face changed for he had recognised the handwriting. He read the letter from Eleanor twice before carefully slipping it, together with the black and white photographs of Jenny, into the back of his pay book wallet.

He caught a glimpse of the note Nelly had given him in Malta. He could not bring himself to ditch the flimsy scrap with the almost illegible pencil message.

At 0405 next morning, after an uneventful middle watch, Jamie wearily hoisted himself into his hammock. At 0415 he remained stubbornly awake.

He couldn't blame the noise; he had grown accustomed to the sniffing, snoring and the sleep talking of dozens of men. It was not the airless humidity; he was used to the sweating; accustomed to the dhobi itch between his legs and the prickly heat rash. The solution was to sleep naked beneath a light sheet; to spread a towel beneath his head to save his pillow from the damp.

None of these things kept him awake; the blame lay with the black and white pictures of his pen friend nurse. The bathing costume, held up by the dynamics of thrusting breasts; by nipples, maybe as large and as swollen as Gina's, played their part too – a supporting role. Black and white legs turned to long beautiful, Prince Charming legs, in full colour – legs that went up to a dark triangle, open and inviting in a bed of sand.

At 0425 Jamie quietly lowered himself to the deck with one hand. In the other he contained the spillage that threatened to run from between his fingers. Grabbing his towel he padded quietly, barefoot, to the bathroom.

Pedlar stepped out of the shower and dried himself. "You?"

Jamie turned his back and stepped into the shower cubicle. "Yeah," he replied. "Bloody nurse. She wouldn't leave me alone. You?"

"Yep. Bloody Wendy. She did her striptease again. Black stockings, suspenders – the lot. I didn't stand a chance."

"Ah, well. If we go blind, we go blind."

CHAPTER 24

PORT SAID

From the date of the 'Ceasefire', inactivity fell like a wet blanket over the ship. Day merged into day with no let-up. From her anchored position the view of the shore appeared to remain the same, except to the discerning eye. If one looked carefully one could detect changes in the colour of the sand, depending on the weather. Through November and into December clouds persisted, interspersed with brief appearances of the sun to brighten the coast and to change the colour from ochre to a white gold. One breezy day Pedlar spotted a sand cloud tumbling along the water's edge. Excitedly he called Jamie to take a look.

The Captain called a special Heads of Department meeting.

"What is going on?" he asked.

"Going on, Sir?" repeated the First Lieutenant.

"I am detecting an attitude among the men."

"An attitude, Sir?"

"An attitude, yes. And please, Jonathan, resist repeating what I say."

"Yes, Sir. Resist repeating what you s…"

"By 'attitude' I mean a certain…" the Captain searched for the appropriate word, "slovenliness. Yes, that's it, slovenliness." He seemed pleased to have found the description.

The officers self-consciously straightened and adjusted their clothes.

"I believe we are seeing the result of inactivity, Sir," said the gunnery officer. "All this waiting around after the assault. It's a big anticlimax, Sir."

"Well, give them something to do. Captain's rounds – that takes days of preparation."

"We had that last week, Sir," said Joystick.

"Oh, yes. Well, there's cleaning; painting."

The engineer piped up. "With respect, Sir, everything that can be cleaned is cleaned every day and everything that can be painted has been painted, more than once."

"What about recreation? Tombola?"

"Every night, Sir."

"Films?"

"Seen them all. More than once."

"Quiz?"

"What about football, Sir?" said Sub Lieutenant Graham. The conversation stopped.

"Football?" The Skipper studied the pale face of his communications officer, wondering if the young Subby had gone round the bend after weeks of long hours in the radio shack between his watchkeeping duties on the bridge.

"Yes, Sir. A few days ago we overheard a conversation between some marine units ashore. They were organising football. They have a pitch in Port Said, apparently. Perhaps we could challenge them."

"It means getting them ashore," mused the Skipper. "A few at a time. Yes, that could be done."

"What about snipers, Sir?" said the gunnery officer. "Remember, we had reports of snipers in the town."

"Ye-es. But that was some weeks ago. It's quietened down since then. No, I think it worth the risk. Good for morale. That's it then, Subby, you get it going. Jonathan, I'll leave it to you to ensure safety."

A mixed bag of players piled into the pinnace for the football game. Despite pressure from Grundy, the Misc. mess failed to find eleven players for their turn ashore, so Little Jock, the chef, Grundy and two other senior rates made up the numbers. Jamie volunteered for goalkeeper; his school experience of playing rugby made handling the ball more natural than kicking it. Joystick borrowed a whistle and lanyard from the gunnery officer and from deep within his locker he unearthed a bright horizontal white-and-green-hooped rugby shirt. He hoped to be invited to be referee.

Slapping through the disturbed eddies at the entrance to the Suez Canal, the boat rounded a long breakwater and entered calm waters. The scene that met them gripped the men's senses and silenced the banter. Like drowned Leviathans, sunken ships filled the wide expanse of Port Said harbour. The bright, clean paintwork and newly painted symbols and designs on the funnels and superstructure protruding above the surface emphasised the wantonness of the waste. Further into the port a large white ship sat high in the water, a red cross emblazoned on her round stern. Zigzagging between obstructions, the pinnace reached the quay.

"They're new." Reluctant to pull his eyes away, Grundy stared at the foundered vessels. "Not even rusty."

As they climbed out onto the quay the destruction of the town took their attention away from the wanton waste in the harbour. Dockside buildings, though pockmarked by artillery fire, seemed more or less intact. Further back, surviving blocks of concrete tenements looked down on their more unfortunate neighbours; many buildings reduced to heaps of rubble. Heavy machines, producing huge dust clouds, noisily piled up the debris from roadways. To Jamie the clinically clean war he had waged from miles at sea had little to do with this.

A group of armed Royal Marines, lolling un-marine-like against the large statue of a studious-looking delesseps, came forward to escort the shore party.

"Football?" A sergeant scanned the unlikely assortment of men for signs of footballer-like tendencies.

"Lt Jollyman," said Joystick. "And yes, Sergeant, we are the football team."

A short walk through wide streets brought them to a wide expanse of sandy ground. The football pitch, a square of uneven sand, had been marked out inside a fenced compound. The opposing team had arrived, gathered at one corner, looking threateningly fit and healthy. Green berets and a smattering of red berets identified the opposition; trepidation quickened the heartbeats of the navy team. The escorting marines posted themselves at each corner and relaxed.

"Bloody 'ell," exclaimed Mick. "I'm glad I'm not playing. That's sand, that is."

"Sod the sand," said Little Jock, the chef. "They're commandos, they are. Geed job I brung me boots."

A good pair of galley boots are a chef's treasured possession. Galley boots should always be two or three sizes too large; for easy donning in the early fog of morning; and for swift doffing for the afternoon kip – the extra size also facilitates the galley shuffle. Maturity comes from years of being pickled in dropped grease, providing the boots with immunity from hot water splashing around tiled galley decks.

As the naval team entered the compound gate a Royal Marine PTI complete with blue edged singlet, whistle and bulging muscles came bounding across the pitch. "Good afternoon, gentlemen. No boots or other footwear if you please."

"Och, sod it," said Little Jock.

"This is sand football," continued the PTI. "Thirty minutes each way; normal rules apply."

The first half resulted in seventeen goals to the marines, one to *HMS Demon*. The one was a penalty given away by a large corporal who buried Little Jock's head in the sand with one huge foot for calling him a big thick bootneck. Joystick, also a rugby player, took over from Jamie at half-time. Being a university player, not merely a grammar school player, Lt Jollyman figured he could stop the onslaught.

During the game a small group of locals appeared from the rear door of a block of tenements fifty yards away across the rubble strewn ground. Showing mild interest in the game, the group of three men joined a gang of boys outside of the wire-mesh fence marking the football pitch boundary. The boys, dressed in pyjama-like trousers and shirts, shouted noisily, reserving the loudest applause for the Navy penalty. The older men, dressed in the long white garments favoured by the locals, solemnly clapped every goal. Within minutes of the start of the second half, a crack like a branch breaking from a tree echoed around the compound. As one the marines dropped to the ground. As one the naval contingent stood and stared.

Another crack caused the marine PTI to shout. "Hit the deck, you idiots. Sniper."

This time Jamie and his shipmates lost no time in burying their faces in the sand. Suddenly the three men dressed in the long white garments broke away from the group and sped towards the tenement blocks. Immediately, the escort marines, weapons at the ready, stood and raced through the gate. Before their pursuers were halfway across the open space the fleeing locals reached cover and melted into the dark of a doorway. As the last of the attackers disappeared into the building he defiantly raised a black weapon, a rifle that must have been hidden beneath his garment. The group of boys nonchalantly dispersed, laughing among themselves.

No one sustained injury and the escort party returned empty handed. The PTI declared the game over and the naval team mustered for the return trip to the quay.

"Pity," said Joystick. "We were just getting the hang of that sand."

Taking a different route back, the marines were much more watchful. The sergeant deployed his men further in front, checking each doorway and window as they passed.

"Why didn't you shoot back, Sarg?" Jamie asked as they kept to the cover of a row of trees on a wide avenue.

"Not our way, son," he replied. "The Frogs would have blasted the lot of them, no questions asked. The trouble is, we wouldn't do that and they know it."

"Nobody told us there would be snipers."

"It's been quiet up to now." The sergeant's eyes darted to every dark arch and each possible hiding place as he spoke. "There's talk of withdrawal. It's made 'em brave, I expect."

An approaching Arab woman moved onto the street to avoid the party. Dressed completely in black, only her face remained visible through a tight head covering. Her eyes, spitting venom, met with Jamie's as she passed. With an almost undetected movement her mouth dropped to a sneer, then she was past and had regained the path.

Back at the quay the party, relieved by the sight of gun-mounted vehicles, relaxed.

Joystick checked his watch. "We're early. Settle down for a while. The pinnace will be here in half an hour."

Jamie spotted a barge with a number of men busy on deck tending wet suits and diving equipment. After a quick word with Joystick he wandered along in its direction.

"Ahoy," shouted Jamie to a diver working on a scuba set, "do you know Latch?"

"Pardon?"

"Latch. Derek Latchbrook. One of your lot. Do you know him?"

A head appeared from a cabin near the stern. "It's no use asking him, he's French. Who did you say?"

"Derek Latchbrook. A navy diver from *HMS Demon*."

"Sorry, no idea. Try the office; it's in that building." He pointed to a more or less intact office block across the wide quay. "They'll know."

Following the instruction Jamie entered an arched opening in the block. Untidy heaps of diving equipment lying around on the floor identified the office as the correct place. A huge map of the Canal Zone took up most of the wall behind a desk covered with office paraphernalia. In a corner, against the rear wall, a naval rating sat with earphones connected to a radio set. A tall man dressed in civilian clothes entered from a back room. He carried a mug in each hand.

"Hi, can I help?"

"EM Latchbrook, from *HMS Demon*. He's working with you lot. I'm just passing – thought I'd see how he is."

"Latchbrook? Is he a pal of yours?"

"You could say that."

"A good pal?"

"The best."

"Sit down, lad – here." The athletic-looking man with fair, thinning hair offered Jamie a chair and delivered a mug to the radio operator. The fair-haired man sat himself behind his desk and offered Jamie his mug of steaming coffee. "Have this."

Jamie sipped the coffee, black, bitter and sweet. A glance back through the open doorway confirmed that the football party were still waiting at the jetty.

Jamie tried to place the accent.

"I'm Jerry – co-ordinator here. Cigarette?" The North American drawl came through stronger.

Something about the atmosphere, the way both men looked at him, created a stir in Jamie's stomach. "What's up?"

"You haven't heard?"

"Heard what?"

"Latch. He got himself into a bit of bother yesterday. You haven't heard?"

"No I have not," said Jamie. "What's happened?"

"He, er, got himself injured." The American paused, assessing the effect of the news. "He caught a stray bullet. Nobody seems to know how or why."

"Snipers, I expect," said Jamie with the authority of a veteran. "Where is he?"

"He was at the field hospital, but I think they've taken him to the French hospital ship. Our injured are usually air lifted to Cyprus, but he was too poorly for the trip."

Jamie pulled deeply on his cigarette and asked quietly. "How is he? Really?"

"He's alive," responded the co-ordinator. "His oppo on the job isn't. They got him through the neck."

Jamie involuntarily reached to the crinkled letter stuffed into the top pocket of his shirt. For a brief second he felt tempted to give it to this man, but instead he thanked him and left.

CHAPTER 25

LATCHBROOK'S BULLET

The mid-December desert sun, orange in a red horizon, dropped slowly behind the western sand dunes bordering the Suez Canal. Derek, sitting on the edge of a diving barge, felt the heat go as shadow enveloped him. Out near the centre of the waterway a dredger's lifting arm marked the position of a sunken hulk. Towed to the narrow canal entrance from its resting place at Port Faud, the old working ship was the last obstruction. Pointing skyward from the water's surface, her rusted lifting arm held the sunshine a few minutes longer, illuminated red by the sun's dying rays. Underwater, Derek's team fought against the fading light, setting charges to separate the arm from the bow. Clearing this final obstruction would allow passage to sizeable vessels; restore some normality to the route.

Derek had never been happier. His team of French and British clearance divers had worked long and hard from the day of the ceasefire in difficult conditions. Visibility beneath the surface was better than tomato soup but worse than scrumpy. Derek tended the generator on the makeshift platform and provided lighting, swimming alongside the demolition divers whenever required.

Concentrating on opening the centre of the waterway, the team had worked their way south from the breakwater, demolishing and clearing the worse of Nasser's vandalism until only this last obstruction remained. The remarkable progress was achieved despite a minimal understanding between the team's two nationalities.

"Froggie," Derek would say, addressing his French colleagues.

"Froggie?"

"Froggie; it is short for Frogman."

Within days the British members of the diving parties revelled in hearing the French addressing each other as, 'Froggie'. The French gave as good as they got and took the mick but mutual respect and common purpose created an effective team.

As he sat and waited, Derek watched the antics of a group of boys as they played at the water's edge, fifty yards down the canal. The scene reminded Derek of unending summer days spent splashing around in the Grand Union Canal. Feeding lighting cable from a reel between his legs, he watched the group to ensure they kept a safe distance from the detonations about to be set off. It had been a long day but with this one remaining major obstruction the team had decided to work on.

Enjoying the peaceful evening, Derek thought of his future. Increasing talk of withdrawal had led him to hope that he would be home before Christmas – maybe sooner if the work here was finished. Perhaps he and Nell would be married before the baby arrived; he would apply for married quarters; maybe join submarines. With a smile he remembered Jamie's dream of Hong Kong; finding a Chinese girl to live with 'like a wife'. Perhaps they could sign up for boats together; go out together, maybe, all four of them. Nelly would like that. For some reason she liked the little Taffy. And that father of hers; maybe he could accept the inevitable; be happy for his daughter. For a brief moment a frown wrinkled his brow; he had not received mail from Nell for weeks but he was sure a bundle lay somewhere – perhaps back on board – waiting for him.

Derek did not hear the rifle shot. The bullet passed through the bone at the very top of his head. It did not do too much damage. The impact caused him to lose consciousness: to topple into the canal. Being submerged too long did the damage. Some Egyptian boys, playing at the edge of the water, pulled him out.

288

A French colleague, hearing the shot, ran out of the barge's cabin. He took the second bullet. It entered through the back of his neck to exit through his open mouth. The French officer knew nothing of his demise – it happened too quickly.

Minutes later Derek's divers surfaced. They did all they could to support Derek with oxygen. They saved his life, but they failed to bring him round.

The next day, if he had been conscious, he would have heard the *Demon's* pinnace pass beneath the hospital ship's ample stern on her way back from the football. Armed with the information of Derek's whereabouts, Jamie had asked for permission to visit the hospital ship, but Joystick had turned down Jamie's request on the grounds that he would have no way of getting back on board. From the hard wooden seat of the pinnace, Jamie scanned the rows of windows along the hospital ship's side wondering which one Derek would be lying behind; wondering with increasing trepidation how he could get to see him; how he would tell him about Nelly. Again he felt for the letter in his shirt pocket. Removing the blue airmail envelope he once more read the neat handwriting on the single blue sheet.

My Dear James,

I hope this letter reaches you, but I suppose you would not be reading it if it had not. From what Derek tells me I think your ship is somewhere close to him but censorship has prevented him telling me more.

I am writing to you because I want you to do me a great favour. I have tried writing to Derek but the words won't come. Anyway, you are his best friend and you will find a way to say the things I cannot.

I don't know if he has told you but Derek thinks that I am having a baby. This is not the case. There is no baby and I cannot tell him. He was so happy, mapping out our future. There is no future for us and I think you could see that, couldn't you, James? I always felt you disapproved of us. Don't judge too harshly, I did think Derek and I had something special – we did – but it has taken me a while to realize that our lives are so different. Daddy and I had a long talk and I see now that he is right.

Please forgive me for asking you to do this but I need your understanding between us. Please tell Derek how sorry I am and try to convince him that this is for the best and tell him not to try to get in touch. Daddy may do something if he does.

Thank you and have a good life, I will always remember our lovely picnic,

Yours, Eleanor.

"Well, that takes the biscuit," said Jamie to himself as he folded the letter and stowed it away. "A Dear John, by proxy."

CHAPTER 26

DEAR JOHN

"You're a slippery bastard, Pedlar," said Jamie.

"And I love you too, Jamie."

"No, I mean that as a compliment. I need your advice."

Pedlar put down the little round shaving mirror he had been studying his face with and listened.

"I need to get to visit Latch. He's in hospital, ashore."

"Just request it." Ginger, lying prone on the mess bench, lifted a corner of a dog-eared copy of a mountain climbing magazine from his face.

"Thanks, Ging. I've tried that."

"Get yourself ill, 'pendicitis or something," interrupted Mick.

"Can't I have a quiet word with my mate Pedlar without you lot interfering," said Jamie.

"No, he's right," said the thoughtful Pedlar. "Something you can fake but something they can't treat on board."

"Yeah, sorry," said Jamie.

"I know," piped up Winkle. "A deadly disease like cholera or something."

"Scarlet fever," said Scouser.

"Sheepshagger's Clap," said Badger, from the other table, "or Wanker's Doom."

Jamie groaned, but resisted responding to the jibe.

"Toothache," said Pedlar. "Say you have raging toothache."

"Brilliant," said Mick. "Now all you have to do to visit Latch is to lose a tooth."

"Just pretend," continued Pedlar. "And say it's much better when you get there."

"Triffic," said Jamie. "How did you think of that?"

"One of the Tiffys is going tomorrow. Bloody great abscess, he's got."

"I haven't got an abscess." Jamie rubbed his jaw.

"I can fix that," said Badger, shaking a fist.

"Tell 'em it burst. Say you can't eat or speak."

"How can I tell 'em I can't speak if I can't speak?"

"Worry not – I'll take you to sickbay in the morning."

"There you are. I said you were a slippery bastard, Pedlar."

"Yeah, thanks, Taff."

The following morning Jamie was called to the office where the problem was simply resolved by Joystick.

"I've had a word with the Captain. Tidy yourself up. ERA Harris has to visit the dentist. Go along with him and if he has gas, look after him. The boat will wait. You may get the chance to see Latchbrook but you are there for the ERA, understand?"

"Yes, Sir, and thanks."

"Davis." The Lieutenant turned in his chair to look directly at his young charge. "Latchbrook is not well. We had a report yesterday that he is critical. By some miracle he survived a long time under water, probably the oxygen from his diving friends saved him, I don't know. If you do get to see him, wish him a speedy recovery from us here."

"Yes, Sir. I'll do that. Thank you."

The wide-open foredeck of the hospital ship indicated its former status of passenger liner. A French naval guard directed them to a reception area. Jamie reported to the desk, settled his suffering shipmate on a comfortable sofa, and enquired the whereabouts of the British diver brought aboard two days ago.

Following the receptionist's directions, Jamie found his way to an ornately-decorated staircase leading to the deck below. Handwritten signs pinned above entrances helped Jamie to find the correct corridor; the soft carpet and wood-panelled bulkheads reminded him that this was not a hospital.

Willing help from white-coated orderlies and medical staff directed Jamie aft to the open door of a small room. Standing in the doorway a doctor and an orderly talked quietly.

"Excuse me, can I visit?"

"Viseet?" said the older man with a stethoscope.

"Can I see my mate? Latchbrook, in there."

"Ah, zee diver. You are his friend?"

"Yes, can I see him?"

"Do you know what happened to him?"

"Nearly drowned, so I hear. That's all I know. I have a letter for him – and messages from the ship."

The two men briefly exchanged words in French. The doctor beckoned Jamie to a door opposite and sat him down in an office.

"Do you know he is very ill, your friend?"

Jamie nodded his head.

"Your friend has suffered a wound to his head – and he is not conscious. A rifle bullet passed through the top of his head but we do not think his coma is the result of that. He was in the water a long time. We think the lack of oxygen has damaged him."

"You mean... his brain?"

"Yes. The extent of the damage is not yet clear. He is a very fit young man but I have to tell you that it does not look good. That is all I can say." The doctor shrugged and stood. "Please, see him if you must, but he will not know you are there."

In the small room a single bed, surrounded by medical equipment, stood beneath an open square window. A breeze ruffled a sheet of graph paper hanging on a clipboard at the feet of Derek Latchbrook. A light sheet covered his body to the neck, the white linen as neat and uncreased as their beds at Collingwood had been when made ready for inspection. An oxygen mask hid his mouth and a swathe of bandages covered his head. Only a quiff of blonde hair, protruding from the head dressing, identified the still figure.

"Hiya, Del," said Jamie, quietly. "What the fu— what the Dickens have you been up to."

Almost surprised at the lack of response, Jamie stared at the closed eyes. With effort, he resisted the urge to reach out and to shake the arm of the unconscious patient. "Come on mate," he said quietly, "look lively – it's me, Jamie. I've come to see you."

The orderly half-entered the room, looked quizzically at the British naval rating and left.

"The fellas send their best and old Joystick…" he paused. "Old Joystick, he's alright really, for an officer… and Gordon says to get better soon. Oh, and yes, I have a letter for you here – from Nelly. It came to me by mistake. I'll read it to you, shall I?"

Jamie removed the letter and spread it on the bed. He licked his dry lips and swallowed. The neat writing was no longer neat; the thin paper, crinkled and sweat stained, took an age to straighten.

"My darling Derek."

The words came out in a croak. Jamie glanced at the unconscious figure, cleared his throat and started again.

"My darling Derek, this is just to let you know that everything is okay. The baby is getting on now, growing fast, kicking and shifting like a good 'un. He's going to be strong and brave like his dad. He's going to be a Valentine baby, just like I said. Ask that best mate of yours, Taffy, to be godfather when we have him christened. Maybe we can call him Jamie too – James Derek Latchbrook… that would be a grand name."

Jamie stared at the letter.

"My father, old Hoppa... my daddy says everything is alright..."

Jamie stopped. He rubbed his eyes.

"My daddy says..."

Jamie sighed – deeply – but the pain in his constricted throat remained. He looked at the silent, unmoving figure on the bed. He wanted desperately to say a prayer, but the words would not come.

"Got to go now," he said very softly. "I love you... Nelly."

CHAPTER 27

WITHDRAWAL

The darkening sky formed a backdrop behind the busy lights of Port Said. In the harbour, craft of all kinds loaded up men and their machines and prepared to leave. From the south, tracer bullets scratched trails into the blackness like a gruesome Hadean firework display, following the Allied forces withdrawing along the canal to the harbour.

"Bastards, bastards," mouthed the Skipper. Quietly, but with deep feeling, Captain De-Fotherinham voiced the anger of his crew as they watched, unable to act except to be there, ready to escort the small, vulnerable vessels on their journey west. With lights blazing, the hospital ship nosed out past the breakwater to come under the protection of the waiting destroyers. She passed close on *Demon's* port bow, sedate and dignified and unhurried. Jamie, watching from the flag deck, heaved a sigh of relief. Guessing at the position of Derek's room, he focussed on one of the square lights and wondered if he was awake yet; awake and watching in return.

With three days to go to Christmas the odds stacked up against a celebration ashore as the escorts were forced to match the speed of the slowest craft. By Christmas Eve it was obvious that the Lucky Horseshoe would have to wait a day or two longer for the return of her favourite sons. Christmas Eve was also the day that Jamie learned of the death of his best friend.

Christmas Day dawned to a sense of anticipation on Miscellaneous mess. For a change the chefs made a special effort with the eggs, and the bacon looked crispy and inviting. Jamie ate nothing, finding himself incapable of joining in with the usual banter; unable even to return the Happy Christmas wishes all around.

"Cheer up, Welshy," said Badger. "It's Christmas."

"Piss off." Jamie, with great effort, restrained the anger welling in his throat as he watched the man he hated most in the world stuff food into his grinning mouth.

"For Christ sake, leave him," said Micky, aware of the hurt stirring the emotions of the young man. With automatic, unthinking movements Jamie turned to at his cleaning station, sweeping and polishing silently. Unable to join the celebrations gathering momentum on the messdecks, Jamie made for the battery shop, preferring to be alone; preferring to hide away and allow the memories of his best mate to fill his mind without interruption. Sitting on the sill of the familiar workshop door he looked across a choppy sea to the many slow-moving craft ploughing along like chicks following their mother home. Pug-nosed tugs; landing craft; transports of all kinds laboured through the short waves. They reminded Jamie of dogs returning home from an illicit jaunt, their tails firmly between their legs. He hated them for allowing his friend to be killed; despised them for being a part of something that had taken his best friend's life before it had hardly begun.

"Davis."

A sharp voice jarred into his consciousness – a voice he had learned to loathe. Before the square bulk of Badger had thrown his shadow on the green anti-slip deck in front of Jamie, the Welshman had risen to his feet. With his fist clenched tight, he brought his right arm back and released a wicked punch into the stomach of his tormentor. Jamie felt no danger; could see no threat — he did it just for himself and for his mate. Resentment and hate blurred his vision; his eyes filled with tears and with an involuntary "bastard", he followed the first blow with another. As if in slow motion the look of surprise on the older man's

297

face changed to agony. He dropped, robbed of the ability to breathe, to land with a bounce on the steel deck.

Shaking his head and lifting his free hand to ward off further blows, Badger scrambled backwards to sit against the guardrail.

"Alright, enough, enough," he gasped. "I didn't come here for a fight."

Jamie, breathing hard, remained standing over his grounded adversary.

"I came here to say sorry."

"Sorry? You? What for?"

"Your mate, Latch. I heard."

"Yeah, well," Jamie relaxed and moved back. "What would you know about mates?"

"More than you think." Badger ruefully rubbed his solar plexus. With a sideways look at his assailant, the older man heaved himself to his feet and sat on a deck locker. "Sit down, you stupid Welsh Sheep… sorry. Sit down Taff; you look like a prizefighter standing like that."

"Why don't you fuck off and leave me alone?" Jamie suddenly felt tired. "Go and bother someone else. I've had it with you."

"Sit down. I told you – I've come to say sorry."

Jamie eased himself down, still watchful and reluctant to give up his distrust. Breathing easier Badger waited until the pain had subsided enough to speak. "So, you've lost a friend. I am deeply sorry about that, but you're not the first and you most certainly will not be the last. By your age I had lost a shipful."

Badger paused, glancing at the young man before continuing. "You wanna know about me?"

"Not particularly."

"Well, I'll tell you about me. Acting PO I was – during the war. I got made up at sea, after a poxy Nazi dive-bomber hit us.

One hit, that's all. We lost eighteen; mostly senior rates. The bomb reached their mess before going up. I thought I knew everything, just like you. A cocky little cunt, I was. They put me in charge of the department. I'd only held the job a day when, bugger me if we didn't get hit again. About here it was, off Alexandria, 1941." He squinted up at the clear sky. "A Junkers screamer; dropped on us before we had a chance to shoot back. At first it didn't seem too bad, but a fire caught hold." Again he paused, the sweat on the high, freckled brow beading and running down his face.

Jamie waited.

"The thing was; the pumps failed – one after the other. Water pressure dropped and the damage control parties couldn't fight the fire. I tried, God, I tried. I couldn't fix the pumps, I didn't know enough to get electrical supply to the motors; I didn't know where the breakers were; didn't know how to get alternate supplies. In short," Badger laughed, a hollow mirthless laugh, "I didn't know fuck all."

Badger closed his eyes tight, reliving the nightmare, remembering for the umpteenth time the panic; the useless running around that had produced nothing.

Jamie watched as sweat mixed with tears rolled down the mottled, lined cheek. The sea quietly slid by and Badger opened his eyes to stare at its surface as if to penetrate its depths.

"It's okay…" started Jamie. Badger stopped him with an upraised hand.

"The for'ard magazine went up first; 'A' Boiler followed. Out of 250 only twenty-nine of us got picked up. That bastard Jerry pilot came back and strafed the ship even as she was sinking. I can still see him grinning and waving to us in the water as he passed."

"Bastard," whispered Jamie.

"I found myself with two mates; in the water; on a float. Nearly three days it was – before they found us. No water; no food; nothin'. I thought we would die."

Badger paused; Jamie sat quietly staring at the guardrail.

"I still see them two old boys. They stayed in Malta after the war. Pansies they are, though I didn't know that at the time. They've got a piano bar in Malta."

"Floriana." interjected Jamie.

"Yeah, Floriana," agreed Badger. "I see them now and again. We have a laugh… but mostly we cry."

Badger looked old and tired; his head dropped, his chin resting on the greying hairs sprouting from the neck of his shirt.

"I've never wanted responsibility after that. Gave up my rate and I've been this," he touched the badge on his sleeve, "ever since."

"But what did you have against me? What was all that about – sheepshagger and stuff?"

"I dunno. You were a cocky little bastard. I wanted to put you in your place, bring you down a peg or three. 'Sides, you're Welsh."

"So?"

"I, er, I had a wife once – Welsh she was." He took a deep breath. "She left me before I got back home – survivors' leave. She went back to her parents. I reckon they encouraged her to leave – just when I needed her the most. They never liked me… and I've never liked Welshmen ever since."

"Well, you can be a little hard to like sometimes," smiled Jamie.

"Yeah, I know it."

The two sat for five long minutes, each silently lost in thought.

"He wasn't yet twenty-one," said Jamie. "He thought he was going to be a dad."

Badger patted the youngster's knee but withdrew his hand self-consciously.

"And what was all this fuckin' lot for?" Jamie, with a broad sweep of his hand, pointed out the craft all about.

"What is any war for?" said Badger. "This one was spectacularly useless but so are they all. The best we can hope for is that them making the decisions know what they're doing, and if they do send us to be killed, it's for something worthwhile."

"I don't think Latch died for something worthwhile."

"Don't you think like that, young man. He was doing something to put things right. That's as useful as it comes."

Jamie nodded, surprised that this man who had done so much to keep him down was now helping him.

"I had an oppo, you know. Not one of the puffs – they're great but this was a special oppo – he helped me through the bad days."

"Where's he now?

"He was killed. Strafed to buggery – just walking through Malta dockyard..."

"I'm sorry."

"Yeah, so am I... Well, come on then, Welshy. Christmas dinner will be served shortly. We can't miss the only day of the year when them lot in the wardroom serve us, now can we?"

Standing, Jamie said, "Why don't you leave – the Navy I mean?"

"Leave? No fear. Where else can I be looked after; fed; cared for; morning and night? No Sir. The Navy is full of people ready to look after dropouts like me. Let 'em. Civvy street dropouts don't get nothing. No, I'll stay as long as they'll have me."

Jamie followed Badger for'ard with mixed feelings. The short, square figure leading him back to the mess still called up a reservoir of revulsion, despite the kind words. Jamie felt a little more respect from the old man and the insight into his past had explained a lot about his attitude, but he knew there would never be friendship.

As the two entered the Canteen Flat the muted tones of a Christmas carol reached them. The messdeck, full to overflowing, reverently rang with 'Silent Night'. Following tradition the officers served dinner and a party, fuelled by extra issues of beer, lasted all afternoon, finishing with The Death of Nelson. Badger, complete with eye patch, took the lead but could not persuade Taps, masquerading as Hardy, to give him a kiss.

Later *Demon*, relieved of escort duties, peeled off and headed for Malta, arriving at Grand Harbour late on Boxing Day morning.

The first liberty boat left the ship at 1600. Jamie, aching to get away from the mess and all the familiarity, joined the noisy liberty men on the pinnace. For the first time in more than three months he stepped ashore at Custom House. Also for the first time, he bought his drinks in a bar on the quay, sitting alone as sailors and marines jostled to get served. Three beers later Pedlar and Mick appeared.

"Are they yours?" Micky eyed the half a dozen Anchor bottles lined up on the table.

"You were smart away," said Pedlar. "We're off to the Lucky. Are you coming?"

"Not just yet. You go along – I'll see you later."

For a moment Mick seemed to be about to say something but instead he tugged Pedlar away and the two left. Preferring his own company, Jamie moved to an outside table and sat on a chair well worn by the old men usually to be found there. In the cool of the late afternoon, as shadows lengthened turning day into night, Jamie sat alone and drank beer after beer. Fewer liberty men passed by to make their noisy way up the hill to the town.

"Davis?" The voice of Gordon Grundy interrupted Jamie's thoughts.

With difficulty Jamie focussed on the PO and his two senior rate companions.

"PO?"

"Are you on your own, lad?"

"Yup. I've got a bit of thinking to do."

"A bit of drinking too, by the look of that lot," he said. "Take it easy or you'll land up in the paint locker. Where are your mates?"

"Dead," said Jamie, matter-of-factly. "Dead or dying."

Gordon waved the others on. "I'll catch up." Sitting, he took a draught from one of Jamie's half-empty bottles. "What's up, Jamie lad?"

Caught unawares, Jamie studied the face of the man he had never really recognised as a man, only as a boss.

"What's up? Not much. My best friend is dead; my second best friend is on crutches somewhere – waiting to be thrown out on the scrap heap. What for? What for, PO? Can you tell me? Everybody is dead. My Mam, my Dad, my friends…"

"You've got a shipful of friends," he waved over his shoulder, "out there."

"They're not friends. They just work there, like me. I thought this life was supposed to be good…"

"It is good, Taffy, but it isn't everything. It's not your family."

"That's easy for you to say. You have a family."

"I made a family. Just like you will. This is a job, but a fucking great job if you're single. Make the most of it lad, but it is no substitute. Enjoy yourself, with your mates, but don't expect too much from them – they all move on sooner or later."

"Mates?" Jamie determined to remain unconsoled. "What about blokes like Badger?"

"We knew what's been going on. You sorted it, didn't you?"

"You knew?"

"Of course we knew; and that includes Lt Jollyman. And we knew you sorted him. Nobody else could have done."

"Bastards," said Jamie.

"I think you should pull yourself together, young man." Grundy emptied one of Jamie's beer bottles. "You have a future, you have. Why do you think you were moved to work with the Chief EA?"

Jamie shrugged, the beer preventing good visual focus.

"He asked for you, that's why. You, my boy," Grundy stood and replaced his hat, "are considered, in naval parlance, to be 'bright'. Happy Christmas."

Gordon Grundy hurried off up the hill to catch up with his oppos. Jamie tried to make sense of Grundy. Failing, he downed the last of the beer and stood shakily.

"They could have told me," he said to no one in particular as he made his way up the hill to the town. The few people passing by prevented him pissing against a wall. Falling into a gap he found as much cover as he could want. Large, broad-leafed plants and shrubs, low palms and beautifully manicured flowerbeds bordered a winding path. Out of sight of the street, he satisfyingly watered a rough-barked palm tree. Continuing along the path he came to a stone wall beyond which a panorama of the harbour opened up. *Demon* sat far below, benign and glowing in the last of the day's sunlight.

"There you are, you bastard," said Jamie, theatrically. "I used to like you. I couldn't wait to get back to you." He slumped down on a wooden seat and grunted. "Huh. What a stupid prick I am."

With great self-control he managed to keep the beer inside, where it belonged. He lit a DF.

"Well, that's okay with me. I'll get meself a wife, like the PO says. I'll marry my nurse; she'll look after all my needs. Maybe I'll volunteer for submarines. Take her to Hong Kong. Wives can come along if you're in submarines."

Jamie lay out on the bench, tipping his cap over his eyes.

"Bright? Get meself a family, that's what I'll do."

The cigarette fell from his fingers onto the short grass and he slept.

Almost two hours later Jamie found himself at the entrance to the Gut. From his vantage point he looked down the length of the narrow street across a heaving mass of uniforms – blues, browns and shades in-between. Jamie sniffed the air, remembering the first time Dusty had introduced him to this place, but the pounding in his head dulled his senses. Starting down the street, he bumped, like a ball-bearing in a pinball machine, from bodies to buildings until he recognised a familiar entrance. Elbowing his way in he stood at the door of the Silver Dollar and shouted, "And you lot can go stuff yourselves too."

The greeting raised a cheer but Jamie found himself back outside.

At the Lucky Horseshoe he halted at the entrance. A group of Royal Marines, jackets undone and singing along to the music of the jukebox, filled the doorway. Jamie stood outside, swaying and reluctant to go in. Suddenly an overwhelming tiredness robbed him of his legs. Losing control, he stumbled backwards to sit in a heap against the wall opposite. The marines cheered and raised their glasses to toast the fallen hero.

From the crowd a pair of black, high-heeled shoes appeared and stood straddling his legs.

"What you do? What you do? You peessed and not come see Carlotta?"

305

Jamie focussed on the woman above. "Happy Christmas to you, Carlotta."

"What you do? Why you not come see me?"

"Sorry. I'm pissed."

The woman crouched down and helped Jamie to his shaky feet. The marines cheered again and made way for the two.

"You come," said Carlotta. "Dahleeng boy, you come weeth me."

Inside the bar, Carlotta pulled Jamie through a tight pack of revellers. Apart from a few sorry specimens crying into their glasses, most of the others had formed a terraced arena around a fight. In the gap around the juke box Jamie spotted Pedlar rolling around the floor, locked in mortal combat with a seaman. He recognised the seaman: AB Raymond Crouch. Pedlar, whose collar, silk and lanyard flapped in the air, held his opponents wavy hair in a grip of steel. Raymond, hanging onto the flapping collar, lanyard and silk tried to bite the hand pushing his face back.

Jamie resisted Carlotta and stopped.

"Pedlar," he said. "That's my mate Pedlar."

"Oh, it ees love," said Carlotta. "Thees one have a letter with the other one's name."

Through his alcoholic haze Jamie saw that each man held a letter in their free hands. Battered, ripped and stained the sheets appeared identical – and coloured pink. Jamie smiled to himself, knowing that both sheets would be perfumed.

Up the stairs, past the toilet, Carlotta guided Jamie along the first floor and pushed him through a door. Inside a sparsely-furnished room she moved some clothing and deposited Jamie onto a sofa. Lifting his legs she laid him back onto the settee. With effort Jamie made out a wall bereft of decoration but for a faded picture of Christ complete with halo. A mirrored dressing table stood in the recess of the window and a single bulbed light hung in the centre of the ceiling. Jamie closed his eyes but before he'd drifted off Carlotta had returned with a steaming mug of coffee. As he sipped the hot drink he caught the sound of muffled cheers and groans emanating in waves from the room below.

Carlotta moved Jamie's legs and sat beside him.

"Why you get peessed – why you no come see Carlotta?"

"I was fed up, Carlotta – couldn't wait. Anyway, you didn't keep your word. You told me you would save your daughter for me."

"No dotter, I lie to you – for you to buy dreenk." She laughed – a throaty, cigarette hoarse laugh.

"What, no tits like water melons; no eyes like black cherries…"

"I told you friend to tell you, no dotter."

"My friend?"

"Yeah – you friend – a beeg dahleeng boy; a dirty boy." Carlotta extended her nicotine-stained fingers to indicate large hands. "He come here one day. I say – where my dahleeng boy? He say your father die." She quickly crossed herself. "I say, 'you tell my dahleeng boy Jamee – Carlotta, she haf no dotter'."

Jamie thought back to the field hospital in Cyprus. He pictured the big man's dirty, smiling face. "Dusty, the bastard," he exclaimed. "The dirty, dirty old bastard – he knew and he lied to me."

A huge smile lit up the face of the young sailor.

"Come on Carlotta," he said. "It's Christmas. Let's go and rescue Pedlar. We'll drink to absent friends and get pissed – again."

THE END

POSTSCRIPT

On December 29th 1956 a Telegram boy returned to a semi-detached house in a street in Harrow, North West London for the third day in a row. He had attempted to deliver a telegram addressed to Mrs Ivy Latchbrook, but could get no reply. The policeman detailed to accompany the GPO man recognised the house. He had visited it before – almost a year before – along with two Naval Patrolmen. Something told him to walk around to the back of the house. He found the back door unlocked. Making his way through the cold kitchen, he passed through a hall stacked high with books. Beneath the front door letterbox a pile of newspapers dated back more than two weeks. The smell as he opened the front room door confirmed his fears. Two weeks later the remains of Mrs Ivy Latchbrook were buried at Harrow Cemetery along with her adopted son, Royal Navy Diver, Derek Latchbrook.